Praise for THE LAST PHOTOGRAPH

'Evocative, harrowing . . . Chapman, author of the much-praised *How To Be A Good Wife*, has an enviable lightness of touch and tackles the big subjects of love and war with aplomb. This book pays tribute to the sixty-three journalists killed during the Vietnam War and asks important questions' *Tatler*

'Chapman's book follows a war photographer and gets under the skin of a character more at home in the pursuit of professional action than in his normal life . . . the knack of evoking time and place without wearing research too heavily or earnestly is something for other writers to aspire to' *Metro*

'Its guilt-ridden hero is hugely sympathetic' *Mail on Sunday*

'Chapman has a taut, economical style that proves immersive' *Sunday Times*

'Ambitious . . . tension-filled' *Daily Mail*

'Elegantly constructed . . . successful in its thoughtful depiction of a man who prefers to look at the world through a viewfinder and its exploration of ageing, memory and time, the hold the past has over us' *Observer*

'Her tale of marriage, vocation, war and friendship shows how intricately these things can become intertwined in a psyche and a life'

Sydney Morning Herald

'No second-book wobbles for Emma Chapman, who has achieved something admirable with *The Last Photograph*. Starting with a death, the following narrative weaves past and present against a backdrop of the Vietnam War and London in the 60s. Two conflicting worlds, writ large within the soul of our protagonist. Authentic and compelling, this is a novel that delivers as a piece of art can, revealing itself in reflection and leaving a lasting impression'

Ruth Dugdall, author of *The Woman Before Me*

'*The Last Photograph* is a novel of the highest calibre – absorbing, moving, and acutely insightful'

Lottie Moggach, author of *Kiss Me First*

The Last Photograph

EMMA CHAPMAN was born in 1985 and grew up in Manchester. She studied English Literature at Edinburgh University, followed by an MA in Creative Writing at Royal Holloway, and now lives in North Yorkshire. Her highly acclaimed debut novel, *How To Be A Good Wife*, was longlisted for the Dylan Thomas Prize. While researching *The Last Photograph* in Vietnam, Emma set up a charity called Vietnam Volunteer Teachers (www.vietnamvolunteerteachers.com) to bring native English speakers to remote areas of the country.

Also by Emma Chapman

How To Be A Good Wife

Emma Chapman

The Last Photograph

PICADOR

First published 2016 by Picador

First published in paperback 2016 by Picador

This edition first published 2017 by Picador
an imprint of Pan Macmillan
20 New Wharf Road, London N1 9RR
Associated companies throughout the world
www.panmacmillan.com

ISBN 978-1-5098-1656-9

1 3 5 7 9 8 6 4 2

A CIP catalogue record for this book is available from the British Library.

Printed and bound by CPI Group (UK) Ltd, Croydon, CR0 4YY

To Benjamin Mosey,

for teamwork and adventures and

who always makes sense

Life can only be understood backwards; but it must be lived forwards.

Søren Kierkegaard

Someday there will be novels about that hardy band of correspondents covering the war in Vietnam.

Time, August 1963

ONE

He walks into the living room and June is dead.

No soft movement across her chest, no quivering eyelid. The sunlight from the window catches her lashes and greying blonde hair. Her painted red nails rest on the arm of the faded chair.

He centres her, checking the light. Focusing, he clicks the shutter.

He'll ask himself later, if he knew. Now, it's easier for him to think that he is acting without thinking, out of instinct.

*

Rook had been out that morning, as usual. Across the fields, through the woodland, despite the rain. He lay for a long time on the damp ground, pointing his camera up through the bark towards the white sky until his bones ached. When a branch snapped, he jumped, despite himself.

He returns to find the house quiet, no gentle movements in the kitchen: a knife on a board, the scrape of china as she pulls a plate out of the cupboard.

She'll be at a WI meeting, a community forum. She'll be back before one to prepare his lunch. But when he walks into the front room, he sees her straight away, in her old armchair, the *Radio Times* across her lap.

After he takes the photograph, he sits down in the other chair, watching her. Eventually, he steps across the sun-marked carpet to the whisky decanter and pours himself a drink. When he's finished his glass, he rests his shaking fingers on her inner wrist, smooth like a polished pebble. Nothing.

What do you do when your wife dies?

He calls an ambulance.

'What's your emergency?' crackles the voice on the line.

'It's a little late for that,' he says.

They come to take her away.

*

When they've gone, leaving him instructions, he pours another whisky. He carries the glass and bottle through the house, across the patch of grass, towards the studio. The clouds have cleared now and it is a bright day: the first after the long winter. Birds are singing and there is the sound of farm machinery far away. The green hills stretch around the house, towards the village.

Once inside, he stops, catching himself in the mirror through the door of the makeshift darkroom. Thinning silver curls, deep lines across his forehead and cheeks.

He's almost surprised not to see the outline of a young man, with bushy brown hair and sloped shoulders.

There's a clutter about this room: the miscellany of objects collected. Battered boots, army issue: never cleaned. The World Press Award, framed and hanging on the wall.

He moves away, towards his photo board. His favourite images, pinned up over the years. There are many more in the filing cabinets that line the room. The negatives, of things he doesn't want to see again, and sees anyway.

June's face smiles out at him. She is gone, he tells himself, but the words seem to hold no meaning. He keeps expecting to look up and see her there, a cup of coffee in one hand. The feeling arrives then: a bulge in his throat, a tightness around his eyes. Sadness, at his loss. Regret, that he can never put things right. He always thought there would be more time.

It wasn't supposed to happen like this. If the situation were reversed, June would know what to do. She'd call the right people and organize a fitting funeral. He's never been the one in charge of the practicalities of life. There was always a plane to catch, a story to follow. Always something more important.

When he looks ahead, he sees blackness, stretching forward. He can't imagine her not being here. He can't bear the thought of this house, with only the past to placate him. All that is left, waiting.

He knows he should call his son and tell him his mother is dead. He imagines picking up the receiver, waiting for Ralph's voice on the line.

He walks back across the garden. The air is fresh and it has grown dark. In the kitchen window, he thinks he sees June's silhouette in the dimness, and feels a searing relief. But when he reaches the kitchen, no one is there.

In the hallway, he stands in front of the telephone. He lifts the receiver to his ear, dials the number. The phone rings. Rook waits until the ringing turns to a dial tone before he replaces the phone.

He goes to the old computer on June's desk, surrounded by her things. An electricity bill sits on top of the keyboard, and he moves it aside, powering the thing up. The screen opens onto their email inbox: the one they use for everything. There are ten new emails: invitations to events in London, to exhibit, questions from his agent. He ignores them, opening a new message, typing the words before he can stop himself. His nerve is holding out, but he isn't sure when it might fail him.

Dear Ralph, he types, *Sorry to tell you like this, but your mother is dead. I tried to call. I have to go away for a while. I'll write when I get there. Don't be angry. Dad.*

He hits send. His hands shake as he climbs the stairs towards the attic. He finds his kitbag, dusty underneath an old lampshade. Opening it on June's bed, everything is just as he left it. His combat trousers, his flak jacket. A mosquito net. A smell swims towards him, of his old hotel room, of the past. He knows what he will do. It is time, at last, to return.

*

He doesn't wait until the morning. He packs anything he can think of into his bag, swinging it into the boot of the car.

The roads open out before him, quiet tunnels of darkness, glowing white lines. The motorway is deserted. He knows his euphoria is not appropriate. But he can't deny it: this feeling of being unbound at last.

When was the last time he travelled this far from the village? His retirement party at Tate Modern, ten years ago. Organized by the newspaper: a parting gift, an apology. The lights across the river had trembled on the black water, expanding across the surface like stars. The Millennium Bridge, newly built then, had hung suspended – a glowing line leading towards the dome of St Paul's.

It was a nice party: sparkling wine with all the appearance of champagne, black-bow-tied waiters with trays of tiny, perfect canapés that all tasted the same. *Not afraid to spend money now I see*, Rook had wanted to say to the new editor, who'd told him they couldn't afford him any more.

'Your work is art,' he'd said, his smile making Rook's muscles tighten. 'And we've been lucky to have you. But times have changed. We can get a freelance shot for a tenth of one of your images.' He'd put his hand out to shake Rook's. 'We wish you all the best.'

What could he say? *I'll take less, too. Just let me keep on working.* He'd been stalemated by his own experience. As if all the stripes he'd earned through the years were shackles. As if a World Press Award was a bad thing. So he'd nodded, shaken the man's hand, and attended the party, where they talked about his career as if he was dead.

And he'd felt it, hadn't he? The days when he could follow the story, taking off on a whim, were over, his world contracting around the house and the village. He'd walked the fields and woodland, trying to carve out a routine. But staying still was as alien to him as walking on the moon. It made him irritable, turning him into the sort of man he didn't want to be. A man like his father, prowling their terraced house like a caged tiger.

At the airport, the desks sit under a midnight hush. He still remembers the words to use, to get onto a flight and into the best seat. The woman he speaks to is calm, listening to his destination, finding him a reserve spot on a flight leaving soon. He glances at the swell of cleavage under her blouse and wishes, again, that he was still a young man.

He finds the bar and orders a whisky. The old ritual – a stiff drink, a newspaper, an equipment check – is comforting in its nostalgia. He smiles as he looks out over the waiting planes, glowing in the spreading blue of dawn.

As they ascend, Rook looks down at the shrinking airport, at the cars crawling along grey roads, cutting through the patchwork fields of England. Like a toy town. Sitting in his wide, business-class seat, he wishes the hostess hadn't made him stow his cameras. He wants to take a photograph, of the world he is leaving behind.

*

Rook must have fallen asleep. A woman's face swings across his vision: the air hostess, her hair pulled back into a bun, her eyebrows too high.

'Are you all right, sir?' she asks. 'You were shouting out, in your sleep.'

'I'm sorry,' he says. The passenger across the aisle looks away.

'It's fine. Let me know if you need anything at all.'

When she is gone, he tries to draw his dream towards him. June, trapped in frozen glass. He was trying to break through to her, but she couldn't hear him.

After the war, when he would wake up from a nightmare, June would always be waiting. She'd draw him towards her, and feeling her slow, calm heartbeat through her chest, his muscles would loosen, his dream dispersing.

In the dark cocoon of the aeroplane, surrounded by sleeping people, Rook feels his loss keenly. Every version of June is gone. The woman who'd stood with arms folded in the kitchen window, her resentment like a language only he could understand. But also the one who'd still loved him: who'd tried so hard to fix what couldn't be fixed.

He pushes the thoughts from his mind. He cannot think about her now, about all the things he will never be able to say. He longs to close his eyes and meet nothing, only darkness, only silence. But he sees June there, standing at a train window, turning and stepping towards him, and he knows he can never escape.

1961

The day June and Rook finally left their home town for good, it rained: streaks slashing the windows as they pulled out of the station. June stood in the train corridor, peering out, catching her last glimpse of Backton. The high steel of the pithead hanging over the town, and below that, the shadow of the buildings.

Rook raised his camera and caught her side-on in the viewfinder: her pencil skirt and white shirt, her hair neat. At the sound of the shutter, she turned and grinned, and he lowered his camera and stepped over to kiss her.

'It's really happening,' she said. 'We're really doing it.'

He put his arms around June, feeling her breathing in and out as they stood in the gap between the carriages. He felt it again: a gratitude that she existed, that she was here with him.

He'd wanted to buy tickets, but June had shaken her head.

'We can hover in the corridor,' she'd said, 'and hide in the toilets. It'll be fun.'

Rook had agreed, though the money for the fares was in his pocket, just in case.

June had wanted to leave Backton earlier, but Rook was determined to do things properly. To marry her first, to save money.

'None of that matters,' June had said, her eyes bright, 'as long as we have each other.'

But people talked behind their hands in the town, and he didn't want June to be gossiped about. Even if she didn't care, he did. He tried, daily, to see things with her boundless optimism.

They had finally married that summer, on a cloudy, windy day. June had made the dress herself, and they'd picked wild flowers together along the main road for her to wind into her hair and carry as a bouquet. Watching her walk down the aisle of the small stone church towards him, he hadn't been able to stop smiling. He said his words without hesitation, thinking of his father and his brothers and how they'd see he was different now, stronger and better than he had been before. A beautiful wife, a move to London: his life was not going to be like theirs. He couldn't help feeling proud.

His father had been moody at the reception, drinking too much. His mother had found Rook, had seen his clenched fists and tight jaw. *I'll take care of it*, she'd said and managed to drag his father towards home. Rook had been grateful: he didn't need that, not at his own wedding.

Even after they were married, Rook was still hesitant to commit to a moving date. June brought it up at every opportunity. *When we move to London. In the city. The big smoke*. She'd researched areas to live in: showing him advertisements in the national papers for apartments in areas with lovely-sounding names. *Bloomsbury*, *Belgravia*, *Knightsbridge*.

'They look a little out of our price range,' he'd said, gently.

'Maybe now,' she said. 'But not once we get ourselves established.'

She'd already made her *London wardrobe*: dressing up for him one evening in her new dresses and skirts, in every colour imaginable. He'd wanted to ask where she had got the money for the material when they were supposed to be saving, but he couldn't risk her broad smile slipping, the quick irritation he'd seen on her face when she spoke to her mother flashing between them like a shield.

'I can't wait to wear these to castings,' June said. 'I really need to stand out.'

'You don't need a dress to do that,' Rook said, and June smiled as if she didn't quite believe him.

Sometimes, Rook wondered what he'd be doing if he hadn't met June at that dance all those months ago. Would he still be working in the chemist's, taking pictures of the coal-smeared town, of the people who lived here, who'd never really accepted him? He'd still be on the outside of things, looking in. June had pulled him from behind his camera, which had always protected him: she'd made him feel he could live his life like a normal person.

She was so certain that everything would work out in the big city. 'We have to make things happen for ourselves, Rook,' she'd say, unable to entertain the idea that there was any risk in what they were doing, refusing to listen to Rook's doubts that he would find a job. Sitting on their favourite bench at the top of the hill, she'd tell him stories of what their life would be like, as if he was a child at bedtime.

'One day,' June said, 'I'll be acting in the West End, and you'll be having your first exhibition. But – oh no – the opening nights fall on the same day. We'll argue, and then get one of them to change the day, because we'll just be *so important*.'

Rook couldn't imagine it, not really. His photos, in a gallery. Photography felt like his way of seeing the world, of digesting it, and the effect it had on other people always thrilled him: the idea that they might see things the way he did. June's desire to act felt different: not so much a compulsion but a desire to do something exciting with her life, to stand out.

He didn't want to go without some sort of job opportunity, without some way of knowing they'd be OK. When June came to the chemist's to find him, he'd been preoccupied, sitting behind the counter and flicking through a *Life* magazine sent over from America. He wasn't thinking about the photos themselves, but the person who had taken them.

He heard the bell: June's familiar silhouette was outlined in the doorway. With the light behind her, she was in darkness. When she stepped forward, an odd, bright smile hovered on her face, as if she couldn't keep it away. She was holding a large brown envelope: Rook could see the smeared ink of the stamp in the top right-hand corner, and the address – June's – written in neat cursive letters.

'I have to show you something,' she said.

She opened the envelope, fumbling in her gloves to pull out what was inside. A slip of paper: short and fat. She handed it to Rook. It was a cheque for almost twenty pounds, made out in Rook's name.

'What's this?' he asked.

June grinned, walking across the room to examine something in one of the cupboards, still holding the envelope. 'I knew it,' she said. 'Didn't I always tell you?'

'Tell me what?'

She held out the envelope. 'You should see for yourself.'

Rook opened it. Inside was a flat piece of paper, the layout of a magazine spread. The paper was wrong – too thick – and the images and writing were only on one side. On the right-hand page was something that made Rook's heart stop. One of his own photos, of his father in the pit showers. His face was coal-dark but it wasn't hard to read the expression – disdain – in his tight lips and the whites of his eyes. The light marked out his thinning hair and the white-tiled wall behind him. His muscular arm was pulled across his chest – it made him look defensive, angry.

There was a block of text next to the image, with the

title 'A Hard Day's Dirt'. The lines and letters blurred together. Rook couldn't take his eyes off the photograph: how different it looked, how *real*, now it was embedded into a newspaper page.

'There's a letter too,' June said. 'He asks if you have any more. I only sent one, but you have so many that are just as good. I told you, didn't I?' When Rook looked up, there were tears in June's eyes. 'If you won't listen to me or your mother, listen to him.'

'Who did you send it to?'

'The editor of the *Sunday Times*.'

'The picture editor?'

'No, the actual editor. But the man who wrote back is the picture editor.'

Rook felt his mouth open. *You can't do that*, he almost said, *you can't just send things to the editor of the* Sunday Times. He imagined some thick-jowled, red-faced man, opening June's letter, passing it on to the correct department. He could have been blacklisted, he wanted to say. But he wasn't, was he? And her plan appeared to have worked.

'When did you send it?' he said.

'Last month,' she said. 'I kept thinking you were going to miss it. It'll be in this weekend.'

Rook watched the paper in his hands begin to shake. June was still talking. 'We can show everyone, Rook,' she said. 'Think how—'

Rook reached for her, kissing her right in the middle of the shop. Her body sank into his.

They broke apart. 'Thank you,' he said.

'Can we finally go now?' she said, and he nodded.

So here they were, on the train to the city. Outside, a ribbon of river ran through a field.

When they saw the ticket man coming along the aisle, June pulled Rook into the toilet, shutting the door and locking it, pressing her finger to his lips. They stared at each other, June's blue eyes crinkled at the corners. Rook put his arms around her waist and squeezed, trying to make her laugh, but the man didn't even try the door. When they were sure he'd really gone, they burst out of the toilet. Rook pressed June up against the window, kissing her hard, until they heard the tutting of a passing woman.

June held up her hand, her ring glinting. 'We're married,' she called. But the woman still shook her head.

*

They stayed in a lodging house until they found the apartment. *Crouch End*: not exactly one of the glamorous locations June had been dreaming of. Only two rooms: a kitchen and a bedroom, large enough for furniture but not much else. When they'd looked around, Rook had been sure she would say no. But she'd squeezed his hand. *It'll be a great adventure*, she said.

And it was. Living together, alone, was an exciting experiment. Everything they did together – going to the greengrocer's, buying sheets for the bed – was new. He loved to watch June complete small tasks around the apartment: the slapdash way she would wash a tea cup, how odd she looked in a turban, scrubbing the bathroom floor. For the first time in his life, Rook felt like he was where he was supposed to be.

They went to bed each night in the same bed. Waking up in the mornings and seeing June beside him, her face crumpled with sleep, was wonderful. Sometimes, he'd wake in the night and think he was in his bedroom in Backton, the one he'd shared with his brothers. It was the same dream that had always startled him from sleep: falling through the air. His body lying frozen on the concrete, his arms and legs immovable. But waking up in London, beside June, the dream would leave him more quickly. He'd reach for her, curling his body around hers, closing his eyes again.

Despite how well everything was going, he was starting to worry. When he'd first visited the *Sunday Times*' office on Fleet Street – a tall black and white building, buckled with age – the picture editor, Tony Matthews, had been surprised to see him in person.

'Who did you say you were?' he'd asked.

'Rook Henderson,' he'd said. 'You accepted my photo of the coal miner. A few weeks ago.'

Tony looked blank. Rook had the magazine with him, and he spread it onto the table.

'Ah,' Tony said. 'That one. I remember now. Great shot.'

'I was wondering if you had any work.'

Tony frowned. 'Don't you live up north somewhere?'

'I've moved to the city,' Rook said, feeling foolish.

He smiled. 'I have to say I admire your balls, old chap,' he'd said. 'Sending your photo to Denis, and now coming down here. But we've already got someone on staff. An Oxford man. Best I could offer would be to take a look at your images on a freelance basis. We do take a few outside shots. You're welcome to use our darkroom.'

Since then, Rook had been there every morning, developing anything that was left in the basket, and trailing the streets each afternoon, looking for stories. The new environment offered up a strange alchemy of things that made him raise his camera. Gulls dipping into the river, the long boats further up. His cold, trembling fingers, capturing a man, walking along the path, the rigmarole of the industrial area looming behind him.

It was like it had been at the beginning, when he'd first got his camera. Looking through the viewfinder and seeing the familiar living room, the battered armchair and the rag rug marked out, separate and important in the frame. He remembered holding the heavy machine up to his face and playing with the silver dials. Catching the blackened terraces; a woman on her front step, beating the dust out of a rug. His father, his hands ingrained with coal, sleeping by the fire.

Ever since what had happened when he was a child, he'd always felt most at home behind the camera: as if he was both visible and invisible. Now, the camera around his neck made him feel like a real photographer.

'These are impressive shots, Rook,' Tony said when he

took a few in to show him. 'But they're more social commentary: we don't have stories to go with them. You need to think more about our readership.'

Rook had nodded.

'I'm sorry I can't offer you more,' Tony had said, and Rook could tell he meant it.

June was trying too: going to castings, meeting directors. At the beginning, she'd managed to keep her spirits high, but they'd been here almost a year now and recently she'd been coming back quiet, her face pinched and tired-looking. She'd started smoking too.

'There's just so many people,' she said, sitting on the kitchen counter. 'Queues and queues of girls, all dressed so nicely and well turned out. I feel like a stray dog who's wandered in by mistake.'

'You're beautiful, June,' he'd said.

He was shocked to see tears in her eyes. 'I just didn't think it would take us this long,' she said. 'I know it sounds stupid, but I thought we'd take London by storm.'

Rook took her hands, bringing his face close to hers. 'We will,' he said. 'Just wait.' It felt good to be the one who was buoying them along, for once.

She wrapped her arms around his waist. 'It doesn't help that it's so bloody cold,' she said.

They clung to each other at night in the small bed, smothering themselves with blankets to keep the cold out. June would shriek if he pressed his foot against her, shuffling closer to his warm torso. Then suddenly they would be kissing and the moment would turn to something else. They'd make love with a sort of fervour, as if to remind themselves of what they had, that it was all they needed. After, they'd lie in the darkness, talking about everything they hoped would happen.

'Tell me a story,' he'd say, and she knew what he meant immediately.

He'd close his eyes and listen to June telling stories about meals in fancy restaurants, about people asking for her autograph. Even when the doubts crowded in about his own career, he could always imagine June's. Her name on a billboard outside a theatre near Piccadilly Circus, going to find her in her dressing room with a bouquet of flowers. She was the propulsion behind them: it only seemed fair that she would be rewarded. And she cared more about those things than he did. He just wanted to take photos, to feel he was doing something important.

'Tell me another,' he'd say, into the darkness.

*

It was nearly two years until anything changed. If they'd known it would be that long, would they have kept going, would they have stayed? By then, June barely left the fifth-floor apartment, with its low ceilings and walls splattered with greeny-black clouds of damp. It was too cold, she said, and there was too much to do. Usually, he'd find her at the sewing machine in the bedroom. The familiar rat-tat-tat, her presence in the apartment. Or in the kitchen, her bare feet on the lino. Scraping together a meal for two from a leek, a potato and an onion.

Tonight, he'd come home early for the first time in weeks. The city was finally thawing: it felt strange to no longer see the snow, hanging over rooftops and cars, crowning the tops of walls and fountains. The Coldest Winter Since Records Began. June worried about the spring flowers – how they would ever make it through these harsh conditions, her brow crinkling in a way that made Rook's chest ache. The cold and the darkness, hounding them for months, had finally given them a reprieve.

By the time he reached the black door with the wonky numbers and climbed the five flights of raggedly carpeted stairs he was out of breath. Despite the chill of the streets, he was hot under his coat and he pulled it off. When he first pushed open the door it was dark, and he thought the apartment was empty. Had the electricity gone out again?

The street lamp outside threw a square of orange onto the peeling wallpaper. There was a line of light underneath the kitchen door.

June was sitting on the end of the counter, swinging her legs against the Formica cabinet, smoking a cigarette. She was facing the sash window, which was open about an inch, letting the freezing air into the room. She turned, her knobbly spine protruding. How loose the old white dress from Backton was on her now, how faded it looked. She'd been begging for new material for weeks.

'We can't afford it,' he said, the words used so often they'd been stripped of their meaning.

Her eyes were ringed with black liner and she was wearing powder: she'd even pencilled in her eyebrows.

'I didn't expect you this early,' she said. 'I haven't made dinner yet.'

'Don't worry.'

'There's some gin on the table,' she said, lighting another cigarette.

'How was your day?' Why didn't he just tell her? Put her out of her misery.

She shrugged, examining her chipped fingernails. 'I had a casting.'

'You did? Why didn't you tell me?'

'It was last minute. I didn't get it. They said they'd keep me in mind.'

'That's good.'

'It's not,' she said. 'I'd rather they said nothing.' Her eyes were glistening, the anger hovering just below the surface.

'You'll get something,' Rook said.

She smiled tightly. 'I hope so.'

'I got a story today.'

'A real one?'

Rook nodded. 'The Aldermaston march,' he said.

'What happened?'

'I was in early. Tony sent me out.'

Going in to the office every day had finally paid off. When he'd got there, all the desks were empty, and the contract photographer, William, was nowhere to be seen. He often came in late, smelling of old beer and after-shave, leaving his rolls of film for Rook to develop before heading out again for an 'appointment'. Rook had been developing some blurry shots, hardly any of them usable, when he'd heard the knock on the darkroom door.

'Just a minute,' he'd called.

When he emerged, Tony's secretary was waiting. 'Tony wants to see you, Rook,' she said. 'He's in his office.'

As Rook entered, Tony stood up, pushing his glasses back. 'Oh, it's you. Good. The Aldermaston march starts today. We need to get someone down there.'

'What about William?'

'He's not in yet, is he?' Tony grinned. 'It's your lucky day. You'd better take the train.'

'Thanks, Tony. I really appreciate this.'

'No time for that.'

Rook made it to Paddington for the 8:43 train towards Aldermaston. He had an idea to intercept them at Reading, and when the train arrived he rushed out of the station onto the main street. He spotted a crowd outside a coffee shop; Rook could see a sign: 'Reading University Against Nuclear Weapons'. The woman holding it was wearing a bright red coat and a tartan scarf.

'Excuse me,' he asked her. 'Are you waiting for the Aldermaston march?'

The woman nodded.

Rook stood outside a cafe, taking a few photos of the

waiting crowd, which increased in size as time passed. Eventually, a child wearing a blue hat pointed towards the horizon. 'They're coming!'

The marchers were approaching, the sounds of their singing filling the air. Something about Hiroshima and children dying. Rook remembered the march from the year before: the photos he'd developed for William had been of a much smaller crowd. This one was huge: ten people wide and snaking back almost as far as he could see.

Rook readied his camera, checked the settings again, patting the pocket where he kept his spare films. He tried taking some photos from ground level, but only the first few rows of people were visible. He spotted a tree at the edge of a little square of grass and levered himself up the trunk. On the left was a row of tall narrow trees with feathery branches. He got some shots of the banners and signs, people massing below them. He shot as many as he could, hoping the exposure would be right: the upper branches were darkening the shots.

A song had started up again further up the line. The sound of it spread up and down the road, in time with the beat of their steps on the tarmac. Rook felt like the ground was humming, like the rough bark of the tree he was clinging to was vibrating with their music. From the ground it had sounded tuneless: just people's voices. But from up here, the song sounded beautiful.

He imagined them all, lying on the polished floor of some community centre or town hall tonight, drinking soup that someone had heated up for them and handed round, making jokes and singing. Perhaps one of them would stand up and give a speech, and they'd all listen and nod to each other, and they'd get a warm strong feeling that they were doing something important.

He wished he could go with them. But he had to get the photographs back to the office. If he wanted them in tomorrow's paper, he knew he must catch a train as fast as he could. He climbed down from the tree, bracing his knees for the drop, returning to the station.

Back at the office, he developed the shots and took them in to show Tony.

'These are great, Rook,' he said. 'Really great. We'll definitely use these five. Get the others out on the wire. There's got to be some benefits to being freelance.'

Rook wanted to thank him, to shake his hand. Instead, he left the room, heading straight for the Wirephoto machine. He'd only used it a few times, and it took him about fifteen minutes to wrap each of the remaining images around the cylinder and get them transmitted onto the news wire. As he watched his photos spin faster and faster, he felt a frisson of excitement that they would be travelling all over the country, and across the sea, re-emerging in news rooms he himself had never visited.

It was almost dark by the time he left the office and made his way home to tell June.

'When will it be in?' she asked.

'Tomorrow, I should think.' Rook felt his excitement again. He knew this was it, what they'd been waiting for.

June leapt off the counter and lunged at him. 'Rook, that's amazing,' she said. 'We should celebrate.'

'I haven't been paid yet,' he said.

'But you will be.'

'What about the rent?'

'It's not due for ages,' she said. 'Please, Rook. I really need this. *We* need it. Can't we go out?'

Rook nodded again. June jumped out of his arms. 'Let me get ready,' she said. 'Though I really don't have anything to wear. Nothing fits me any more.'

'You've lost weight,' he said.

'I know,' she said. 'It's marvellous, isn't it?'

I liked you the way you were, he wanted to say, as she turned to go to the bedroom. What June looked like was nothing to do with who she really was underneath. She was strong – much stronger than him – and brave. He couldn't stand to see that part of her beginning to fade.

*

For a few weeks, things seemed better. Rook sold eleven photos of the march to four different papers. He managed to buy a heater and they went out for dinner to a local Italian, eating everything they'd been dreaming about for months. June seemed to be enjoying the challenge of cooking on a budget again, and she'd made herself some new outfits. She started to go to more auditions too. Rook was able to convince himself that it had only been the cold that had been getting her down.

It seemed that it would go on like this for ever, but of

course, the money started to run out. William was in the office early every day, determined not to miss another lead. They were back to scraping together meals and exchanging false, fair-weather smiles, and Rook was tired of it. He began to realize that he'd been more use to the paper when they'd been in Backton, offering photos of northern life that no one could be bothered to get on a train to take.

On the day that Tony called him into his office, Rook wondered if he was going to let him go. There didn't seem to be anything for him, after all, and goodwill could only get him so far. Tony told him to take a seat without looking up. That couldn't be a good sign, Rook thought.

'We want to put you on contract,' Tony said.

Rook inhaled. 'What about William?'

'Oh, he'll be staying on too.' Tony rested his hands on the desk. 'There's absolutely no obligation to take the new position. We'll still keep you on freelance, and something else will come up eventually. You know we love your stuff: the Aldermaston shots really impressed Denis.' He paused. 'Have you heard what's happening in Vietnam?'

Rook remembered seeing some photographs in *Time* magazine. The greens and browns, the murky water, the taut faces of the people. The stiffness of olive green uniforms.

'I've read a little,' he said.

'Well, things seem to be heating up out there. Not many papers have someone on the ground yet, not even in the US, and we want a head start.' Tony took out a gold cigarette case and slid one out, gesturing the rest to Rook, who shook his head. 'What do you think?'

He imagined himself emerging from a plane onto a dusty airfield and his heart sped up. 'I'd have to think about it.'

'Of course,' Tony said, 'we'd pay you a wage here, and all your expenses in Vietnam would be covered – food, hotel, car, whatever. So your salary could essentially stay here, untouched, for your wife. It would be fairly generous, too – due to the nature of the assignment.'

'I'll need to talk to her. When would you want me to leave?'

'As soon as possible,' Tony said. 'It's not showing any signs of slowing down. Short term at first, and we'll see how it goes.' Tony stood up and brushed down his grey suit. 'Go home. Think about it. But I can't see you staying here for ever, Rook. You're just not that kind.'

Rook shook his hand and walked out of the office, past the clack of typewriters, past the darkroom, down the dimly lit staircase and out onto the rush of Fleet Street. The sunlight was muted by the haze over the city, the sky still holding on to blue. He stood for a moment on the steps of the office, watching the glimmer of cars and taxis leading down towards the river. Turning the other way, he could see the domed outline of St Paul's. He turned and walked towards the tube.

He found June in the bedroom, standing in front of the wardrobe wrapped in a towel.

'You're back early,' she said, turning.

'Tony's just offered me a job.'

'That's great news,' she said.

Rook sat on the edge of the bed. 'It's overseas.'

'Oh,' June said. 'Where?'

'Vietnam.'

'Isn't there a war there?'

'There's not much going on yet,' Rook said, though he wasn't sure this was true.

June was looking down at her hands. 'It sounds like you want to go,' she said.

'They'd pay for everything, so the salary would be here for you. We could move somewhere nicer, and we'd have more money. It would solve a lot of problems.'

'But you wouldn't be here.'

'I know. It wouldn't be for ever.'

'I need to think about it.'

Rook took her hand. 'So do I,' he said. 'I don't want to do anything we're not both happy with.'

Rook wasn't able to think of anything else. At night, he lay looking at the orange edge of the blind, listening to the traffic rumbling along the street below them. He imagined himself getting on a plane: leaving England for the first time, heading to a war. He saw himself clad in grimy army fatigues with the beginnings of a beard, traipsing through a jungle. Was he really the sort of man who could do that? He wanted to find out.

He was pretty sure June was awake, lying beside him, her mind shuttling back and forth over the decision too. He knew he couldn't try and persuade her. What would he do if she said no? He didn't let himself think about it.

Three days later at dinner, June brought it up.

'I think you should go.'

Rook looked at her, her face open, as if she was offering him a gift. 'Are you sure?'

June nodded. 'It's a great opportunity. Maybe you being gone will give me the incentive to get out and do more auditions.'

Rook grabbed June's hand across the table.

'Thank you, June.'

'No,' June said. 'Don't thank me. We came here for this, to make something of ourselves.' She raised her water glass. 'Congratulations, Rook.'

*

Tony invited them for dinner at his club before Rook left. When he asked, Rook was flattered, finally mustering up the courage to thank him, not just for the invitation, but for all the opportunities he'd offered.

'Don't be silly, old chap,' Tony said. 'You've proved yourself. I'm not doing you any favours.'

June fussed over what to wear, adjusting and readjusting a new blue dress. She'd bought it with a chunk of his first proper salary: the first one since they moved she hadn't made herself. When she finally emerged from the bathroom, dress just above the knee, her hair out of its rollers, her face bright, Rook re-experienced, if only for a moment, the feeling he'd had when he'd first seen her on the steps of the town hall.

'You look beautiful,' he said.

June smiled. 'I didn't want to show you up,' she said.

They took a taxi. June quizzed him on the name of Tony's wife, which Rook couldn't remember.

They were shown to Tony's table, in a bay window looking out over a darkened garden.

Tony and his wife stood up, her pearls gleaming in the soft lighting. 'You must be June,' Tony said. 'Just as lovely as I imagined.'

June blushed, and they sat down. As they ate, Rook watched June, aware of her carefully playing the part of the graceful wife, of someone who fitted in in these luxurious surroundings. When she knocked over the salt, Rook saw her hands shake as she righted it, and he wanted to put his own hand over hers, to tell her she was behaving perfectly.

'We got you a gift,' Tony said after they had finished their desserts. His wife slipped a large paper bag out from under the table. 'The least we could do, for a man heading off to war.'

Rook opened the bag. 'This isn't—' he started, looking at Tony.

'Just open it,' Tony said.

Rook lifted out the gold box, revealing the letters embossed onto the side. *Nikon F.*

'I can't believe you've done this,' Rook said.

'We can't have you using that old thing out there,'

Tony said, indicating the old Rolleicord on the table, the one that had been his grandfather's. 'You'll be laughed out of the country.'

'This is too much,' Rook said. But he wanted to open the box and lift the camera out, to hold it in his hands.

'Now you've got no excuse not to get the best pictures out there.'

Rook smiled inwardly. He was really going.

TWO

As they descend into Saigon, Rook's palms begin to sweat, trepidation looming like a memory. He remembers this feeling, from the first time he arrived in country, decades ago. His first war; his first real assignment.

Saigon was the greatest love I've ever had, and the greatest I ever will. He remembers saying that in an interview once: then looking up and seeing June, waiting next to the cameraman. The hurt on her face, quickly covered with the appropriate smile. Had he said it to injure her or because it was true?

Ears popping, he moves to look out of the window, at the sway of the river looming through the cramped patchwork of buildings, tracing its way towards the coast. Below the clouds, the blurred lines of monsoon rain are lit silver. The land around is all dazzling greens: the banana trees, the rice fields, the rubber plantations.

Rook shuts his eyes, remembering the sound of whapping rotors. His knees ache as if he is back there, ready to bend and jump: he feels, for a moment, the splash of cool water, the heavy cling of wet material against his legs. He can already taste the air in his mouth, thick and dense with moisture, and he swallows, reaching for the last sip of his whisky.

He opens his eyes. A baby is crying, and the passengers around him sit still, staring straight ahead.

When they're told it's safe to disembark, Rook stands but he is breathing too fast; he sits and waits for the feeling to pass. The stewardess moves to help him, but he bats her away.

'I'm fine,' he says and she shrugs and turns away, back down the narrow aisle.

*

Outside on the runway, people are in his way, pushing to get onto the already overcrowded bus which will take them to the terminal. An image shuttles towards him: the mesh windows of the military bus, the smell of other men and the sound of singing. A dusty airfield surrounded by odd trees, their branches blown horizontal. The heat, the air shimmering on the horizon.

When the bus stops, he follows the other passengers towards the double doors of the brand-new building. Inside, the air conditioning thrums. He is relieved by the arrival procedure, by having instructions to follow. And he is glad of the wait for his bag, disappointed when it arrives early. There is nothing left for him to do but walk through the exit doors.

Palm trees stand unmoving before the grey tarmac; the rows of car roofs wink. There is a crowd waiting: the rush before the post-lunch lull.

Men shout, surging forwards. 'Taxi, sir. Taxi.'

Automatically, Rook starts walking, letting them trail him. 'How much?' he says.

He halves the price the man gives him, keeping his pace. One man falls away, shaking his head, leaving only two. They barter it out, and Rook walks with one towards his car.

In the taxi, rushing through the wide streets swamped with motorbikes, he is afraid to look out of the window. When he does, the place he knew is unrecognizable, hidden behind neon signs and tall new buildings, reflecting the harsh light. Even the street names are different. The city name.

Fear'll keep you alive. Henry's voice, in his head.

As they drive closer to the centre of town, vines wind their way around lampposts, ancient tree roots buckle the roads. The old facades rise up among the new: the cathedral with its two turrets and large circular window, like a ghostly Notre-Dame. The presidential palace squats behind vast gates, bordered by the perfect lawn. A park, where people play music and drink coffee under trees.

The same streets he walks in nightmares are now here before him. In his mind, he's suddenly running. Quickening breaths fill his chest. The others are still with him, up ahead. He calls out, telling them to stop. But the car comes out of the darkness, headlights off, the moon bouncing on the windscreen. The windows begin to roll down, and Rook's eyes snap open.

He is there again, in the square with the opera house at the centre. The tall frontage of the hotel is like a mirage. Fresh white paint, columns in the colonial style: reinstated grandeur. For a moment, Rook cannot move. It is only when the driver gets out and opens the door for him that he steps out into the blinding sunlight.

1963

Rook waited in the shade outside the dirty Continental Palace. He couldn't get used to the heat, pressing into him at night, moistening the hotel sheets. There was the smell too, of things growing. He stood in the shade of a wonky tree, watching a lizard clamber up the bark. The square ahead of him was already alive, the beeping of horns becoming louder and more insistent as vehicles circled the grand old opera house.

Three white-uniformed concierges stood at his side, leaning against the shutters at the street-facing bar and talking in Vietnamese. They laughed as the car arrived, the engine struggling. As the driver passed over the keys and took the money, he grinned, his bottom teeth blackened. Rook knew then he'd paid too much.

Inside, there was the smell of damp and burnt rubber. Dirt, embedded into the creases of the leather. The petrol gauge was almost full, and despite a sputter when Rook first turned the key, it started. He twisted the dials to get some air flowing. No luck.

Weaving through bicycles, motorbikes and pedicabs, he pulled out of the courtyard. Leaving Saigon, he took the straight road towards the Delta, cutting through paddy fields that glowed under the hot, cloudy sky. He passed dilapidated concrete towers from the French war, empty now. Crouching in nearby fields were the tilted triangular hats of women working the land. He'd had dreams last night of narrow roads teasing their way through jungle: but out here, everything was flat and open and he could see for miles.

Henry, the American journalist he'd met in the hotel bar last night, had drawn him a hurried map on a paper napkin, showing him where he'd find the Seminary. 'Keep straight on Highway 4 and you can't miss the turning,' he'd said, his voice gravelly from cigarettes. He'd come over from a laughing group of white men on the other side of the room and introduced himself, pushing his round glasses back onto his nose as he offered his hand. He had smooth dark hair in a side parting and looked more like an accountant than a journalist.

Later in the evening, Henry had even organized a collection of bits and pieces from the other journalists: whatever they had left over from that day's patrol or found in their rooms. A mosquito net, a cased canteen, a jackknife, a few cans of food, toilet paper, brown water-purification tablets and aspirin. He'd need more for an overnighter, and Henry promised to take him shopping. Someone had even lent him a battered copy of *A Short Guide to News Coverage in Vietnam*, written by Saigon's longest-standing correspondent.

Rook had been so relieved to have some help he'd

almost hugged him. When he asked Henry how long he'd been in Vietnam, the man grinned. 'Not as long as you might think. I'm a fast learner.'

'Can I buy you a drink?' Rook said. 'I owe you.'

'If you're back tomorrow night, you're on. It might be a small one, but it's still a war.'

Rook still wasn't sure if he'd been joking. He'd read the guide in his room last night: there were warnings, particularly under *Some Pointers on Guerrilla Warfare*, that had made his bowels loosen. *Lie prone under fire, and move only on your belly. When possible, step in exactly the same places as the soldier ahead of you. If he wasn't blown up, you probably won't be.*

He hadn't yet ventured further than Saigon airport since he'd arrived the week before. He'd spent the first few days in his hotel room, sleeping off the jet lag and trying to get used to being so far from home. Each time he'd woken up, his body recognized the new environment before his mind: the beeping of horns outside the window, the clamminess of the air. Gradually, he'd remember where he was: that June wasn't beside him, that he was completely alone.

He'd known, of course, that he was heading for a war zone. But before arriving, he'd started to believe his own reassurances to June and his mother that it was safe. The idea that it was temporary, that he could leave at any time, had made it seem easier to deal with. But when he headed out into the unfamiliar city each morning in the hope that the war would present itself, his fear had become more and more insistent. A low churning in his stomach, a ghostly feeling that made him think of the cramped house where he grew up.

Passing underneath some umbrella-shaped trees with startling red flowers, a quiet voice told him to turn back. Was it June's? He'd written to her last night, telling her he'd arrived safely, but who knew when his letter would reach her? He'd longed to call her, to hear her voice on the line. He missed her more than he'd expected: her laughter, the way she talked to him. Without her positivity, his doubts surrounded him.

Henry had told him they could make international calls at the radio station, but they were expensive and the lines were bad. He'd laughed when he'd mentioned calling London. Only Paris or Tokyo, and only for serious business.

Rook's fingers clenched around the steering wheel. He took the next left as Henry had said, flipping the indicator, though the road behind him was empty except for the clouds of red dust thrown up by his tyres. A barbed-wire fence surrounded a concrete border wall topped with jagged shards of glass. Ahead, he made out a long orange-roofed building. The telltale military jeeps were lined up outside, along with mountains of sandbags.

As Rook parked the Citroën, jerking the gear stick as he tried to get it in reverse, he felt the eyes of a group of barefoot Vietnamese children on him. He wiped his forehead on the sleeve of his new khaki shirt, opening the door onto the courtyard. The children didn't move. Their faces were smeared with grime, their eyes bright. Rook wondered what the hell they were doing out here. But this was their country, after all, not his. He raised his new camera, half-expecting them to scarper like startled animals, but their expressions didn't change.

The building was raised a little from the ground: Rook could make out some figures moving in its shadowy underbelly. As he got closer, he saw they were carrying sacks of something towards two of the parked jeeps.

Most of the men were Vietnamese, which Rook hadn't expected. There was the tall outline of a white man with broad, muscular shoulders. He was facing Rook: had he seen him?

'Excuse me,' Rook said. 'I'm looking for John Friday?'

Stepping forward into the light, the man wiped his hands on his mucky combat trousers. He had high cheek-bones, quick-shifting eyes and a square-edged crew cut. His shirt sleeves were rolled up neatly above the elbow, revealing an expanse of brown skin brushed with golden hairs.

'I'm him,' he said, in a deep Southern drawl.

Rook swallowed. 'Rook Henderson,' he said, putting out his hand.

Friday's handshake was firm to the point of being painful. 'Interesting name.'

'It's a nickname,' Rook said. 'From childhood.'

The man folded his arms across his chest. 'Press?'

'Photographer. For the *Sunday Times*. Henry Peters from the *New York Times* sent me down.'

Friday smiled, revealing a row of perfect white teeth. 'Henry's cool,' he said.

'I just arrived in Saigon last week.'

'Brit?'

Rook nodded.

'Well, welcome to the Seminary,' Friday said. 'We like to make you folks feel at home down here.'

'Thanks,' Rook said, hoping he was being sincere.

'We're headed to a suspected Cong village further south if that sounds like your bag?' Friday said. 'We'll be out all day, back here by nightfall.'

'I'd love to come along, if that's all right,' Rook said.

'I just invited you, didn't I?' Friday laughed. 'I love you Brits. Always apologizing for sweet fuck all.'

They made their way to the airstrip, a six-mile walk. There were at least a hundred Vietnamese soldiers, flanked by fifteen or so towering Americans, all weighed down with more stuff than Rook could imagine carrying in this heat. The bulge of grenades in their combat jackets, weapons slung easily across their chests.

They walked fast along narrow roads bordered by high vegetation and Rook struggled to keep up. He remembered the patter of his brothers' feet, always ahead of him.

Friday fell into step beside Rook.

'First time out?' he asked.

'I've been trying to get my bearings.'

'Where did you try?'

'The MACV, the press meetings.'

Friday waved away a mosquito. 'There's your problem,' he said. 'You won't get much out of those creeps in Saigon. Lips tighter than their assholes.'

'They don't seem to like journalists,' Rook said.

'They're just very wary. Don't want to give you guys a good look at what's going on here. I keep telling them, if you act like you're hiding something, people are only gonna get suspicious.'

'And are they?' Rook said. 'Hiding something?'

Friday threw him a cryptic smile. 'I guess you'll see for yourself.'

Tan Hiep airstrip was a vast clearing of patchy land, surrounded in the far distance by banana trees. Just next to the strip itself, the grass was pooled wet from the monsoons, and beyond that, miles and miles of paddy fields spread, stalks of rice sticking up above the surface of the silver water. The huge blue sky above them made Rook lightheaded.

The men lined up in neat formation, ten Vietnamese and one American to each chopper. The Vietnamese had their sleeves rolled up, in the manner of Friday. As they straightened their too-large helmets and readjusted their ammo belts, Rook thought how much they looked like children, playing at war.

Friday was whistling beside him, his broad forearms crossed over his chest, rocking back on his booted heels.

'They look scared,' Rook said.

'They're fucking terrified,' Friday said. He clapped his hands, startling a nearby soldier. Rook raised his camera:

Friday's broad torso was silhouetted, his gesticulating arms dwarfing the small fearful faces in front of him. 'That's the whole problem. They don't want to fight. If they're scared of me, for fuck's sake, what are they going to do when they meet the Cong?'

Rook looked through the viewfinder, the blood rushing in his ears. He wanted to do justice to it all: the sounds of cicadas from the paddy fields; the dense, maddening heat; the wide-eyed blankness of the men's faces.

They could hear the dull roar of the engines long before the helicopters appeared, flying in a long curved line towards the runway, like musical notes. As they came closer, the thwack of rotors filled Rook's mind, blowing his hair back. They lowered themselves one by one. As he looked at the gaping door where they were supposed to climb in, Rook felt vertigo.

Friday was shouting, the words lost. Whatever he was saying, the soldiers seemed to understand, jogging in a neat line as the helicopter jerked to an almost stop, its three wheels kicking up wet gravel.

Rook watched as the men ran forward, grabbing at a handle on the inside of the door and pulling themselves up. He copied, and after a brief moment of almost-calamity when his arms felt too weak to hold him, he was in the belly of the thing, crammed back against a thin metal wall, alongside a crowd of trembling soldiers. They pulled out extra flak jackets to sit on, dropping their packs at their feet.

There were already three Americans in the helicopter: the pilot, co-pilot and one other in the crescent of shadow behind the door hole, his upper arms holding onto a gun that pointed out. He was chewing gum, his jaw tense. Friday and he made eye contact, and the man took one hand off the gun to shake Friday's.

As the helicopter rose, Rook looked out at the flat mirage of greens, oranges and blues, lifting his camera instinctively and catching the trail of helicopters rising behind them. His fear was changing into something else: exhilaration.

He took a step forward, directing his viewfinder towards the cockpit of the machine, where two long-bodied American pilots had their eyes trained straight ahead.

Someone tugged on his arm.

'Try not to get the round-eyed pilots,' Friday said. 'We're supposed to be "advisors", not running the show. First time in a chopper?'

Rook smiled. 'That obvious?'

Friday shrugged. 'You'll get used to it. You should see the little things they have up North. Barely hear 'em coming. Not like these clunky things. Korea issue. Not much chance of sneaking up on the Cong in these.' He tapped the wall with a meaty fist.

'You must have them running scared,' Rook said.

'They were. Shit scared, last year, when we brought them over. But they've started digging in and fighting back. At Ap Bac, we had some shot down. Officially two, but I was there, and we lost eight.' He gritted his teeth. 'They're tough little fuckers, the Cong. Sometimes, I think us and them'd make a stellar team. Don't quote me on that though.'

Rook was about to tell Friday that he was only a photographer, that he wouldn't be quoting anybody, but the man had turned to yell at a soldier whose drooping head suggested he was falling asleep.

'Un-fucking-believable,' Friday said.

Rook wiped sweat off his brow again. 'You'll get used to it,' Friday said. 'Make sure you drink plenty of water.' He slapped Rook on the back hard and hooted with laughter. 'Fuck me, I sound like your mother. The village we're headed for is Cong. We're pretty sure of that. Enemy fire reported. Problem is, the men only return there at night, and if by some stroke of luck they're there, they'll hear the 'copters and flee. Most of these missions are a fucking write-off. Just how these guys like it.' He gestured to the row of silent eyes watching them. 'Don't you, fuckers? No action, make happy, yeah?' Friday waved his hand in front of one of their faces, provoking a stuttering of blinks, like butterflies' wings. 'See, nada.'

'Do they understand English?' Rook asked.

'How the fuck would I know?' Friday said. 'If they do, they never let on. I could dance around this chopper in my birthday suit and I swear they'd act like nothing was happening. The only time they do react is under fire, and that's to crawl on the ground and cover their asses. Fucking useless.'

Rook looked again at the row of stationary soldiers clutching their guns to their chests, looking past Rook and Friday, or through them.

Once on the ground, Rook followed Friday and the men through calf-deep water. The wind was strong, and he kept his head down, watching the now horizontal blades of rice grass, all rushing in one direction, like water flowing towards a plughole.

As they moved, the water got deeper, until it was up to Rook's waist. Holding his camera higher, he waded on. The men were faster than he thought they'd be and he was glad he only had his two cameras, flak jacket and a small pack to worry about.

Now, there was only the wet mud, the open land all around him, and the other soldiers. They were completely exposed. Hearing Friday's sure step behind him, he forced a blankness to fall over his features and felt an odd rush of something familiar; the fear and the tense strain of having to hide it. He let himself close his eyes for a second, and behind them, he saw his father's hands. The fingers white around the knuckles, the fingernails – short and square – still ingrained with coal dust.

Ahead lay a dense mesh of vegetation. Among the greens, Rook could see some straw roofs. A village. Following Friday – like some oversized cartoon figure with his long legs and big booted feet – they moved around the edge of it in a long line. There were only ten men with them now, the others having split off to surround the houses.

At Friday's whispered instruction, one of the Vietnamese soldiers ducked through the narrow space in the trees, slashing through the densest sections with a long, curved knife. It was painfully slow: every snap of a twig, every footstep, sent echoes into the surrounding foliage.

There were markings scratched into some of the trees closest to the houses, and Rook raised his camera and took some shots. A red square with a star in the centre. Slogans in Vietnamese, and one in English: *Down with Diem*.

Outside the first house, butterflies circled over the broad, slanted roof; a barking dog was chained to a post dug into the ground. Friday shoved one of the men forward, who resisted, shaking his head until Friday cracked him over the back of the helmet with the butt of his gun. Rook focused and clicked the shutter. The man moved slowly towards the doorway, his arm tensed around his weapon: the door swung upwards, like a cat flap.

Inside, the house was dark, exuding the smell of damp straw. The man's green legs disappeared inside. There was a woman's cry, a long torrent of shouting from the Vietnamese soldier, then the sound of a child wailing. Unable to see what was going on, Rook felt his insides pull together in preparation.

The door opened again: an old woman emerged, bent over, her arms held crookedly above her head. A wiry ponytail hung across her stooped shoulders. Following her was a shirtless boy of five or six with a distended belly and grimy feet. He was sucking his thumb, his wet eyes darting. The soldier followed them, his gun trained on the back of the old woman's head.

When the woman saw the greeting party, she dropped to her knees and began keening, her hands clasped together. The little boy crouched too, pushing his head into her concave stomach, his eyes closed.

Rook looked at the boy through the viewfinder. He was sucking on his fist, his belly lifting and falling, and looked like he might be sleeping, but Rook recognized the way his eyelids fluttered and his fast, shallow breaths. Then, the boy opened his eyes and for one sharp, harsh moment, Rook felt the boy's terror as if it was his own. In an instant, a memory flashed before him, of his father's angry face, the fear that had marked his own childhood. His finger shook as he clicked the shutter, hoping he caught him in time. He wanted to capture that feeling, to make sure the boy's ordeal was not in vain.

Friday said something in Vietnamese, the unfamiliar words barbed. The soldier shouted at the woman, shoving at her temple with his gun. She was shaking her head vehemently, tears falling now across her sunken, age-spotted face. Whatever she was doing wasn't enough: the soldier was becoming agitated. The boy's fists clenched around the bunched, loose material of her trousers. Rook had a pointless desire to step in, to slow down the escalating situation.

Then gunfire started up, at first with no determinate direction. The other soldiers fell to the ground, and Rook followed, his nerves electric. Friday, still on his feet, was shouting something. His rifle was trained on the trees they had just emerged from and he was firing, the tendons in his neck tensed.

'Return fire, you useless fuckers!' he yelled. 'Don't just lie there.'

Rook hadn't been expecting the terrible noise of the guns, and his immediate reaction was to flee. The men lay on the ground, pressing their cheeks into the wet dirt. Slowly, they began to inch their way towards the house. One or two of them raised themselves enough to position their guns, firing low useless shots from where they lay. The dog was still barking.

The VC had been behind them. Did that mean they'd followed them, all this time? Rook dragged himself towards the open door of the house. Cast-iron pots on a low table, a picture of Ho Chi Minh, surrounded by flowers. This was it, he thought, this was what he'd come here to do. He edged around the corner. Friday was crouching behind a pile of rice straw, protected, still shooting out towards the vegetation. Return fire whipped back, slowing now.

Rook raised his camera. He saw the old woman, crawling towards the trees where the fire was coming from, tugging at the little boy, who was lagging behind her. She jerked his arm harder: he cried out. The woman's eyes widened as Friday's head turned. Then his rifle swung round and he shot the woman, three times, in the back. She dropped to the ground with a heavy thud.

Through the viewfinder, it felt unreal. Rook tried to

press his finger down, to capture the scene, but found himself frozen, holding his breath, watching. The boy's mouth was a dark hole in his face, his eyes wide and black with terror. He was screaming, his fingernails scraping at his grandmother's clothing, where blooms of red spread slowly across the material.

Rook found he couldn't look any more. He sank back behind the door, shutting his eyes and telling himself to breathe deeply. What was he doing here if he wasn't going to take photos? Losing it wasn't going to help anyone. But his heart and his breathing were moving too quickly. This was what he'd feared: that he wouldn't be able to do this after all.

The gunfire had stopped, but the barking continued. Rook wondered how much time had passed. When he could move again, he edged around the doorframe. The dog's pink-gummed jaws were snarling at Friday, who was standing nearby shouting instructions into his radio. The woman's body still lay in the dirt, but the boy was gone.

'Medevac. We've got one down,' Friday was yelling. 'We'll get him out. I'll let you know the coordinates when we find an LZ.'

Friday was already moving off, around the other side of the village. When he passed one of the Vietnamese soldiers, groaning on the ground, he stopped and stared down at him.

'Didn't know you could get shot down there, did you?' He spat, a big wet globule curving outwards from his taut lips. He gestured to the two nearest, trembling men. 'Grab him, you two.'

He kept going, without looking back. The other soldiers followed sheepishly, their eyes on the ground. Rook stepped out into the clearing. An eerie silence had fallen. He stumbled along the edge of the houses, at every moment expecting to hear more gunfire. Following the crashes of vegetation, he caught up with the others as they made it to another clearing.

'Here's good,' Friday said. He watched the men lay down the wounded soldier. 'Where's our medic? Med-dic. Where?' One of the soldiers raised his hand. 'Well, what are you waiting for?' Friday said. The man knelt next to the soldier, beginning to unbutton his sodden shirt. Rook took a shot. His third film was almost finished.

Friday looked back at him as if seeing him for the first time. 'Glad to see you're still with us,' he said. 'Got a little more than we bargained for.' He pulled out a crumpled map tucked inside his fatigues and traced his finger along it. He lifted the radio receiver to his mouth. 'Good to go.' Then he turned to Rook again. 'Well, that was a ride,' he said. 'You're looking a little grey, man. You all right?'

Rook felt a tremor of anger. 'Why did you shoot that woman?'

Friday's face darkened. 'She was VC.'

'How did you know?'

Friday gave him a wry smile. 'What did you think that firefight was about?' he said. Then he slapped Rook on the back. 'You'll get used to it. I'll get you out on this chopper.'

There was a far-off beating, like a fan in a hot, still room. Rook looked up. The helicopter was smaller than the ones that had brought the men in, with a round nose.

'Huey's here,' Friday shouted, looking around at the men for some trace of his own excitement. Most of them were sitting or crouching, smoking cigarettes, and didn't even look up. One was running the red dirt through his fingers, which clenched into a fist at the sound of Friday's voice.

The helicopter circled back around and returned, dropping slowly into the clearing. Once it was low enough, two Americans climbed out carrying a stretcher, nodded at Friday, then helped the wounded man onto the bed and turned to carry him back to the waiting copter.

'Wait,' Friday yelled and the guys stopped. 'Room for a press guy?' He gestured at Rook.

They shrugged. 'Sure,' one of them said.

Friday reached forward and shook his hand, his skin rough. 'Looking forward to seeing your shots,' he said. 'Come and see us again some time.'

As the helicopter rose, Rook knew he should be feeling relieved. He was out of there, he was safe. But he couldn't help thinking of those most crucial moments, when he'd turned to stone. And now that boy was still out there, somewhere in the paddy fields or clumps of trees below them, terrified, and Rook hadn't done him justice at all.

As he looked down at his hands, clasping his camera, Rook felt his heart, still beating hard in his chest. The sweat at the back of his neck, the wind of the chopper. He was really here, he thought. He'd done it. He wished his father and his brothers could see him now, at the centre of everything at last. No longer left behind, or deliberately forgotten. He thought of them: in that boring house in their boring town, shuttling between the pub and the pit. As he looked down at the foreign land below him, he felt as if he was clinging on to the eye of the storm, and despite his failure he didn't want the feeling to end.

THREE

At reception, Rook asks for a room, giving his full name. The people behind the desk are too young to remember him, or the war.

He follows a young man up the dim stairway, along a corridor of polished dark tiles. Despite the hum of the air conditioning, fans still hang from the white ceiling. He makes himself look at the old photographs on the walls, the light streaming dustily through the window. It's as if he's holding his breath underwater, seeing how long he can last.

His room is on the floor below the one he had all those years ago. As the man lets him in, he hears a creak from above and wonders if there are tourists up there now, watching television, unaware.

The fittings in the bathroom are unchanged. A basin the shape of a seashell; old brass taps. He turns on the shower, pulling off his clothes, bracing himself for cold water. But of course it runs piping hot now.

Wrapping himself in a towel, he makes himself go to the window and step out onto the balcony. Clutching the filigree barrier, he looks down at the white arches of the opera house. Through the trees, the evening sun glimmers from the glass frontage of the art deco Caravelle Hotel, as if the old building is winking at him.

Beneath the wonky tree, he thinks he sees Henry's long, spindly silhouette, the glow of a cigarette in his hand. His grin, flashing in the stifling sunlight. Like some detective, staking out the place.

When he blinks, the man is gone, and Rook feels uneasy. What is he doing here, so far from home? The sound of the traffic outside, the world that is turning on without him, makes him feel nauseous. He is afraid, to walk out of the hotel, to pace the streets, where so much of the past is lurking. Like his last Saigon days, when he been unable to leave his room while the city was torn apart outside. Except now, there is nothing tangible to be afraid of.

He needs a drink. Opening the minibar, he empties the miniatures into his mouth, one by one. It isn't enough. He dresses and leaves his room, walking out of the bar and the hotel entrance. The streets are still buzzing with traffic: the headlights of motorbikes and taxis glowing in the dusk as people snake their way home. On the pavements around the hotel, stalls are set up, selling bracelets made of shells, scarves, leather handbags. Rook watches a woman reach forward and pick something up, turning it over.

He walks along the main thoroughfare, past the bustle of the indoor markets, towards the winding streets where the locals live. His legs ache and his knees creak, but he keeps going, turning the shadowy bends of narrow lanes, crammed with houses.

The rubbery smell of melting tarmac greets him. He remembers it from other assignments: past rain drying on hot pavements, associated in some way with freedom. He smells frying chicken with fish sauce too, and here and there, there is an open door: a glimpse into a living room or a steamy-aired kitchen, catching floral-wreathed pictures of dead relatives on the walls and the blaring of televisions. Two cats chase each other across Rook's path, and he raises his camera, but is too late to capture them.

This feeling, of being an outsider, is familiar to him. He remembers it from his early days in Vietnam, when he would catch glimpses into lives from the back of Henry's motorbike, and long to understand them. Before that, in the town where he grew up, where he always felt like he didn't fit, as if he was speaking a different language to everyone else. As he walks through the streets, it is as if nothing has changed, as if he has failed, entirely, to find his place.

Soon, he's standing in front of one particular house. The yellow paint is peeling: the door is slightly ajar. Rook steps forward, then stops. He raises his hand to knock. What is he doing here?

The door swings open, and a woman is there. She has grey-black hair in a neat bun, high cheekbones in a lined face.

Her brown eyes widen and her hand flies to her mouth. 'Rook?' she says. The 'k' is absent, as it always was.

He nods. He watches her face change. Then she reaches forward and embraces him.

She beckons him inside. The tiled floor. The metal spiral staircase that Rook has never climbed. A small kitchen: a freestanding gas hob on the sideboard, a pot of coffee beans waiting to be ground. There is a refrigerator now, looming in the corner.

The television is on, without sound. This house was always full of bustle, people chattering in Vietnamese.

He sits on a low plastic stool.

'Tea?' she says.

'Yes please.'

She stops, and turns. 'Or beer?'

'OK. Beer.'

She brings a can of Ba Ba Ba and sits next to him. She opens her mouth to speak, then puts her hand over it. 'English, finish,' she says, laughing. 'For-get.'

Rook smiles too. 'I came to see if you were all right.'

'All right?' she says, confused.

'Yes. You,' he says, pointing at her. 'OK?' He does a thumbs up.

She points at herself. 'Me, OK.' She points at him. 'You?'

Rook sees June, lying in the armchair, the sunlight drawing a line across her face. 'OK,' he says.

Linh's smile fades. 'You sad?' she says. 'Henry?'

Rook takes her hand. 'Always.' He realizes she hasn't understood him. 'Yes,' he says. 'Sad. You?'

Linh nods, placing her free hand over her chest. 'Sad,' she says.

*

Rook keeps expecting the door to open, for people to come crowding into the room. Linh's family, her friends. Even the hammock slung across the corner of the room is empty. She was never alone when he knew her, and this house was never silent. He can't bring himself to think that it is only Linh here now.

He imagines his own stone house in the countryside: the empty rooms, the wardrobe crammed with June's clothes. Her bureau; her handbag, still sitting on the hall chair.

There is the sound of the streets outside, dark now. Linh gets up to make tea, busying herself in the small kitchen, filling the room with the whistle of the kettle. She places a chipped cup in front of him, and he drinks.

She goes to a kitchen drawer, coming back with a stack of photographs, badly faded. Shuffling through them, she hands him one. There he is with Henry and Tom, grinning into the camera, the overexposure of the shot somehow conjuring up the heat of the day.

'Tom,' Linh says, her finger tapping his face in the image.

As Linh says the name, it comes to him: where he has seen the photograph before. It was the cover of Tom's book, the one he published after the war. Rook remembers seeing it in a bookshop. The title – *The Last Photograph* – had made his anger return again. How dare Tom write about what had happened, how dare he make money from it? Some part of him knew he was being unfair: he understood better than anyone the need to preserve a single moment, to make it mean something.

Rook looks at the photograph again, trying to conjure up how he felt, standing between the two men. He looks into his own eyes, looking for some trace of foreboding, but of course there is nothing there.

Linh's finger is still covering Tom's face. 'You see Tom now?' she says.

'No,' Rook says. 'Not for almost fifty years.'

Her face changes, and she takes his hand. 'Here. Friday. Tom.'

She can't mean what he thinks she means. 'Tom is here?'

She nods. 'Friday. Lunch. Tom.'

1963

Driving fast in the impending twilight, through the fields, spread under the fading orange light. Henry's words in his head. *At night, the countryside belongs to the Cong.* But when, exactly, was night time? When was he in danger?

The bustle of the city embraced him. At a junction, the eyes of the street sellers made Rook turn his head: they whispered behind their hands. Battered wooden carts took up the pavements, surrounded by small groups of people sitting on low wooden stools. Off the main street, Rook caught glimpses of lanes humming with activity. Chickens pecking their way down alleyways, skirting the open sewers; children on their way home from school. He longed, for a moment, to know what their lives were like. But then the traffic moved on, and struggling into gear, he followed.

Somehow, he found his way back to the hotel. The cool of the marble reception made him feel dirty. Catching sight of himself in the mirrored lift doors, his dusty, worn-out reflection looked like someone else's.

His room was still there, just as he'd left it. He sat at

the creaking desk and pulled out a sheet of hotel writing paper. His fingers shook around the pen, his mind's eye flashing over the 'o' of the boy's mouth, the way the old woman's body dropped with a thump onto the red earth. How could he explain that to June? He wished that she was here. He'd tell her how he'd watched it all through the viewfinder without doing a thing, how he wasn't sure he wanted to go back out there. Was this what his job was now? Was this what he'd longed for?

He squeezed his eyes tight shut and tried to imagine what she'd say, how she'd reassure him. *Of course you feel out of your depth, dummy, you're in the middle of a war!* He saw her smiling at him, making light of things in a way that took him out of himself.

The sheet of paper was there before him.

June, he wrote, *I don't know what I'm doing here. I went out on my first patrol today, and I was terrified. I froze, darling. I didn't take a single shot. What kind of photographer does that? I'm a fraud.*

He was sweating, the words not quite right. As he slipped the letter into an envelope, he stopped. He imagined June opening the letter in London, saw the crease that would appear on her forehead. She'd worry about him, wouldn't she? It would be months before he was home again.

He took the letter out and started again. *June, Other than missing you, everything is fine here. I met another journalist who is helping me and I went on my first patrol today. I didn't get all the photos I wanted, but there's always next time. I hope all is well there. I miss you, darling. All my love, Rook*

He put the letter in the envelope, then showered and left the room for the bar. A crowd of white men in civilian clothes sat at a table: Rook pretended not to see them. He thought of the first time he'd gone to the pub in Backton, how he'd stood amongst the crush of bodies, hoping that his father would turn and acknowledge him. That hovering feeling of not fitting in.

Henry was standing at his table, a hand on the back of the empty chair. 'How was your day?' he said. 'Did you head out?'

'I found a patrol. With Friday.'

'He's a character.'

'You could say that,' Rook said.

Henry pulled out the chair and sat down. 'Any action?'

'There was actually.'

Henry slapped the table. 'Damn it,' he said. 'Wish I'd come now. See any Cong?'

'Depends on your interpretation. We saw some Cong-sympathetic villagers.'

Henry smiled slowly. 'They all are,' he said. 'Apparently.'

'I don't think I understand,' Rook said. 'The US is protecting the Cong against themselves?'

Henry waved over the waiter and ordered a beer.

'It's complicated. We don't want the Cong's power to spread. But this is their country, and they're protecting it.

They see us as a new version of the French colonialists. It's ironic, really.'

'I thought the US was fighting Communism.'

'We are. But the Cong are really nationalists, and that's a lot easier to sell to the locals. A lot of them *are* the locals. Doesn't help that the government in Saigon is so dodgy. We've got our money on the wrong horse, you might say.'

'President Diem?'

'You haven't met him yet, I take it? His brother's the one you want to look out for, or his brother's wife. It's a bit of a family affair.'

Rook rubbed his temples, his head aching. He wished there was a way to leap forward to a time when it was all clear to him. June's parting gift had been a book about the French involvement in Vietnam, which took the history up to the siege of Diem Bien Phu and the French defeat in 1954, but that seemed antiquated now, outdated.

Henry lit a cigarette, inhaling deeply as the lighter flared. 'You'll get used to it,' he said. 'You don't need as many of the details as us hacks anyway. What is it they say: if your pictures aren't good enough, you're not close enough?'

Rook swallowed, thinking of the woman lying in the dust. How he'd failed to click the shutter. 'Something like that,' he said.

'Have you found anywhere to develop your shots?' Henry asked.

'My office suggested Associated Press?'

'Come to UPI,' Henry said. 'It's just me and Tom. It's a bit of a squeeze, but we have a darkroom.' He smiled. 'I'll swing by and pick you up tomorrow morning.'

*

They set off on the back of a motorbike, zipping down a wide, tree-lined boulevard, ducking and weaving between bicycles. Here and there, hidden beneath irrepressible greenery, were traces of French elegance: the cathedral, shuttered villas with columned facades, a 'town hall' in the traditional style. Plants covered once-white walls. Everywhere, colour and light glimmered.

They pulled into a dusty entrance amongst a row of buildings – a shop selling tyres, hanging like odd earrings; a noodle restaurant, crammed with people; and nestled in between, what looked like a closed shop with a dusty venetian blind covering the front window.

'This is it,' Henry said, pulling off his helmet. 'Our humble abode.' He pushed the door and sighed. 'Tom's always leaving this open,' he said. 'And I've told him I don't know how many times that we should block up that window: it's a security risk.'

The room was long and thin. A sagging brown sofa with a dented pillow stood in front of a low table covered in used mugs. Behind that, two desks faced each other, deep with piles of papers, receipts, detritus and a half-hidden typewriter. The blind blocked out most of the light, casting strange shadows across the far wall onto a wrinkled map of Indochina. A bare bulb hung from the ceiling.

A man was slumped over the far desk, his face pressed onto the typewriter keys, his messy blond hair catching the muted light. Henry walked over and tapped him on the back of the head. The man sat bolt upright, replacing his hands on the keys, his hair sticking up around his face, eyes darting.

'Morning, Tom,' Henry said. 'Working late again?'

Tom cleared his throat. 'I had a deadline,' he said, turning the watch at his wrist. 'Fuck! I still do.' He rubbed his neck, noticing Rook through the gloom. 'Who's this?'

'Rook Henderson,' Henry said. 'Photographer. He just arrived. Was on his way to AP, but I told him he could use our *facilities*.'

They smiled at each other, as if this was a joke.

'Is he any good?' Tom asked.

'Guess we'll find out.'

Rook stepped forward and reached out his hand. 'Nice to meet you.'

Tom sighed. 'You didn't say he was a fucking Brit.'

Henry shoved Tom's arm. 'Be nice, Tom.'

Tom shrugged and turned back to his typewriter.

'I'll show you around,' Henry said.

He pushed open a door Rook hadn't noticed. Inside was a small bathroom: the toilet lid stacked with various plastic trays, a small shelf cluttered with bottles. Above the sink, a clothes line had been strung up.

Henry flicked on the bulb in the ceiling: red light suffused the room. He shrugged when he saw Rook's face. 'AP's is no better,' he said.

'Suppose I'll get to work then,' Rook said, patting his pocket for his films.

Rook sat on the toilet lid in the dim red light. He'd spent the night waking too hot under the sheets, sure he'd heard the sound of the woman's keening, the little boy's scream. He didn't want to see those images again.

He thought about leaving the darkroom, about stepping out into the office and telling the guys he couldn't do it. He imagined taking a taxi to the airport, getting on a flight and returning to June and to London. He could be there in a day, wake up in their bed the next morning. But he'd be back to freelancing, with no hopes of anything else coming up. And he imagined Henry's face, if he admitted he wasn't cut out for all this.

Rook stood up, pulling the negatives from the film before he changed his mind, holding them up to the light. The view from the open helicopter door: a machine-gunner in the foreground, above a patchwork of greens, oranges and browns. A bold line of helicopters marked ARMY in huge white letters. The men splashing through the paddy fields, careless ripples spilling out around their legs. A soldier with a dusty hat and gun, tensed as he kicked at the door of a small rice-straw house. The old woman and the little boy, clutching each other, crouching on the ground. The boy's face, his terror.

As he moved between them, he felt a strange sense of

clarity fall over him. When he looked back on his first patrol, his mind whirred with chaos, with the panicked feeling that he'd held back. The images were better than he'd imagined, focusing everything he'd experienced into a series of still pictures, without the distractions of the moment itself.

As he picked the best ones for the enlarger, and before he lost himself in the process of bringing the images to their full potential, he smiled to himself. The doubts he'd had last night seemed overdramatic now. He was glad he hadn't sent that letter to June. He heard her voice, ringing in his head. *These are really good, Rook. You should show them to someone.*

*

Some time later, he re-emerged to find Henry and Tom at their typewriters: Henry tapping out word after word, as if they were all there in order in his head; Tom hammering the typewriter keys, stopping every few moments, sighing, then starting up again.

Henry glanced up. 'How're they looking?' he said.

'All right.'

'Mind if I take a look?'

'Help yourself.'

Henry opened the door and stepped inside, pausing at each image.

'Tom,' Henry said.

'Just a minute,' Tom murmured, without looking up from his page.

'Tom.' Henry's voice was sharper. 'Get over here.'

Tom sighed. 'I'm on deadline,' he said, 'and I'm already late.'

'Just give me two seconds.'

Tom pushed back his chair and strode towards the bathroom, his hair bouncing. He peered in, then exchanged glances with Henry. 'What paper did you say you were from?'

'I didn't,' Rook said. 'The *Sunday Times*.'

'And you're on contract? They get all your shots?'

Rook nodded.

'You can't sell them on the wire?'

'If the *Sunday Times* don't want them, I can.'

'But they get first dibs?'

'Yes.'

Tom slapped Henry on the back, so hard he coughed. 'Well, let's hope they don't take them all. With you on side, we might win this fucker after all.'

Henry grinned. 'Tom isn't a fan of AP,' he said. 'He sometimes forgets which war we're actually here to fight.'

'AP've got two writers and a photographer,' Tom said. 'My editor at UPI – Ernie – won't send me anyone else, and believe me, I've begged. Henry's *New York Times* of course, but we share everything. You could be our photo man.'

Rook looked at them: Tom with his dark-ringed eyes and wrinkled shirt, and Henry, standing pristine beside him. He thought of a photograph he'd once taken of his brothers, standing side by side, fresh from the mines. He felt more fondness for these two near-strangers, like he finally fitted in. But he'd imagined himself working alone. 'Let's see,' he said.

Tom's face fell. 'Guess we'll have to work on our pitch,' Henry said, grinning.

*

That night, there was a party at the boys' villa. It was big enough to hold hundreds of people: two storeys, from the French colonial days. A columned porch, a huge open-plan living area, wide patio doors looking out onto a crystal blue swimming pool. There was even a hired caretaker, Thinh, who'd pushed open the gate for them, a smile spreading across his face.

'The *New York Times* pay for it,' Tom said. 'Lucky for me – there's no way UPI would swing for this. They don't even give me accommodation allowance.'

On the kitchen counter, several bottles of liquor were laid out, along with a collection of chipped glasses. All the furniture had been pushed against the wall.

'Who did all this?' Rook asked. They'd all been at the office all day.

'Thinh,' Tom said.

Henry was standing by the patio doors, his arms folded, looking out. 'Gotta love him.'

Tom poured three whiskies. 'There's no phone line,' he said, 'but we've got hot water now: courtesy of our friend Friday.'

'Rook was confused. 'Friday from the field?'

Henry nodded. 'Contraband heater delivered last week by some of his men.'

'Why would he do that?' Rook asked.

Tom shrugged. 'He scratches our back, and we scratch his. We have a very mutually beneficial relationship. He takes us out, shows us the real war: the one the officials don't want us seeing. In return, he gets his stories in the newspaper. The *New York Times* is a much quicker route to the President than his superiors in Saigon.'

'Sounds like a win–win situation,' Rook said.

Tom gave his arm a playful shove. 'If you're on our team, we'll share our sources, don't worry.'

'Leave him alone, Tom,' Henry said, opening the patio doors. 'I'm going in the pool.' He pulled off his shirt and trousers and dropped them onto a rain-damaged sun-bed, diving into the water. Rook found himself doing the same. The cool water was the perfect antidote to the accumulated heat of the day. Tom bombed in, sending cascades onto the patio, splattering over the assortment of plants: huge waxy leaves sheltering smaller plants, all stock-still in the hot air.

'It's our little jungle,' Tom said, his blond hair slicked back against his head, droplets hanging in his fair eye-lashes. 'Whenever we get a hankering for the field, we sit here. Waiting for VC.'

Henry splashed him. 'He's joking.'

The sky was fading. Evening sounds started up: frogs

and the unrelenting beat of insect legs, rustling in the undergrowth. The tall concrete wall seemed impenetrable.

'Prime mosquito time,' Henry said, slapping at his freckled forearm.

'They won't get us in here,' Tom said. 'Henry's paranoid.'

'A French journalist got dengue and had to go back to France,' Henry said. 'And malaria is everywhere.'

'Not in the city,' Tom said.

'I know people who've had it in Saigon.'

'You believe too many tall tales.'

Henry shrugged. 'I don't want to be out of action. You should watch yourself too. UPI'd go crazy if you got it.'

Tom laughed. 'They'd fire me. If I can't work, I'm no good to them.'

'How many journalists are out here?' Rook asked.

'Not many,' Henry said. 'There's the AP lot, probably five or six of them, and then me and Tom. A few others swing by from time to time from other foreign bureaus. Big shots from the US: given the royal treatment.'

'You'll meet most of the gang tonight,' Tom said.

The towels were already laid out for them. Tom ran back into the house like an oversized child, his wet feet slapping the paving stones. Rook could hear the patter of the shower. Alone, he washed off under the outdoor one, enjoying the darkness and the water on his skin in the warm air. He looked up at a sky tattooed with clouds, and felt a surge of contentment: he was really here.

Inside, Tom was pouring himself another drink. His

hair was already drying, long around his face and at the back of his neck.

'Want one?' he said.

Rook nodded, watching whisky fill the bottom inch of the tumbler.

Tom took a big sip. He walked over to a record player balanced on a hip-high shelving cabinet stacked with LPs and began flipping through them. He slipped one out of its sleeve and opened the glass case, positioning the needle. From the two huge speakers, the jangling of a guitar filled the room. Tom jigged a few steps as he slid across the marble floor back to the counter.

Henry emerged from upstairs, taking a glass and holding it aloft. 'Welcome to 'Nam, Rook,' he said.

'And to our team,' Tom said. 'We'll crush those fuckers at AP.' The doorbell rang. 'Just in time. Looks like the party's starting.'

Henry took the two steps up into the entrance hall. At the door was Thinh, next to a beautiful local girl, wearing a figure-hugging dress. Her dark hair was cut to chin-length, her eyes lined with thick black kohl.

Thinh said something in Vietnamese, and Henry laughed, putting his hand on the girl's lower back and drawing her into the house, muttering something into her ear.

The couple stepped across the room together, still entwined.

Henry grinned at Rook. 'This is Linh,' he said. 'My girlfriend.'

The girl held out a small hand and Rook took it. A girlfriend? 'Nice to meet you,' he said.

'She's a singer,' Henry said.

There was another knock. Tom shouted out for them to come in. A crowd of white men stood at the door, four or five of them: Tom whooped, slapping each of them on the back. 'Drinks?' he said.

One of the men spotted Rook and came straight over. He was short and barrel-chested, with sandy hair. 'I love new blood,' he said. His accent was European – German, Rook would have guessed. 'I'm Hans,' the man said, holding out a hot, meaty hand.

'Rook.'

'You're English?'

Rook nodded. 'And you?'

'German. How long have you been in-country?'

'A week.'

'How're you finding it?'

'Good. Still getting my bearings.'

'Been out yet?'

Rook nodded, taking a sip of his whisky. 'Once.'

'Writer?'

'Photographer.'

Hans grinned. 'Me too. This place is overrun with writers. It's nice to meet someone of the same breed.'

Rook was uncertain. Surely they were competitors?

'Are you with a paper?' Hans asked.

'The *Sunday Times*.'

He nodded. 'I'm freelance,' he said.

The man's eyes were still warmly focused on his face, with no trace of malice. 'I'm confused,' Rook said. 'About the way you guys do things. Working together to get stories, sharing sources. I thought it would be every man for himself.'

'Needs must,' Hans said. 'It's hard enough to get real info on what's going on out here, so we need to pitch together. Team work, I suppose you'd call it.'

Tom bounded up to them with a whisky and handed it to Hans. 'Don't you be trying to take him over to the other side.' He turned to Rook and mock-whispered. 'He's one of the enemy.'

Hans laughed. 'We're all in the same game, Tom.'

'Don't pull that shit with me, Hans,' Tom said. 'I know you want to win just as much as me.'

'I'm saying nothing.' Hans turned to Rook. 'So you're working out of UPI? You know we have a better dark-room?'

'Bullcrap,' Tom said. 'Why would you want to share with this German monkey when you can have our dark-room all to yourself?'

'I haven't decided yet,' Rook said, and Tom's face dropped. 'Joking, Tom.'

Tom punched Rook on the arm, then turned to greet another group who'd just arrived: a combination of white men and their Vietnamese girlfriends.

'He cracks me up,' Hans said. 'Takes it all so seriously.

The way I see it, us guys have got to stick together. There's not so many of us, and we're all in the same ship.'

Rook lifted his glass. 'Let's drink to that,' he said.

*

The girls danced, their slim hips moving, their eyes semi-shut to the music, sweat making their faces glow. Rook tried not to stare, but when he looked around, he saw there was a crowd of men, standing with drinks in their hands, watching the women who took up the makeshift dance floor.

Rook knew he'd had too much to drink. He stumbled outside, where some wicker garden chairs had been set up in a circle on the patio: people were passing around a joint, their heads tilted up towards the sky, the same stupid smile on their faces. Rook sat down and shut his eyes.

When he opened them again, the other men were gone and Henry was sitting beside him.

'Have you seen what's going on in the pool?' Henry said.

Rook blinked, looking down at the lit-up water below them. It seemed to be full of entwined people, the bottom halves of their bodies lost from sight.

'Wow,' Rook heard himself say.

'You should get down there.'

Rook thought of June. No matter how he looked at

it, she was still out there, waiting for him. He shook his head. 'I'm married.'

Henry raised his eyebrows. 'Well, I didn't expect that. Is your wife in London?'

Rook nodded.

'What's she like?'

Rook fought the desire to say she was beautiful: she was so much more than that. 'She's wonderful. The bravest person I've ever met.'

Henry smiled. 'You must miss her.'

Rook nodded. 'Where's Linh?'

'She had to go home. Her father likes her back before midnight. There's a curfew.' He lit a cigarette. 'How does your wife feel, about you being out here?'

'It's supposed to be temporary,' Rook said.

'The job, or the war?'

'Both.'

'I don't think it's going to be ending any time soon.'

Rook's mind moved slowly. 'Didn't JFK say it'd be over by Christmas?'

'Yeah, I'd call bullshit on that one.' Henry waved the smoke away from his face. 'There's already twelve thousand troops here – all hush-hush – and it doesn't show any sign of slowing down. Poor Kennedy. It's a nightmare, really. The government down here is rotten to the core: without the US, it might just collapse. And then it'd be open game for the Commies. Washington's shit-scared the rest of South-East Asia will follow suit.'

Rook thought about that. 'Do you think they should pull out?'

'No way. Without us here, the whole place will fall apart.' He finished his whisky.

'Where are you from in the States?'

'Kansas/Oklahoma border. The most boring place on earth. Just the horizon and flat yellow fields. An hour's walk to school. As soon as I could, I got the hell out of there.'

Rook thought of the house where he grew up, of that trapped feeling. 'I know what you mean,' he said. 'Your family's still there?'

Henry nodded. 'Three brothers, mother and father. They're all a lot better suited to the rural life than me. I'd never heard of a "hick" until I got to the city, but that's what they are. What about you?'

'I'm from a coal-mining town in the north of England. My father and brothers all went down the pit, but I didn't want to. I moved to London and, somehow, I've ended up here.'

'Lucky for you. I've got a feeling about this story. I think it'll be good for all of us.'

Rook looked around him: at the tropical gardens, the swimming pool. 'It's certainly different,' he said.

Henry laughed. 'You could most definitely say that,' he said. 'It's like we've finally found our treasure island.' He turned to Rook, suddenly serious. 'I hope you stay for a while, Rook. We're enjoying having you around. And your shots are really something.'

Rook felt his face heat up. He looked at Henry, his face pink from the alcohol, his glasses still neat on his face. He grinned. 'Me too,' he said.

FOUR

Rook tries to imagine seeing Tom after all these years. What would he say?

He finds himself drinking beer on the crowded pavement of another bar. Above him, the neon signs cluster around a narrow strip of sky.

Once again, he hears American accents, watches lumbering bodies blinking slowly, as if not sure why they are here. Loud shirts, smoke and grimy deckchairs. The tourists gaggle around him, eating burgers and slices of pizza, faces charred by the day's sunlight. The locals push carts selling everything from sunglasses to counterfeit tourist guides, and the beggar children hobble with mutated hands outstretched, feigning blindness.

Linh must be mistaken, he thinks. Tom can't be here. Rook followed his career, in the beginning. He knew he'd remained in Vietnam, covering the American pull-out in 1972, and three years later, the official Communist win. He'd finally won his World Press Award, and a Pulitzer. His name was still synonymous with the war: his book about it, about them, had been a bestseller. But Rook had assumed he'd returned to America, and after a while, he'd stopped looking for him. In all his years of working, their paths had never crossed again.

A broad man in a sloganed vest is shoved into his table by one of his friends. Rook's beer sloshes over, his jaw tensing. The man laughs, pushing his friend, not even turning to apologize.

Rook finds himself on his feet, the man's collar in his clenched fists.

The man smiles. 'All right, old man?' he says, his accent unmistakably Australian.

'You spilt my drink,' Rook says, his fingers trembling. His voice sounds different to how he imagined, weaker.

The man laughs again. 'Sorry, mate. I'd better get you another.'

Rook thrusts his arms against the man's chest, but he can't seem to muster any power.

'Calm down, grandpa,' the guy says. 'There's a lot more of us than there are of you.'

The man's friends are behind him. Soft paunches and bare arms: there's nothing threatening about them except their number. They are trying to hide their smiles, as if they're already retelling the story later, of the old man who tried to start a fight with them.

Rook lets go, sinking back. The man waves over the waitress and orders him another drink.

'I am sorry, mate,' he says. 'Mind if we sit down? It's a bit crowded in here.'

Rook looks around them at the other tables, all busy with people. 'All right.'

The men surround the table.

'You on holiday?' the man asks.

'Not really.'

'You live here then?'

'I'm visiting.'

'Oh, right,' the man says. 'Who?'

When Rook tries to ask himself what he's doing here, a fog falls. He sighs, wanting to tell the man that he doesn't need to make conversation. 'Some old friends,' he says.

'We're on Biffo's buck party,' the man says, pointing at a tanned man with a small goatee. 'We're from Perth.' He puts out a hand. 'I'm Rob, by the way.'

'Rook,' he says, shaking it. 'Long way to come, for a stag do.'

'Not really. We went to Vegas last year, for mine. Are you married?'

Rook starts to nod, automatically, then stops. 'My wife died recently,' he says.

The man's face falls. 'Sorry, mate,' he says. 'How long ago?'

Three days, he thinks. 'A while.'

'That can't be easy.'

Rook doesn't want to talk about this. 'When did you arrive?' he says.

'Tuesday. We went to the war museum today. Pretty full on, but Biffo's a bit of a war buff.' Rob leans in. 'He's special forces. Was in Afghanistan last year.'

Rook looks at Biffo, wiping the beer from his chin

across the table. He feels the words before he's aware of them. 'I was here in the war.'

'Really? You were a soldier?'

'A photographer.'

'Hey, Biffo,' Rob shouts, and Rook feels hot. 'This guy was in the war. He's a journo.'

'How long were you here?' Biffo says.

'Five years, give or take,' Rook says. All of the men's eyes are on him now. He feels like he's at the top of a diving board, about to leap.

'In Ho Chi Minh City?' Biffo says.

'All over,' Rook says.

'Out on patrol?'

'All the time,' he says.

'I wonder if we saw any of your shots, in the museum,' Rob says.

Rook thinks of the burning man. He isn't used to talking about his work without June there, to fill in the gaps for him. *He won a World Press Award*, she'd say, *for the immolation of the monk. You must have seen it?*

'Perhaps,' he says.

The men are watching him, waiting for him to say more.

'Have you done the tunnel trip yet?' one of them says.

Rook shakes his head.

'That's worth a look,' Biffo said. 'A tour of the North Vietnamese tunnel complex. About an hour from the city.'

Rook sees an army boot, kicking away leaves from

the forest floor. The hole that appeared in the undergrowth ahead. 'Maybe I'll try that,' he says.

Walking back to the hotel, he wishes the night had not yet fallen. In the darkness, it is easier to be thrown back into the past. The looming outline of the twin-headed cathedral, the shadow of trees cast by street lamps. When he sees the lights of the hotel, he moves as fast as he can towards them.

He stares up at the turning ceiling fan. On the precipice of sleep, the jungle is there with him. Covering him with layers of green as if he is in a grave. He's never forgotten that feeling, of being at the bottom of a well, trapped yet protected by the trees. The nights when everything fell silent, except his heartbeat: as if all the animals and birds knew something he didn't. The rains that would come suddenly, out of nowhere, filling the sky with walls of water. Rook would long for saturation point, for the morning light which made the water steam from their clothes and bodies. On the mountain passes, mists would cloak everything in a matter of seconds, leaving them disorientated, with only the shadow of another man's boots to follow. His terror a huge, looming thing, bearing down on him. The exhaustion of it, that could last for hours or days. That is still with him, even now.

1963

The first time he went out in the bush with Henry, the marines warned him.

'Don't take it personally,' a black soldier told him. 'We're not risking our lives for you.'

'I'm ready,' Rook said, and Henry smiled: he'd already passed the test.

They were dropped into the middle of the rainforest: the chopper circling down to avoid enemy fire. It was a clean landing into a clearing of hacked trunks and charred land. They found cover at the edge of the dense trees, which offered a darkness that made Rook think of the mines, the claustrophobic weight of the earth above.

There were eight of them: three thick-shouldered marines, three stocky Montagnard tribesmen, and Henry and Rook: *Bao Chi*, the Vietnamese for journalist. It was stitched on their fatigues, in case it might save their lives. The marines had sung in the chopper, their own tuneless barbershop choir, but they were silent now, their faces still. Orang-utan, with ginger hair and freckled features; the black guy who'd warned Rook; and the blond-haired sergeant who seemed serious until he smiled. The

Montagnards' silence was the heaviest of all, a deep calm that laid itself across their features. The jungle was their place, and they were comfortable here.

'We'll go in that way,' the sergeant said. 'Four hours or so, and we'll dig in for the night. That'll be base, then we'll patrol the area. It's ripe with NVA, so keep your eyes peeled. And this is reconnaissance: we're trying to observe the fuckers, so don't shoot unless we take fire.'

'Even if they're close?' Orang-utan said.

'No pot-luck shots. We're fucking invisible, all right?' All the men nodded. 'Let's go. Remember, silence. If they're nearby, they'll have seen the chopper.' Sgt Peter turned to the journalists. 'You guys know the drill. If you compromise us, we will leave you.'

'Got it,' Henry said.

Rook focused on the jungle floor ahead of him, on the dark hair at the base of the closest Montagnard's neck. The forest was everywhere: the heaviness of it inside his body, slowing his movements. The far-away sounds of lizards and monkeys made him start. He kept his face as flat as he could, practised at keeping his fear hidden. *Ripe with NVA*, he thought, as he looked out through the branches and leaves, through a sea of vegetation. They could be all around him, waiting to strike.

The key to it was letting his mind go blank and still, focusing only on the next step, the next moment. They would pass, he told himself, whether he was scared or not. And when they stopped for a short rest, he looked for his fear and couldn't find it, couldn't find anything except an excitement that thrummed through his nerves. He was surviving, he thought, as he looked around at the other men: they all were, together.

Henry grinned at him, his brown eyes magnified by his glasses.

Rook framed the men inside his camera as the sun broke through the trees behind. This moment would be gone soon too, but he could take it away with him.

*

Coming back to Saigon, there was the thrill of having made it out. In the darkroom, Rook always felt a shadow of his fear return, and he'd spool the negatives out into his hands before he could think about it, losing himself in the careful washing of each chosen image until it did justice to the moment he'd captured. He knew that half of the work was done in the darkroom, and there was a strange satisfaction in seeing the images, separate from the experience he'd had, hanging up on the line.

Once the job was done, he'd walk out onto the baking streets of the city, feeling as free as he ever had. He'd find the boys at the villa or the bars. Henry, dark-haired and serious, sarcastic, with a sense of humour that could make light of anything. Tom, with his almost white blond hair, who always looked like he'd just climbed out of bed, always rushing from thing to thing, skirting the edge of deadlines.

They showed him everything. The city. The best places to pick up tips: waiting in the right noodle bars and coffee shops, learning to read body language, teaching him a few words of Vietnamese and falling about laughing as he tried to get it right. They invited him along to the odd social engagement in the city, telling him which dignitaries were the most useful and which were just up for a good time (the former were the Japanese, the latter, the Germans). Soon enough, Rook's name started appearing on the invitations too, and he didn't feel so much like an intruder.

The Friday Follies were the 'official' weekly military news briefings, where all the journalists would turn out to raise their grievances, or watch the Tom and Henry show. While the voice of the announcer stuttered over body count, numbers of men and blood trails, they'd sit in the back row like naughty kids on a school bus, nudging each other when they spotted a discrepancy. *I was there*, one of them would scrawl on a piece of paper as they announced a skirmish in the Delta, the DMZ or the Central Highlands. *That's not how it happened.*

On one occasion, a general was visiting Saigon from the White House. He stood in neatly pressed fatigues, his chest puffed out.

'Do you have any questions for the general?' one of the aides announced after the briefing had finished.

Tom raised his hand. 'We're not getting enough news,' he said.

The general laughed. 'Well, that's certainly not how it appears to me when I read your dispatches every morning.'

'Let me rephrase my statement,' Tom said. 'The news we're getting, we're having to work too hard for it. We're never given a straight answer. Your colleagues seem incapable of telling the truth.'

'You can't expect us to tell the press everything. For security reasons.'

Henry stood up. 'We've been there, sir. There's a vast difference between what we've seen and what's announced by the MACV.'

The general smiled. 'Do you really think I'm going to take your word over those of my own men?'

'We're all on the same side here.'

'It sure doesn't seem like that to me,' the general said, his face turning pink. 'Your negativity is not helping us win this war.'

'It's not negativity,' Henry said. 'It's the truth.'

'Everything I've seen since being here tells me we're winning this war. Why can't you get on board with that?'

'We're trying to do what's best for the country,' Henry said. 'Would you rather we didn't point out discrepancies?'

'Yes,' the general said, crossing his arms. 'I would. If you could consider how your writing is damaging what we're trying to achieve, we'd all be grateful.' He gestured to his aide. 'That's it,' he said. 'I'm done here.'

Hans, the German photographer, raised his hand. 'One more question, sir, if you please,' he said. 'What will you be reporting back to the President?'

The general was beet-red now. 'I'll be telling him we

should continue on the path we're on,' he said. 'All our data suggests it is working.'

A groan went up from the crowd.

*

They'd spend hours in the pool at the boys' villa, or in the rooftop bars near the hotel, debating small political details, trying to sift through everything they'd found out between them. Tom and Henry would do most of the talking, but Rook was happy to listen, occasionally weighing in. When he did, they'd swivel round, taking notice, as if the fewer words he spoke, the more attention they commanded. Henry would nod, happily. 'See, Tom,' he'd say, 'Rook gets it.' And Rook would feel like a bit of a fraud. He never really felt he knew things with the depth of these men.

He could see them though, in the field: the moments that seemed to sum things up visually, that moved him. They came at him without warning, sometimes at the most inopportune times. The outline of a father brandishing the body of his child, killed in a firefight, at a group of American soldiers. The grief of a helicopter gunner in the airport storage room, after his comrade had been killed.

Everything would slow in these moments, and Rook was able to dull the chaos all around him, the screaming and the gunfire and the tears, to stay calm and raise his camera. He could recognize the fear and suffering of others, and he could capture it. He was proving rather good at it too: at keeping his cool, at surviving. He'd surprised himself, not only by mastering his fear, but also by the joy he'd started to take from his work. An elation, not in the moment – which was serious and calm and needed all his attention – but in the build-up. He'd begun to feel he was really doing something useful, to look forward to getting on the choppers, to leaping into whatever was waiting for them at the other end.

The longer he was in-country, the more he felt like he belonged here. He still missed June, and their alliance, and there were nights when his need for her was something physical that only a stiff drink would dispel. But once he got used to being without her, he could see a new version of himself emerging. Someone daring, but not reckless, who the others turned to when they were out in the field, trusting his judgement on situations, knowing that he would take only calculated risks. Some of the more gung-ho journalists threw themselves in things with a sort of wilful blindness, as if by shutting their eyes to the danger they were immune to it. But though Rook was often the first on the scene, he knew when to draw back. He wasn't sure how, but he could recognize when the danger might not be worth the reward. He could feel a situation escalating, almost like the swell of a wave coming towards him, and he knew when to step out of the way. He wondered, sometimes, if he had his father to thank for that.

Sources in Saigon and on the army bases seemed to immediately warm to him too. He let them talk, listening to their concerns before pushing them to put him in a helicopter or on a patrol. These preliminaries gave him a good view of the situation, but it also gave them time to trust him. More recently, they'd started to look pleased to see him when he arrived, with a bottle of whisky and all the time in the world. The soldiers welcomed him too, knowing he wasn't a glory seeker, knowing that when it came to it he'd muck in like the rest of them.

*

With the arrival of the monsoon, deluging the landscape in the Delta with even more water, the patrols became less and less fruitful. The race riots in the US were dominating the headlines: Vietnam was still too small and far away to compete.

'I'm not risking my life for a story that isn't going to be printed,' Henry said. 'We might as well enjoy ourselves.'

'President Diem's heading up to Hue for some Catholic celebration,' Tom said, standing over the teleprinter. 'We could try and cover that.'

Henry shook his head, leafing through the pile of paper which the machine had already churned out until he found a photo of a black child being sprayed by a water cannon on a street in Mississippi. 'It's not gonna match this stuff,' he said. 'Linh's family has invited us round for dinner tonight, and I suggest we go. It's always a good feed.'

They arrived a little late, having been lost in the warren of lanes in Cholon. The taxi driver could only take them so far before he shook his head, the edges of the car almost brushing the walls of opposite houses. They had to climb out through the boot, passing doors through which they saw flickers of movement: an old man lying in a hammock, a family crouching around plates of food laid out on the ground.

Linh was waiting on the doorstep when they finally arrived, shirts sticking to backs and hair damp at the nape of their necks. Henry kissed her immaculately made-up cheek, and she turned her head slightly so he wouldn't disturb her beehive. She was wearing long silk trousers and a tight-fitted, floor-length dress, slit up to the waist. Not an inch of her skin was revealed, but the shape of her body was enough to make the boys' eyes water, and for Henry to turn around and wink, clutching her waist as they were shown inside.

The yellow-doored house was small, open to the elements on one side, with a drainage hole in the tiled floor for the worst of the monsoons. Rook had expected something grander: Linh's father was important, a government official, and her mother was a singer: but in Saigon, that didn't mean much. Even properties on these narrow, winding streets were expensive.

They were greeted by three or four family members, who came to the door with eager smiles, nodding their heads and shaking the boys' hands.

'Please, please,' Linh's mother said – the only English word she knew – inviting them to take a seat at the table, which was neatly laid with small bowls and chopsticks, and spread with an array of colourful dishes.

Henry smiled at the others as they sat down on too-low stools.

Linh was called to the kitchen on the other side of the room by her mother, where they both crouched on the floor and made spring rolls, expertly wrapping the rice paper around the filling and adding them to an already huge pile in a basket next to them.

The women wouldn't be joining them at the table, but Linh's two brothers and their father took their seats. Without Linh's smattering of useful English, the time was passed by grinning and nodding, the silence broken only by a confused cockerel somewhere outside. Linh's father stood up and offered the boys beer, which they readily accepted. Once the drinks had been poured, Tom raised his glass and said the usual Vietnamese alternative for cheers, and they drank, laughing at his attempts at the language.

Linh's father began to talk, directing his comments at Linh so that she could translate. Even before Linh had started to explain, Rook could have predicted what he was saying, glancing at the three white men and nodding solemnly.

'My father want to tell you how grateful we are that you come here for dinner,' Linh said, blushing. 'He is so happy that you are here helping us fight against the Viet Cong.'

Tom nodded. 'Thank you,' he said, addressing Linh's father. '*Gam ern.*' More laughter at his pronunciation. 'For inviting us. We love coming here.'

'*Bao chi*,' Henry said. 'We are not fighting.'

'I told him that,' she said.

As Rook looked around at the grateful faces around the table, he felt ill at ease. The longer he was here, the more he felt there was something wrong about the set-up. The way the Americans held up the government and army of South Vietnam was fine in the short term, but it didn't seem to have an end point. With the US to help them, the army didn't have an incentive to fight back against the Cong, who were gaining strength all the time. In Saigon, the government was popular, but everywhere they went in the countryside there were signs of the Cong's influence spreading. Officials who came from Washington seemed determined to see only what suited them: to remain mainly in the city where everything seemed under control. When Rook looked ahead to the future, he didn't like the ominous feeling it gave him.

*

They went back to the office after dinner, to check the service before heading out.

'Son of a bitch,' Tom said, leaning over the machine. 'They've got us again.'

'Who?' Rook said.

'Bloody AP.'

He handed Rook the sheet of paper.

SAIGON, VIETNAM 05/08/1963 18:34

ASSOCIATED PRESS

EIGHT PEOPLE KILLED IN HUE ON THE 2587TH ANNIVERSARY OF THE BUDDHA'S DEATH. PEACEFUL PROTESTS BEGAN AS A RESULT OF PRESIDENT DIEM'S REFUSAL TO ALLOW WORSHIPERS TO FLY THE BUDDHIST FLAG. THE PROHIBITIONS CAME JUST DAYS AFTER THE CATHOLIC FLAG WAS OPENLY FLOWN IN HUE TO MARK THE 25TH ANNIVERSARY OF PRESIDENT DIEM'S BROTHER, ARCHBISHOP THUC'S, ELEVATION TO THE CATHOLIC HIERARCHY.

'We should have covered it,' Henry said.

Tom's face was turning redder. He picked up the phone and put it down again. 'How did we not see this?'

Henry shrugged. 'We made a mistake. The *Times* are not going to be happy.'

'This piece went out three hours ago,' Tom said. 'We need to start making calls.'

Henry picked up the phone and started arguing with someone who couldn't speak English very well. Tom went to his desk and began his stop-start typing.

Rook stood and watched. There was nothing he could do: Hue was half a country away, and he couldn't take photos of something that had already happened.

The score didn't end up too bad. AP took the majority of stories: coverage in fourteen papers; UPI took seven. The *New York Times* ran Henry's story, but not on the front page: it was reserved for the race riots.

'We need something big,' he said, gritting his teeth. 'To knock these race stories out of the park.'

As Rook nodded, he was suddenly aware of what they were wishing for. That the war would escalate, that it would become more serious. He couldn't help thinking of Linh's family: how their gratitude felt like a burden that the Americans could never successfully shoulder. When he was out in the field, he longed endlessly for something to happen too, for them all to be rewarded for risking their lives with coverage. He shook off the idea: they weren't wishing anyone harm, after all. Just that they could be in the right place at the right time, capturing moments that would happen anyway.

FIVE

Rook wakes early, a hard habit to break. The light pushes against the thick cream curtains; a car-horn chorus intrudes from the square below. For a moment, he can't breathe, can't move.

He makes himself get up and go down to breakfast, held in the street-facing restaurant, bricked in now. There are starched white tablecloths and uniformed waiters. Linen-trousered ladies with fake pearls. Men with guts hanging over their cargo pants, the smooth skin on the backs of their balding heads vulnerable. Oversized, over-stuffed adventure backpacks; identical blue guidebooks at every table.

For a moment, he sees the bar as it was, open to the square. Old wooden ceiling fans moving languidly, doing little to lift the heat. The crush of bodies, of journalists, all turning to look at Rook, calling out to him. *Where've you been today, Rook? Got any tips for us?*

Rook collects his plate of food and sits down. He wonders how he will fill the day. The thought of returning to Linh's house, of seeing Tom, brings back the old fear and anticipation he remembers from before a jungle patrol.

He eats his noodles. When he looks up, the man from reception is by his table.

'Your son is here, sir.'

'What?'

'In reception. He wants to see you. Shall I bring him here?'

*

The man returns with Ralph, leading him across the restaurant. He is wearing jeans, a crumpled checked shirt. His hair is too long; his eyes are fixed on Rook, determined.

They stand, never sure how to greet each other. Already, Rook feels June's absence.

'You look as if you've seen a ghost,' Ralph says.

Rook nods. 'How did you find me?'

'I called the hotel. I had a hunch.'

Rook stares at the table, aware of the diners around them, of the buzz of chatter.

Ralph sighs. 'I shouldn't be surprised. You've never been good at communicating. But Mum dies, and you can't even call me? Did it cross your mind how it would feel for me to find out in an email?'

Rook remembers his hand, cocooning the telephone. 'I tried to call,' he says, but even to him, the words feel weak. 'No one answered.'

'You tried once,' Ralph says, his voice resigned. 'And then you ran away.'

Rook remembers driving fast down the motorway as if he was being pursued. 'I did what I needed to do, Ralph.'

Ralph pulls out the chair opposite him and sits down. 'Well, I'm not leaving here without you. Mum deserves better than this.'

Ralph's eyes are full of sadness and Rook has to look away.

'I went to your house,' his son says. Rook feels his skin itch, imagining his son there. 'Mum gave me a key. What else was I supposed to do? You left no information.' His son is still looking at him: Rook can't bear it. 'What happened, Dad?'

For a moment, he thinks Ralph is asking what went wrong between him and June, all those years ago. He doesn't know how to answer. Just in time, he realizes. 'She died in her chair,' he says. 'When the ambulance came, the men told me she'd had a heart attack. They said it would have been quick.'

'And you believed them?' Ralph's eyes dart. 'Where were you?'

'I was out.'

'Taking photos?'

Rook sits, feeling his pain, spreading. His mind won't let himself come close to the thought of June, dying, and him, out in the fields somewhere. 'This isn't my fault, Ralph.'

Ralph sighs. 'Where is she now?'

'At the funeral director's in Relter. They gave me some papers to read and said to let them know when I was ready to arrange the funeral.'

'And when will you be ready? When are you coming home?'

Rook thinks of the cottage, surrounded by darkness. The empty rooms. 'I don't know,' he says.

'I'm not letting you do this, Dad. It's not fair on Mum. You need to organize the funeral.'

Rook imagines leafing through June's address book. Calling June's London friends. Mildred. Jimmy. People he hasn't let himself think about for years. 'You can do that, can't you?'

'I can help you,' Ralph says. 'But this is your responsibility. It's important.'

Rook shakes his head. 'She's dead, Ralph. There's no changing that. It's too late.' As he says it, he re-experiences all those moments he let pass by, when he could have made things right. He stands, his chair scraping across the marble floor. 'Go home, Ralph. Have your funeral. I'm going to my room.'

Ralph gets up too. 'That's right. Leave. But I'm not going anywhere, Dad. I won't let you get away with it this time.'

*

Rook's hand shakes as he waits for the lift. Leaning against the wall, he feels his heart throwing itself against his ribs. When he gets to his room, he shuts the door, sinking onto the bed. He tries to breathe normally, but it is as if Ralph is here with him.

Rook had wanted to be the kind of dad who swung his son around the room, who pulled faces, who made Ralph laugh by tickling his soft belly. He'd longed for it, for a connection stronger than the one he'd had with his own father. He'd known he could be different, that some part of him was capable of overcoming the barriers he'd been unable to get past in Backton. Hadn't he done it before with June, who had accepted and loved him, and with Henry, who'd shown him he could belong?

But even when Ralph was little and Rook was at home he hadn't known what to do. He'd thought it would come to him naturally, but when June popped out to run errands, leaving them alone in the house, he'd watch the boy picking up blocks and putting them together, a fearful feeling rushing towards him. Like a fast train, rattling through a station, leaving an unsettling quiet behind.

Sitting in front of his son just now, that fear had returned. It was as if Ralph had held a mirror up to Rook's face, and shown him all the worst things about himself. He knew he'd failed June and Ralph in so many ways: he didn't need to be reminded.

There is a knock at the door. Rook's legs ache: he can't get up.

The door opens. Ralph is there, standing over him, the light from the hallway bright behind his silhouette in the dim, curtained bedroom.

'Dad?' Ralph is saying. 'Are you all right? I saw you by the lift. You didn't look well.'

Rook tries to answer, but the words tangle together. He hears himself make a noise, a sort of whimper. Pain spreads through his chest: the air can't get through, and he is relieved. His time has come.

Ralph's looming face is frightened. Rook wants to tell him that everything will be OK, but he can't find the words. Just as he was unable to comfort Ralph when he was a child and woke from a nightmare. It felt false to tell his son there was nothing to be afraid of.

He hears Ralph's voice, from across the room. 'We need a doctor,' he says. 'Room 208.'

Rook is fading. He sees June, standing at the airport arrival gate, smiling. He steps forwards, into her arms, breathing her in, and his relief is palpable. He is back there, at the beginning again.

1963

On his first flight back home to England from Vietnam, Rook couldn't sleep. He could think of nothing but June, his anticipation almost as potent as a month previously, when he'd left her at the airport and flown into the unknown.

The first plane was full of American soldiers heading to Manila for R and R. He recognized one or two of them: becoming boisterous with the enthusiasm of those free from danger, laughing a little too hard at each other's jokes, drinking more than was strictly necessary. They invited him to join them but he declined, preferring to sit quietly and wait for time to pass by, each moment bringing him closer to home. He wasn't sorry to wave them off when they touched down, remaining in the airport for his connecting flight.

June was waiting in arrivals, her red lips spreading into the most wonderful smile when she saw him. They looked at each other, and then her arms were around his neck, her body pressed into his. Her smell, which had haunted him for so many nights, surrounded him, and he felt as if all their time apart had been worth it for this one exquisite moment of reunion.

*

They took a taxi to their new apartment in Putney. It was nicer than the old one, but not much larger: one of six in a tall red-brick Victorian building just off the high street. There was a small living room adjoining the kitchen, with just enough room for a sofa and a record player.

'What do you think?' June said.

'It's lovely.'

'You should have seen it when I moved in. You would have laughed at me, in my painting clothes, trying to scrub the place clean.'

Rook looked at the white walls, at the bunch of dried flowers in the fireplace and row of candles on the mantelpiece. 'You've done a great job.'

'I'm glad you like it. It's been my little project.'

June was looking up at him so earnestly he felt his stomach twist.

'I'd like to see the bedroom,' Rook said, taking her hands in his.

She smiled. 'Right this way, sir.'

Everything was so tidy, so unlike the messiness of the previous apartment. Rook wondered if she always kept it like this.

In the bedroom, they stood unmoving in front of each other for a long moment. Then the space between them was closed, her lips on his, his arms around her. They made love slowly, as if it was the first time. There was a sort of reverence about it, as if their desperation made them careful, determined not to take each other for granted.

They lay together afterwards, their bodies entwined, saying nothing for a long time. Rook looked at the curve of June's cheek in profile, and felt a profound joy: that everything he'd remembered was true, that nothing had altered between them.

June turned to look at him, her blue eyes meeting his. 'I've missed this,' she said.

'Me too,' he said, reaching out for her again.

*

That day, they barely left the apartment, lying in the semi-darkness of the bedroom.

'We haven't had any lunch,' June said, checking her watch and showing it to Rook. Just before five, and it still felt like the morning. 'I'll make tea.'

'You don't want to go out?'

'Let's save it, shall we? I've got something in mind.'

Rook went to get up, but June pushed him backwards.

'Stay here,' she said. 'It's a surprise. I'll call you when it's ready.'

Rook took a long shower, enjoying the hot water. June's bottles were lined up along the edge of the bath. Even though he knew she had moved house, Crouch End was where he'd imagined her while he'd been away, and being here felt temporary. He wondered how long it would take for this place to feel like home.

A towel wrapped around his waist, he looked through the stack of books on the bedside table. *Mother Courage and Her Children*, Bertholt Brecht. *The Cherry Orchard*, Anton Chekhov. Rook opened one: June had written in the margins and highlighted sections. Was she acting? In all her letters, she'd only mentioned two or three auditions. He was sure she would have told him if she'd got a part.

He pulled on some clean trousers and a jumper from the wardrobe and went to find her.

She was standing in front of the hob, two pans on the go, the oven lights on.

'You can't come in,' she said.

'I'm lonely in there. Are you sure I can't help?'

'Sit,' June said, gesturing at the kitchen chairs. 'You can talk to me.'

'What are we having?'

'Wait and see.' She looked at him. 'Are you cold?'

Rook looked down at his jumper. June had a skirt and blouse on, her legs and arms bare. 'A little.'

'It's warm! My mother says they've opened the outdoor swimming pool in Backton.'

'How is she?' Rook asked.

'Same as always. Worried about me.'

'Have you been back?'

'I wouldn't want to. Not without you. I call her from

the pay phone every now and then. She always thinks I sound sad. I tell her I'm fine, then I come off the phone in a bad mood, wishing I hadn't rung at all.'

Rook watched June: the fine hairs on her arms, the soft skin on her legs. '*Are* you all right?'

'What do you mean?'

'I'm just wondering how everything has been here, since I left. I get your letters, but – I don't know. I thought I'd ask.'

'Everything's fine. Of course, I miss you. But the house has kept me busy.'

'Are you still acting?'

June looked away, towards the stove. 'I've been to a few auditions, but nothing's come up. I might have finally found a friend at the most recent one, though. A girl called Mildred.'

'That's good,' Rook said. 'I'd like to meet her.'

'You will.'

He wanted her to turn around so he could see her face. He thought about the letters he'd sent her when he first went away, how he could only give her a partial representation of what his life in Vietnam was like. When he looked at the spotless apartment, he felt as if he was outside in the corridor, looking through the keyhole.

He got up and went to the stove, turning her around and holding her to his chest. After a moment he felt her shoulders relax, her body sinking into his.

'I want you to tell me everything,' he said. 'I want to know all about your life.'

She looked up at him. 'You're the one who's been overseas, doing exciting things. You've been in a war, for goodness' sake! That's what we should be talking about.'

Rook thought about the past month, about Henry and Tom, and how warmly they'd accepted him. How could he explain Saigon, with its mishmash of old French buildings and hastily constructed wooden ones? The way it felt like the city was growing, bursting at the seams, vibrant and disorderly in a way that London tried so hard not to be. And then there was the war itself: the dangerous edge of it that Rook skated along, how alive it made him feel.

He opened his mouth to begin. But it felt too much: he didn't know where to start, and his exhaustion fell over him like a curtain.

'We will,' he said. 'We've got plenty of time.'

*

Over dinner, June tried again.

'What's it like out there?' she said.

Rook paused. 'It's hard to describe. There are three of us who knock about together: Henry and Tom and me. They're both Americans. I think I mentioned them in my letters.'

June nodded. 'What's your average day like?'

He told her the basics: the days when he was in Saigon when he had something of a routine, when he was safer.

'Is it very dangerous?' she asked.

He didn't want to lie to her. 'You have to be careful. If you stick to the city, it's all right.'

'And you do that, most of the time?'

Rook thought of the sounds of the jungle, of following Henry and Tom through the undergrowth. 'Mostly.'

'I've been reading the coverage,' she said, carefully, 'and it doesn't seem to be slowing down.'

Rook paused. 'It isn't,' he said. 'I actually want to talk to you about that. Tony wants to extend my contract.'

'I know. He told me.'

'What?'

'Don't be cross,' June said. 'I've been going to the office and reading the wire service. Tony said it was fine as long as I didn't get in anyone's way.'

Rook felt his face heat up. It felt strange, that she'd been reading Tom's stories coming over the wire, seeing his images.

'Don't be angry. Your letters take so long to come,' she said. 'It makes me feel better, if I know what's happening.'

It crossed his mind again, how difficult it must have been for her, since he'd been gone. 'I'm sorry we can't be in touch more.'

'It's not your fault. But I need to know. Tony's been brilliant: everyone has.'

Rook smiled. He shouldn't have been taken aback that June would have the nerve to waltz into his office, to get herself the information to put her mind at rest. It worried him, though, that she knew so much about what the war was really like. 'It's not as bad as it sounds in the stories.'

June reached over, stroking his cheek. 'I trust you, Rook. You're not a reckless person.'

He felt a lump form in his throat. 'And you don't mind? If I go back to Saigon?'

'I'm so proud of you. Of all the things you've achieved. You need to keep going. I understand that.'

'Thank you,' he said, and he kissed her.

*

Before he went back, they went to meet June's new friend at the Rivoli Bar at the Ritz, as a special treat. June spent a long time getting ready, emerging from the bedroom in a red dress with white flowers along the neckline. She looked lovely, but Rook couldn't help thinking of the make-up-free girl of the last few weeks, who'd wandered around the apartment barefoot in one of his old shirts.

Mildred was already there when they arrived, sitting on a high stool at the bar, chatting to the barman. Her red hair was piled on top of her head, and the peacock blue of her dress was striking.

She slipped off the stool as they approached and June kissed her on both cheeks.

'You must be the photographer,' she said, and as she leaned in, Rook smelt cloves. 'Fresh from a war, how exciting!'

'Nice to meet you.'

'I've heard all about you, of course. June never shuts

up about it. Misses you terribly. She's quite the bore, if you must know.'

June laughed, and shoved her arm. 'I am not.'

'I'm glad you've been keeping her busy,' Rook said. 'How did you two meet?'

'At a casting,' Mildred said. 'Hated each other, of course. I took one look at June and thought, there's my competition. We've been firm friends ever since.'

June was blushing.

'I'm starving,' Rook said. 'Shall we find our table?'

They were seated in the window, looking out onto the street.

'Have you been here before?' Rook asked Mildred.

'We come here all the time. Didn't June tell you? In the beginning, she said she couldn't afford it. Until I told her we wouldn't be paying for our drinks. There's always someone willing.' Mildred gestured at some men near the bar, wearing suits and drinking champagne. 'Those men over there. They'd be happy to pay for our dinner. All I'd need to do is ask.'

'That won't be necessary,' Rook said. 'Tonight's on me. It's a special occasion, after all.'

Mildred smiled. 'I won't argue with that,' she said.

*

In the taxi on the way home, June turned to Rook.

'Did you have a nice time?' she said.

'I did. It was nice to meet Mildred.'

'She's a scream, isn't she?'

'She's certainly that,' he said. 'Does she really get men to buy drinks for her?'

June nodded. 'It's only a bit of fun.'

'Doesn't she have someone, then?'

'A boyfriend? No, not at the moment.' June paused. 'She's harmless really. She's been a great friend to me, while you've been away.'

'I know. I'm happy for you.' There was another silence. 'You didn't mention going to the Ritz in your letters.'

'No. I suppose I didn't. We've only been a couple of times.'

Rook looked down at the seat between them, at June's hand resting there, her wedding ring glinting. He felt it again: the narrow space which had opened up between them, blurring their vision so they couldn't see each other as clearly.

June was looking past him, as they passed the Houses of Parliament, lit up in the darkness. He reached across and took her hand, and she smiled at him.

SIX

Before the doctor arrives, Rook is feeling better. He has pulled himself up to a seated position on the bed. Ralph waits with him.

'I'm fine now,' Rook says.

'Just let the doctor check you over,' Ralph says. 'He's on his way now.'

'There's no need.'

'Please, Dad. You look terrible.'

'I'm old. That's all that's wrong with me.'

The doctor, a small Vietnamese man with kind eyes and a medicine bag, is persistent, checking his temperature and his blood pressure, shining a light in his eyes. Rook tries to tell him he isn't needed, but he doesn't listen, and Rook is too weak to physically push him away.

'You need rest,' the doctor says when he's finished.

Rook tuts. 'I could have told you that.'

After the doctor leaves, Rook and Ralph are alone. 'I can't wait to see his bill,' Rook says.

He pulls himself forward to stand up, but his son stops him.

'Where are you going?'

'I'm getting up.'

'You heard what the doctor said, Dad.'

'It's the middle of the day. I'm not staying in bed.'

'What are you going to do, then?'

Rook stops pulling on his shoes. He thinks of Linh, and her promise about Tom. But it is only Thursday, a whole day stretching ahead unfilled.

He can't stay in this room, alone with his son. He remembers the Australian men in the bar, their advice about Cu Chi. 'I heard about a tunnel tour,' he says. 'A few hours from the city.'

'That sounds like a terrible idea. Going out into the heat, walking around. If you're going anywhere, it should be home with me. You should get checked out properly.'

Rook stands, his legs shaking, determined not to let his son see. 'I'm not an invalid,' he says. 'I'm going to try and catch the tour.'

'Dad, please. You can't just pretend nothing's happened.'

Rook isn't sure whether he means his little episode, or June.

He turns for the door. As he approaches the lift, he tries to hear whether his son is following him. When he presses the button, he is alone. Then Ralph emerges from the door, and against his will, Rook is relieved.

*

A dilapidated bus waits in the shade. A small, wiry Vietnamese boy with an earring and thickly gelled hair welcomes them on board, grinning. The interior is crammed with tourists, their knees pressing into multi-coloured seats. A fat man with an NYC baseball cap, his camcorder already trained on the guide's face. A woman wearing a billowing Alabama choir T-shirt, hair damp at the nape of her neck. Two tall, thinly muscular men with tans and the beaky look of Europeans. A Japanese family, clutching their cameras. A honeymoon couple, all inter-twined limbs and whispered conversations.

Most of them hold a camera or phone, snapping pictures out of the window, of the bus, of the tour guide. *These days, everyone is a photographer*, Ralph had said once, as he took a photo of their Sunday dinner. Rook had felt outraged. How was that possibly a good thing?

They sit opposite the Alabama choir woman.

'We leave now,' the tour guide says. 'My name is Duc: I will be your guide to the tunnels. It takes two hours by bus. I will tell you stories, about my country.' He pauses. 'Was anyone here during the American war?'

Rook feels his hand raise. 'I was,' he says, feeling immediately uncomfortable as people's eyes fix on him. He knows he is trying to prove something to his son, after his show of weakness in the hotel room.

'You were a soldier?' Duc asks.

'A photographer,' Rook says.

'Brave man,' Duc says.

Rook is used to this reaction. People are often

impressed by his courage, by his profession. Everyone except his own family. He remembers returning from overseas trips, how Ralph and June's eyes would glaze over as he talked about his experiences. How he always felt like an inconvenience, a hindrance to their ordinary routine, to their closeness. Was it any wonder he was always desperate for the next call, for the next story?

Duc is still talking. 'I am too young to remember the war. But my family tell me many stories, and I will share with you.' He smiles. 'Don't worry: no bad stories. Here, we like to talk about the war.

'At the tunnels, we will see the place where people hid to escape the bombs of the Americans. Very clever. They build many things below the ground because the only place that is safe. We can look at the tunnels, and we can climb inside too: if we are brave enough.' Duc laughs, short and sharp.

They are reaching the edges of the city. The buildings crammed along the roadside and river fall away, leaving only the open paddy fields, where once again people work the land. The glare of the green rice shoots, the sunlight. Rook leans towards the scratched glass, looking out for the red umbrella trees.

'Do you remember this?' Ralph says, and Rook shakes his head. But away from the brash modernity of the city, the country he remembers has become visible again. As if he is travelling back in time.

The entrance to the tunnels marks a clearing in the vegetation. There are low, red-roofed buildings, joined by wide, concreted paths, dotted amongst a sparse covering of trees.

They follow Duc through the path to the first pavilion. Beneath their feet is an artificial forest floor, nothing like the canopied mesh of plants that Rook remembers. The fake jungle is filled with the sounds of cameras clicking.

'Can anyone find the door to the tunnels?' Duc says.

The tourists look around blinking at the ground below their feet.

Duc crouches. He rustles around in the carefully discarded leaf litter, smoothing back a space where a small square hatch becomes visible. He lifts it up: underneath is a hole, perhaps 30cm square.

'Anyone want to try?' Duc says.

The girl from the honeymoon couple raises her hand. Her husband grins and raises his phone as she lowers her legs. Her narrow hips almost become stuck, and she giggles, wriggling free. She raises her arms above her head, ducking out of sight.

Duc places the lid back over the hold.

She shrieks half-heartedly. 'It's so dark!' she says, her voice muffled.

Duc lifts the lid. Everyone claps as she emerges.

Rook feels a heavy nausea as he follows the others towards the next pavilion, where there are a series of punji stick traps. He and Ralph stand to one side as the tourists take photos, pretending to have their legs maimed.

The next pavilion holds guns, a whole room of them, stacked in glass cases and labelled. Rook sees the weapons, slung across the chests of soldiers, held above heads as they crossed rivers.

This is not a tourist attraction, he wants to shout. He can't be here any more: he walks away, towards the bus.

'Where are you going?' Duc calls after him. 'We must all stay together.'

He follows the tourists around the rest of the exhibits: a pavilion with a map of the tunnel system, where they are shown a video about the life of the tunnel rats. Rook focuses on the whitewashed wall and lets the voices run over his head. He feels his hands shake in his lap and he is sweating now, though the room is air-conditioned.

When Ralph touches Rook's shoulder, he jumps.

'We're moving on now, Dad,' his son says.

At the end of the tour, there's a shop, selling old bullets and replica guns. People buy cobs of buttery barbecued corn from a stall. Ralph buys one, but Rook isn't hungry. He's made it, he thinks: they'll be back on the bus soon.

Duc claps his hands. 'One more exhibit,' he says. 'We have weapons here,' he says. 'Many types. The same as in the war. If you like, you can fire them over there. Pay extra.'

He points beyond a dense hedge line at the edge of the shop with a narrow door cut into it. There is a clearing beyond, just visible: a wide space with a series of sun-glared sandbags at the far side.

Rook looks at the other people around him. Surely none of them will actually volunteer. But the man in the NYC cap is already squeezing through the hedge, followed by the honeymoon couple. Soon, the sound of AK-47 fire rings out across the quiet of the enclosure. Rook feels himself sink onto a nearby chair, all the breath knocked out of his chest. He stares at the sandy floor, pain shooting up his arms. Squares swing across his vision. This is worse than the hotel room, and Rook moves towards the pain, embracing it.

Ralph's face looms over him, his mouth moving. He is grasping onto his shoulders and Rook wants to push him away.

The Alabama woman is there too, and she hands him some water. He watches the bottle drop to the ground, the dark stain spreading on the earth beneath his feet. The woman is trying to take his pulse, and he pushes her, managing to stand, to stumble away from the watching group and towards the bus. When he reaches it, he leans against the hot exterior and closes his eyes.

1963

Rook, Henry and Tom were in the office when the phone rang. Rook had only been back in the country for a week. They were all hungover: no one wanted to answer it.

'It's probably Ernie,' Tom said, groaning. 'I can't speak to him today.'

'Maybe he wants to give you a pay rise,' Henry said.

'Yeah, right. He wants stories. I don't know where he wants me to find them: Diem's pulled most of the army back into the city. There's nothing going on in the field.'

Rook picked up the phone.

'The day of activity has arrived,' a voice said.

Rook frowned. 'Hello?'

There was a quick, dry laugh. 'Xa Loi pagoda, nine a.m.'

The line went dead, and Rook replaced the receiver.

'Who was that?' Henry said.

'It was Thich Duc Nghiep,' he said. 'I think. He said, "The day of activity has arrived".'

Tom snorted. 'Not today, Tic Tac Toe,' he said. 'We're not falling for that again. I'm going home to bed. This headache is killing me.'

Rook looked at Henry, who shook his head. 'I'm meeting Linh: I can't blow her off for work again. Are you going to check it out?'

Rook shrugged. 'I don't have anything better to do,' he said.

Thich Duc Nghiep – or Tic Tac Toe, as the journalists who couldn't pronounce his name called him – had been leaving tips for months. Writers and photographers all turned out for the first few, waiting in the heat for an hour. Finally, a young, skinny monk would appear and bow. 'The human sacrifice will happen soon,' he'd say, turning and retreating back into the shade of the pagoda.

The journalists tried to work out what he meant. The monks were peaceful, so the brutality of the wording didn't seem to make sense.

'Maybe they've got President Diem held hostage back there,' Henry said. 'Force-feeding him green tea.'

Hans shook his head. 'They're just trying to shock us. To get a reaction.'

'Well, it's working,' Tom said, looking around at the gaggle of journalists, beginning to disperse.

But the numbers had gradually diminished with each call, and today, when Rook approached the pagoda, there wasn't another white man in sight. Rook's head was ringing with his hangover: the heat wasn't helping, and he was about to turn around and return to the hotel when the air began to hum with voices. Rook made out a mass of yellow- and white-robed people ahead, clustered around the entrance to the holy place. They were surrounding a grey car waiting at the side of the road.

As the vehicle pulled away, the chanting stopped and an eerie silence fell. Rook felt his fingers tighten around his camera: there was an electricity in the air he remembered from the day of the nuclear weapons march, and he felt himself become alert.

The crowd formed two lines behind the car. Rook pursued at a distance, endeavouring to get everything into his lens. Soon, curious locals joined the procession. Up ahead, Rook noticed the two police vehicles, clearing the road.

The car stopped at a junction and the door opened. Three monks emerged, their heads shiny in the Saigon glare. Rook recognized Tic Tac Toe, his lips upturned. He searched the crowd, his eyes resting on Rook, his smile spreading. Again, Rook's internal compass began to spin, and he raised his camera.

The monks led a stooped, elderly monk towards the centre of the junction, forming a circle with the older man at its apex. The murmuring chants of the waiting crowd became louder. Rook watched through the viewfinder as the ancient monk sat cross-legged, his bones like poles under his tent-like robe. One of the others lifted a jerry-can over his head. Pink liquid cascaded off the man's bald head, running into his eyes and mouth, damp patches spreading across his yellow robes.

Rook felt his finger compress the shutter, then wind

on the film. The monk pulled something out of his robes. At the very moment Rook realized what it was – a match – the monk's hands moved in his lap, and the man was ablaze, a tower of fire erupting as a gasp went up from the crowd. People began moaning, lowering themselves to their knees.

Seeing it all from behind the camera, Rook held his nerve as he clicked and wound his film on, again and again. As the other monks dropped to the ground, as their wailing increased, Rook remained in the same spot. He remembered, fleetingly, the old woman and the little boy on his first patrol, how he'd failed to capture what had happened to them. He wouldn't let that happen again. Without his photographs, there would be no evidence. This monk would have died in vain.

Tic Tac Toe spoke over the loudspeaker. 'A Buddhist monk burns himself to death. A Buddhist monk becomes a martyr.'

The man's body melded into flames, remaining upright for far too long. As the wind moved the fire, Rook could see his face contorted in agony. All around him, people were crying, tears running down their faces. Rook moved past them, turning the focuser, until he could feel the heat coming off the burning man, see his eyes staring back at him through the wavering orange. Then, the figure fell to the side, his body heavy and charred, no longer a living thing.

*

After it was over, Rook found Tic Tac Toe, who smiled wanly, his hands pressed together in front of his chest.

'I saw you already,' he said. 'Where is Mister Henry and Mister Tom?'

'They didn't come.'

'They will be sorry, I think.' Tic Tac Toe tapped Rook's camera with a long fingernail. 'Did you get a picture?'

'I think so,' Rook said.

'Diem is the enemy of the Buddhists,' Tic Tac Toe said. 'Perhaps now, the world will listen to us.'

Rook thought of the photos of water cannons firing at black children on the streets of Mississippi. The race riots, which had so dominated the headlines. Surely this would be enough to push them aside? 'I hope so,' he said.

Tic Tac Toe smiled again. He seemed elated, oblivious to the monk's charred body, a few yards away. Rook himself was suddenly aware of it, and of a terrible smell, which made his stomach churn. He needed to get away from here.

As soon as he was out of sight, Rook stopped in the shade at the side of the road, suddenly too hot, dizzy. The smell would not leave him. He took a deep, shaky breath as his nausea returned, his stomach expelling its contents onto the pavement.

*

No one was at the office when he got back. Rook was disappointed, longing to tell Henry, hoping he would be back from Linh's. He went into the darkroom and started sorting through the negatives before the adrenaline left him, distracting himself with the intricacies of developing. His hands shook as he saw again the solidity of the flames, the charred limbs, bent and outstretched in the final images.

Doors slamming, chatter and laughter. Through the wall, lost in the images, Rook heard Henry and Tom get back. Once he'd hung all the photographs up to dry, he opened the door.

'Rook!' Henry said. 'We didn't know you were here.'

'What're you developing?' Tom said. 'Don't tell me that tip was something?'

Rook looked at them. 'See for yourself,' he said.

Tom stepped passed him, his eyes moving from image to image. 'Fucking hell, Rook! Have you got these out yet?'

'No.'

Tom ran a hand through his hair. 'Fuck,' he said. 'Fuck fuck fuck. I can't believe we missed this. Ernie's going to kill me.'

'Was anyone else there?' Henry asked Rook.

'I don't think so.'

'Well, at least that's something, Tom,' he said. 'No one else got the story either.'

Tom's face was red. 'Fuck that,' he said. '*I* didn't get anything: that's all Ernie'll care about.' Tom was pacing now, not looking at Rook. 'This is what we've been waiting for, and I fucking missed it.'

'I got a quote,' Rook said. 'If you want to put together a story.'

'That photo doesn't need a story,' Tom said. 'If you were on freelance, you'd've just made yourself a fucking fortune.' He sighed. 'I need a drink. Coming, Henry?'

Henry looked at Tom. 'We need to write, Tom,' he said. 'Do some damage control. AP won't even know this has happened yet.'

Tom glanced between Henry and Rook. 'Suit yourself,' he said. He walked towards the door. Then he stopped. 'Did no one think to put the fucker out?'

For a moment, Rook couldn't think what he meant.

'The monk,' Tom asked. 'All those people in your photograph, just watching. Surely someone should have done something?'

'He set himself alight,' Rook said, thinking Tom didn't understand, that the photo didn't make it clear what had happened.

'I know that,' Tom spat. 'It doesn't make it right.'

'Come on, Tom,' Henry said. 'You would have done the same thing.'

Tom scowled. 'I hope not.' He stalked out of the room.

There was silence after the door slammed.

'I didn't even think to stop him,' Rook said, eventually.

'Don't worry about Tom,' Henry said. 'He would have done exactly the same. He's just pissed he didn't take the tip. Ernie's never going to let him hear the end of it.'

He pulled out a chair in front of his typewriter and sat down. 'Now let's get this story written.'

*

Once the photos were out, Rook didn't hear anything. It was still night time in London: he'd have to wait until early evening before he heard from Tony. Henry wrote a story and got it out to the *New York Times*, with the caption *Pictures to follow*.

Rook couldn't be in the office, waiting for the sun to rise over London.

'Let's find Tom,' he said. 'Talk him into writing something.'

They tried all their usual haunts: the rooftop bars around the opera house and the street-facing bar at the Continental Palace. They ran into Hans and the guys from AP, but Tom was nowhere to be found.

'Anything going on?' Hans asked.

Henry's face was deadpan. 'Nothing,' he said.

'We're just looking for Tom,' Rook said.

'He was around earlier,' Hans said. 'Drinking and swearing. Have you fallen out?'

'You could say that.'

'What aren't you telling me?' Hans said, narrowing his eyes.

Henry and Rook grinned at each other. 'You'll find out,' Henry said.

'You guys drive me nuts.'

Henry and Rook took a table at the edge of the patio,

looking out onto the square. 'You must be on top of the world,' Henry said, sipping his drink.

Rook thought about the photos, about what they might mean. He'd been holding off his excitement, in case he was disappointed, but it was there: he could feel it.

'You've every right to be elated,' Henry said. 'How many tips have you followed? How many patrols have you been on? This is the pay-off, and you should enjoy it while it lasts. It's gonna be a huge story.'

Rook felt happiness then, as if Henry's permission had released it. He thought of June, imagined her seeing his image on the front page of a newspaper. She'd be so proud of him.

'And don't worry about Tom,' Henry said. 'He's angry with himself, not with you. He knows he should have followed up on that tip. We both should. He'll cool down.'

'I still feel guilty,' Rook said. But part of him thought Tom was behaving like a child who hadn't got his own way. Couldn't he be happy for Rook?

'He could have had the first story,' Henry said. 'If he wasn't so stubborn. You got a quote, and no one's seen the pictures yet.'

'I really wanted to share it with you guys.'

Henry smiled. 'And you did. I'm glad you were there at all. Whoever got the story, it changes everything. This has to get coverage: no one can see that photo and ignore it. Anything that puts the war on the map is all right with me.'

Rook decided to wait until seven to check the wire – nine a.m. in London – when he could be sure Tony was in the office and could respond. He'd had a few drinks by the time Hans found them again, barrelling up to the table with a red face.

'Have you guys seen the wire?' he asked.

'No,' Henry said. 'What's happened?'

'Don't play the innocent with me,' he said. 'It's gone fucking crazy.'

'Looks like Tony got your photos,' Henry said to Rook.

'The *Sunday Times* have sent them out,' Hans said. 'They're going to make a pile of cash.'

Rook grinned. He couldn't speak.

'Look at him,' Hans said. 'So happy.'

'We'd better head back to the office,' Henry said.

They both stood up. Hans put his hand out, and Rook took it. 'Well done, Rook,' he said. 'You lucky son of a bitch.'

*

The teleprinter was clicking and beeping, piles of paper curling out onto the ground below the table. Rook leaned over. His photos, emerging one after the other. In amongst them, a note from Tony.

> KNEW YOU WERE THE RIGHT MAN ROOK STOP PHOTOS IN TOMORROW'S PAPER STOP WE'RE SELLING THEM ON THE WIRE STOP BONUS COMING YOUR WAY STOP

Rook couldn't keep the smile off his face. It was really happening. He wished he could call June.

Henry had a message too, from the *New York Times*. They were running the story, but not the images. TOO MUCH FOR BREAKFAST PAPERS, the desk wrote.

Henry grinned at Rook. 'Typical,' he said. 'I'm the only one with the story, and they're too pussy to print the photo to go with it.'

*

They found Tom back at the villa, drinking vodka out by the pool, slumped on a sunbed. He looked up through the patio window at them, grimacing when he saw Rook.

'He's drunk,' Henry said. 'Let me go out and talk to him.'

Rook waited inside, leaning against the marble kitchen counter. It wasn't long before Tom's voice reached him, through the crack in the patio doors.

'He's a fucking traitor,' Tom was saying. 'Haven't we shared everything? And then he goes and screws us all.'

'We all got the tip, Tom,' Henry said. 'Rook just followed it.'

'I'll lose my job over this,' Tom said.

Henry said something Rook couldn't make out.

'I don't care if he can hear me,' Tom roared. 'Let him come out here and I'll say it to his face. He's too much of a fucking coward.'

Rook stepped out of the doors. 'Here I am.'

Tom stood up. 'After everything we've done for you.'

'It was a tip, Tom,' Rook said. 'I haven't done anything wrong.'

'You've been here five minutes, and you think you're king of the fucking world.' Tom stepped forward: Henry put his arm out.

'Calm down, Tom,' he said. 'Let's discuss this when you're sober.'

'Stop taking his side.'

Henry turned away. 'Let's go, Rook,' he said. 'Leave the man to his drink.'

*

Tom didn't calm down. He'd barely spoken to Rook since his outburst at the pool, leaving the office whenever he arrived. Henry told Rook that Tom was spending a lot of time at the pagoda, sitting cross-legged in darkened side rooms with Tic Tac Toe, talking in hushed whispers, while the smell of boiling cabbage and joss sticks ruined endless cups of green tea.

'He's determined not to miss another trick,' Henry said.

Apparently, Tom was finding it all highly frustrating: the cryptic way the monks used English, their words meaning both everything and nothing at all. *The sky is blue and the clouds move across it.*

When he caught glances of Tom – his grey face and tired eyes – Rook felt guilty, then immediately chastised himself. He'd done nothing that Tom wouldn't have done himself. He wasn't going to apologize for following the tip, for taking the photographs. Tom had blown things way out of proportion.

Rook had other things to worry about. The photographs might have propelled his career forwards, but it had also put him on Diem's blacklist. A few days after the craziness of the photo, Rook's picture appeared on the front cover of the *Times of Vietnam*: the expat newspaper, and mouthpiece for the Diem regime. *Who is Rook Henderson and what does he want?* read the headline. The story accused him of being a Communist sympathizer, of bribing the monk to immolate himself.

The other journalists teased him, and it was easy enough to laugh off. But men in black leather jackets – the uniform of the secret police – started lurking outside the office and the hotel. They'd trail Rook through the streets on motorbikes, helmets obscuring their faces.

Approaching the office one day, Rook overheard Tom. 'He's putting us all in danger.'

'They're not going to do anything,' Henry said. 'They're just trying to frighten him out of taking any more photos.'

'I wouldn't be so sure,' Tom said. 'We shouldn't be taking chances.'

'What do you suggest we do, Tom?' Henry said. 'Kick him out of the office? He's our friend.'

Tom laughed. 'He's not my friend,' he said. 'Not any more.'

Rook took a taxi back to the hotel, afraid to be on the streets. He didn't go back to the office for a few days, lying low in his room. Henry came to find him.

'Where've you been?' he asked, letting himself in.

'Here,' Rook said.

Henry sat on the corner of his bed. 'You can't let them win, Rook,' he said. 'You need to do your job.'

'It's too risky.'

'Don't be stupid. I've had a tip about a protest near the pagoda. Want to check it out?'

The streets were quiet: the midday lull, when most of the locals took to their beds to ride out the heat. Usually, Rook would have done the same, but recently, he'd not been able to sleep. Whether it was day or night, his mind was alive with the fear of the men who could be waiting for him.

As they drew nearer to the pagoda, the streets became busy, crammed with monks and students in plain clothes, holding banners and yelling. The eyes of the crowd flashed and no one was smiling.

'I feel a little uneasy,' Rook said, as his old warning signals began to display themselves. 'We should get out of here.'

'Wouldn't you be angry if you'd been totally dismissed by your own government?' Henry said. 'Did you hear what Madame Nhu called the monk's suicide?' Rook shook his head. 'The barbecue of the bonze.'

Rook looked around at the chanting faces of the

people, taut with frustration. 'I think it's going to turn nasty.'

'That's why we need to be here,' Henry said.

Henry started to follow the crowd through the streets, and Rook stuck close. He could feel eyes on him, and he turned, sure he would see the familiar group of black leather jackets. But it was Tom who was staring at him from across the street, where he was standing with Hans. Henry raised his hand in greeting, but Tom turned away.

'When's he going to let this go?' Henry asked.

Rook said nothing, lifting his camera, losing himself in the moments he saw through the viewfinder. A monk's face as he shouted into a loudhailer. A conical hat knocked from an old woman's head. The arrival of the government police in riot gear and helmets. They forced their way through the crowd, pushing people down as they went.

Suddenly, Rook was dragged backwards by the collar of his shirt. He landed flat on the ground, protecting his camera with both hands. Blows rained down on his legs and arms, and he curled on his side, shutting his eyes. A boot met his face: he heard a crack as pain spread across his cheekbone. He shouted out for Henry.

Feet trampled close to his head.

'Get off him!'

Rook opened his eyes, blinking in the sunlight. He saw Tom, pulling one of the men off him. Henry was there too, his fists up, pushing the people out of the way.

From the ground, Rook saw Tom's fist draw back and meet the stomach of one of the leather jackets.

He felt hands under his armpits, pulling him upright. His legs were loose and weak, and he began to slide down towards the ground, his head heavy.

SEVEN

Eventually, the wash of panic passes Rook by, leaving him standing by the bus, surrounded by a small group of concerned faces.

'I'm calling a doctor,' the woman with the billowing Alabama choir T-shirt says, pulling a mobile phone out of her pocket.

'That's not necessary,' Rook says, though his voice betrays him.

'You don't look well, hun,' she says.

'I told you, I'm quite all right. I just need to get back to the city.'

Ralph and the woman exchange glances. 'I'll make sure he sees someone in the hotel,' Ralph says.

'We'll see about that,' Rook says.

Duc claps his hands. 'Everyone, back on bus. Let's get the photo man home.'

As they climb aboard, the Alabama woman takes a seat near them. 'I'm so glad you're all right,' she says. 'I thought you were having a heart attack. You gave your son quite a fright.'

Rook looks at Ralph and knows he is thinking the same thing, imagining June in her armchair, alone.

'It was the heat,' he says.

'Just make sure you get checked out,' she says. He wishes this woman would leave them alone. He wants to stare out of the window, and forget any of this ever happened.

Twice on the journey back, Rook turns to catch Ralph looking at him. He has said nothing since the tour, and Rook wishes he knew what he was thinking. Is he angry, that he was right about leaving the city? Or resentful, that he is here at all?

When he looks across again, Ralph is asleep, his head thrown back, his mouth slightly open.

There is stubble on his chin, and it makes Rook feel odd to look at it. He remembers returning to the cottage from a trip, and finding Ralph sitting on the rug in the living room, watching TV while doing his homework.

When Ralph heard the door, he looked up, and Rook saw the trace of shadow darkening his jawline, the missed hairs below his nose.

'When did you start shaving?' he'd said, without thinking.

His son shrugged, returning to his workbook, a lock of greasy hair falling over his eye.

When he tried to talk to June about it later, she shook her head. 'What did you expect, Rook?'

Rook imagined his son, his boy, standing in the bathroom, a razor in his hand. Had somebody taught him, or had he worked it out for himself? He felt again that heavy sense of inadequacy. Even when the pictures of the famine appeared in the *Sunday Times* that weekend, even with all the outrage and fundraising that followed, his mind kept shuttling back to his son's stubbly face.

I should have taught him that, Rook wanted to say, but as usual, he said nothing.

*

When they get back, it is already night, the lights of the hotels enclosing the square. Rook goes to his room. Ralph follows him, going to the phone on the bedside table.

'What are you doing?' Rook asks.

'Phoning the doctor,' Ralph says.

'You are not. I'm fine.'

'I wish you'd stop saying that.'

'It's true.'

Ralph pauses. 'You need to take care of yourself.' Rook realizes then: he isn't angry, he's worried. He's treating Rook like an old man, and he can't stand it.

'I am. I'm going to bed right now.'

Ralph slams the phone back onto the receiver. 'We're leaving in the morning.'

'I'm not.' Rook opens the minibar, pulling out a miniature of whisky. 'I didn't ask you to come here. I'm perfectly fine on my own.'

Ralph just stands there, watching him. 'You're being a fool.'

They stare at each other. Rook's frustration thrums through his muscles; his fists clench.

'You can't keep running away, Dad,' Ralph says. 'You need to face what's happened. Come home, and be fair to Mum.'

His son's calm seems to exacerbate Rook's distress. His limbs feel weak, his heartbeat too fast. His body begins to tremble with the strength of it, and he sinks onto the bed, dropping his head into his hands.

Ralph stays where he is. 'I'm scared too,' he says. 'We all are. It's nothing to be ashamed of.'

Rook opens his mouth. He thinks of Tom, calling out to him, that last night. Of his childhood friend, looking up, his eyes full of uncertainty. *I am not a coward*, he wants to say. But the words will not come. Instead, a roar of feeling rushes through his chest, spreading until it escapes from his mouth in a sob. He imagines June in her chair, her body so finally still. Ralph's face, his disappointment etched into his features. The images he has held back flash in front of his eyes, and his body is racked with the strength of his tears.

I'm scared too, his son had said. *We all are.*

He remembers when Ralph was ten or eleven, he had taken him camping, on one of his rare stints home. They drove into the Scottish Highlands, taking roads at random until they found what Rook was looking for: a quiet valley where they could be tested.

Night was drawing in as they set up their tent, the dark forest outlined against the dusky sky. Rook showed

Ralph how to lay the groundsheet, how to pull the canvas tight to avoid leaks, how to use the hammer to peg it to the ground. Every time he asked the boy to try something, he looked startled.

'What are you afraid of?' he asked, when he stood on the edge of the forest, reluctant to come and collect firewood.

The best Ralph was able to do was stand there.

He was quiet by the camp fire, watching the flames flicker as Rook showed him how they'd minimized the smoke from their fires in Vietnam, so they wouldn't be spotted by the Cong.

'Were you scared?' Ralph said, eventually.

'Sometimes,' Rook said. 'But you learn to keep calm under pressure. And you work out that the man next to you is just as scared as you are. Our fear keeps us alert, and alive.'

Ralph nodded, his eyes finding Rook's. For a moment, Rook thought of the boy he himself had been once: the outsider, and how hard it had been. He could help Ralph, he realized, he could show him that there was no reason for him to be afraid. That even when the worst things happen, it is possible to survive.

The next morning, while they were in the town collecting supplies, Rook saw the newspaper: the coverage of the Ethiopian famine. He found a payphone and called the office, his fingers heavy as he pressed the familiar numbers. They wanted him to go, as soon as possible. Rook imagined saying no, remaining here with his son.

But as he looked out of the phone box to where his son was waiting, all he could think about was the time, ticking away.

He left the phone booth, putting his hand on his son's shoulder. 'You wouldn't mind if we went home a day early, would you?'

Ralph shrugged, covering the surprise that had flashed across his face. 'No,' he said.

'There's a famine in Ethiopia. I'd like to cover it.'

'It sounds important.'

June was angry, when they arrived back at the cottage. 'He's waited a month for this, Rook,' she said.

Rook was already searching the wardrobe for his bag. 'If the boy understands, I don't know why you can't.'

A few days later, he made it into the camp on a dusty jeep, bumping through the dark stencil of the surrounding mountains. In the bowl of the valley there looked to be thousands of rocks, clumped together. Coming closer, Rook could see that the rocks were moving. People, clad in rags, some squatting or sitting on the ground, crammed into every available space. There was a sound, too, as they got closer, and Rook wheeled down his window. A sort of moaning, as if the earth was protesting at the weight of the bodies.

As their vehicle approached, some of the figures got up, rushing towards them on spindly legs. They surrounded the jeep, eyes bulbous in their domed skulls, their thin fingers touching the windows.

The driver wheeled down his window and shouted something, and slowly, the people began to drop away.

'What did you say to them?' Rook asked.

'I told them we have no food,' the driver said.

As he raised his camera, to take the photos of these people he had travelled across the world to see, he knew it wasn't just about the photographs. It was this feeling of being at the centre of things, of being important. When he was out on a story, everything else in his life – his distant family, his own sadness – was secondary to what was happening right in front of him.

But now there is no escape. Rook has run again, but this time Ralph has followed him. When Rook looks up, his son is sitting beside him in the hotel room, his hand on his back, his eyes fixed on his father.

Rook feels his heart stretch to breaking point.

'I'm sorry,' Rook says. 'I'm sorry for everything.'

1963

After the fight at the pagoda, Rook spent a week in hospital, with two cracked ribs and a broken cheekbone. He'd been given a private room on an upper floor, with a window overlooking the park.

Within ten minutes of being in bed, he was bored.

'Just don't make me laugh,' he said to Henry when he came to visit.

'All right. I won't show you a mirror either.'

Rook put his hands up to his face, which felt swollen and wrong. Talking was painful, so he let Henry update him on what had been going on: how he and Tom had spent four hours being questioned by the police.

'The *secret police* are accusing *us* of espionage.'

'Are they going to charge you?'

'No. The *New York Times* got on to it and they let us go.'

'How's Tom?'

The door hinges creaked. 'He's fine,' Tom said, stepping into the room, the shadow of a black eye falling across his face.

'They got you too?' Rook said.

'Hardly,' Tom said. 'How are you feeling?'

'All right. Thanks to you two.'

Tom looked down. 'I wasn't going to let them attack you.'

'Well, thank you.'

'Truce?' Tom said, and Rook nodded.

'Thank fuck for that,' Henry said, and they all laughed.

'I've brought something for you,' Tom said. 'From the wire.'

He held out a torn piece of paper.

ROOK STOP THIS IS JUNE STOP YOU MUST COME HOME STOP TONY THREATENING TO PULL YOUR CONTRACT STOP WE BOTH AGREE YOU NEED REST STOP WON'T TAKE NO FOR AN ANSWER STOP

'Looks like you've been told,' Henry said, reading over his shoulder.

'Do you think Tony's serious?' Rook said.

'It sounds like June is.'

'I can't leave now,' Rook said. 'Not with all the Diem plotting going on. What if they overthrow him while I'm gone?'

'You don't look great, Rook,' Tom said. 'You should probably get some rest.'

'You just want me out of the way.'

'That may be true,' Tom said, and they laughed.

'You should probably go,' Henry said. 'You can stay up to date on the latest coup du jour on the wire. If anything happens, just jump on the next plane.'

Rook sighed. 'I'm going to have to, aren't I?'

After the boys had waved him off at the airport, he took slow, painful steps towards the waiting plane, feeling a surge of relief. It would be nice to see June, to be fussed over for a week or so. The last few weeks of constant vigilance had been exhausting. It should have all blown over by the time he returned.

He'd only been away from the UK for a month, but when he saw June standing in arrivals, looking anxious, he knew he'd made the right decision.

He walked towards her and she embraced him.

'Thank you,' she murmured. 'For coming home.'

In the taxi, rushing through the streets of London, he felt her watching him.

'What?' he asked.

'You look terrible. Your beautiful face.' She reached her hand up. 'Does it hurt?'

'Not if I don't think about it.'

'We'll get you rested up.'

Rook took her hand. 'I've been in hospital for a fortnight. I don't want to just stay in bed.'

'Even if I'm there?' June said.

'Well, maybe.'

'I'll make it worth your while,' she said.

*

Back at the apartment, June had everything set up for him. She'd moved the record player into the bedroom and set up a mountain of pillows for him to lean against. Today's papers were on the bedside table.

The sunshine pressed against the blinds. He knew how rare days like this were in London, and though he hadn't slept on the flight, he didn't feel tired. 'Can we get some fresh air first?'

'Are you sure you can walk?'

'Of course I can.'

But even by the time they'd reached the bottom of the stairs, Rook was out of breath, his bruised torso aching. He was determined to keep going.

'There's a park at the end of the street,' June said. She took his arm, and they walked slowly along the pavement. He could feel people staring at him.

'Not much further,' June said, just as he was about to ask if they could turn back. He took the last few steps, and finally they found a bench near the entrance to the park.

'It's a beautiful day,' June said, although the sun had just dipped behind a cloud.

'I'm glad to be back,' he said.

'Are you? I felt like your mother, ordering you to stay off school. I just couldn't stand the thought of you being injured, so far away, where I couldn't do anything to help you.'

'You're so sweet, June.' He put his hand on her knee. 'But I only got beaten up. It's not life-threatening.'

'Beaten up by the secret police. Wasn't that what Tony said? I thought they were on your side?'

'Technically, I don't have a side. But they are fighting with the Americans, yes. The Vietnamese president didn't like the photo of the burning monk. Fleas on the backside of the Americans, that's what he calls us. He thinks we're being disloyal and he wanted to teach me a lesson.'

June sighed. 'If you can't even trust the government, how can you feel safe there?'

Rook thought back over the past month, the tension that had constantly thrummed. 'I think that comes with the territory. It is a war, after all.'

'Well, I don't like it.'

'We knew it was dangerous when I signed up for it. And really, it could be much worse. At least it's not shrapnel, or bullets.'

'Is that supposed to make me feel better? That you could have been shot?'

'It's the reality.' There was a silence. 'I didn't expect to come home to a lecture.'

'I'm not lecturing you. I'm worried. Look at yourself, Rook! Don't you think it's time you took a break?'

'It was hard enough for me to come back now,' Rook said. 'We're getting coverage: things are finally happening. There've been rumours that some of the generals are plotting to oust the President. I need to go back as soon as possible.'

'You're not going anywhere until you're better. I don't care what's happening.' June's face was determined.

'This is my job, June. It's important.'

'Not important enough to die for.'

'You're being dramatic. Who said anything about dying? I've been in a fight, that's all.'

'And it could be a lot worse next time.'

'I thought you trusted me to know my limits.'

'And I thought what we had was more important than the war.'

Rook paused. 'It is. But when I tell you I know what I'm doing, you have to believe me.'

'You can't control everything, Rook,' she said. 'You can't possibly know what's going to happen.'

'I have support. And I get this feeling, when something isn't worth the risk.'

June laughed. 'You're the last person I expected to be superstitious.'

'It's not superstition, it's common sense. Calculated risk.'

'Forgive me for finding that hard to believe.'

A silence fell. Rook had thought he was coming home to be made a fuss of, not to be told what he could and couldn't do. He felt like June was questioning his ability to do his job.

'If you weren't such a cripple, I'd leave you here,' she said, eventually.

'If I wasn't such a cripple, I'd walk away.'

They glanced at each other, and smiled. 'I'm sorry,' June said. 'I've just been so worried about you. Getting word from Tony that you were injured – I just don't want to go through that again.'

'You won't. I promise.'

'It could be worse next time. I can't even bear to think about losing you, Rook.'

He turned her face towards his. 'That's not going to happen.'

She looked down. 'Humour me,' she said. 'While you're here, just rest. I can get the papers for you, go to the office to check the wire. Even if you won't admit it, you look exhausted. The more rest you get, the happier I'll be sending you back out there.'

So she was allowing him to return to Vietnam. Choose your battles, he thought. 'All right,' he said.

*

He did as she asked. He remained in bed, listening to music and reading the papers. Stories about Vietnam were featured more and more: still tucked away at the back in the rarely read 'International News' section, but at least they were there. The Buddhist discontent seemed to be escalating: the police had arrested and beaten eighty protestors downtown; pagodas had been closed, the entrances strung with barbed wire, but still the monks and students kept up their struggle, with protests and more suicides. Reading the stories, a tingle travelled down his spine: he could smell the incense and imagine the chanting, and he longed to be there, his shirt wet with sweat, his camera at the ready.

June went to the office every few days to bring back reams of paper from the wire. A week after he came back, there was a message from the boys.

HELLO STRANGER STOP ARRESTED AGAIN TODAY STOP HELD FOR FIVE HOURS IN SAFEHOUSE STOP YOU MISSED OUT STOP GET YOUR ASS BACK HERE STOP HENRY AND TOM STOP

June watched Rook read it. He could imagine Tom writing it, and Henry laughing, and he missed them and Saigon so much it was painful. He couldn't bear it: the idea that things were moving on without him.

'How was Tony?' he asked June.

'He's fine. Wondering how you were doing.'

'I bet he wants me back to work.'

'He wants you to get better. You're no use to him like this.'

June sat on the edge of his bed and chatted to him in the first few days. But after a while, she had to return to her normal life: she'd been chosen for a small part in a play and couldn't miss any more rehearsals.

'Why didn't you tell me?' Rook asked.

'It didn't seem important.'

'I'm so pleased for you, June. When's the performance?'

'Not until the end of August,' she said. 'It's really not a big deal. It's a small theatre, very experimental. It's pretty much amateur dramatics.'

Rook pulled her towards him in the bed, wincing as she fell onto his chest. 'It's brilliant. Well done.'

'Mildred's in it too,' she said. 'She knows the director: Jimmy. She got me the part, really. It was nice of him to give me a chance.'

She didn't sound like June: always so sure that everything would work out. He wondered whether her difficulties at finding success had affected her more than he thought. 'He's lucky to have you.'

'It's a start,' June said.

June had had a phone line put in and it rang non-stop. He could hear her through the wall, giggling and chatting to Mildred, clearly gossiping about something or other.

'Who was there?' June would ask. 'I can't believe she said that. I wish I could have been there.'

Now that she'd met Mildred, June seemed to have a very busy social life. Mildred popped in to visit one day, perching herself on the end of his bed and making them laugh.

When it was time for her to leave, June walked her to the front door.

'Do you think you'll make it tonight?' he heard Mildred ask.

'No,' June said. 'I'd better not.'

'Well, let me know when he's up for doing something. I miss you, darling.'

Once the door closed, June came back into the bedroom.

'It was nice to see her,' Rook said.

'She's great, isn't she?'

'What were you talking about at the door? About tonight?'

'Oh, nothing,' June said. 'She invited us to the Rivoli for drinks, but I said we're not up to it.'

'I feel a lot better,' Rook said. 'Maybe we should go.'

'I'm not sure. You still seem very weak to me.'

'I need to get out of here, June. I'm going stir-crazy.'

June paused. 'Perhaps we could go for an hour. It would be good to see everyone. You can meet the gang.'

*

It felt good to take a shower and change out of his pyjamas. When they were ready, Rook and June stood in front of the full-length mirror in the bedroom and admired themselves. Him in a suit; her in a red patterned skirt and jacket and black dolly heels.

'Don't we scrub up well?' June said.

Rook kissed the side of her face. 'Thanks for letting me out.'

She pushed him away, playfully. 'You make me sound like a jailer.'

They took a taxi, pulling up outside the Ritz. The doorman smiled when he saw June, and she kissed him on both cheeks.

Rook put his hand on her lower back and leant towards her ear. 'How often do you come here?'

'Not that often,' she said. 'And only ever for drinks. Mildred's quite a fan.'

Inside, June led them towards a group of people at the

bar. Mildred shrieked when she saw them, coming over and winding her arms around both of them, drawing them all together.

'You didn't tell me you were coming,' she said.

'We wanted to surprise you,' June said.

'Well, it worked. We've just opened a bottle of champagne, if you fancy a glass?'

'When have I ever said no to champagne?' June made her way around the group, greeting everyone. Mildred had an arm slung around a tall, dark-haired man, who Rook imagined must be Jimmy.

'You must be the wounded soldier,' Jimmy said. 'I've heard a dreadful amount about you.'

'Photographer, actually,' Rook said.

'You're right, darling,' Jimmy said archly, turning to June. 'He doesn't look well, does he?'

'We're working on that, aren't we?' June said.

'We certainly are,' Rook said. 'I hear you're directing a play?'

'I am.'

'June's happy to be involved.'

'The pleasure's all mine, I assure you. Will you be able to come?'

'I imagine I'll be gone by then,' Rook said, conscious of June watching him. 'It's really heating up out there.'

'You must be sorry to be missing the action.'

Rook shrugged. 'One of those things, I suppose.'

'He's not going back until he's better,' June said. 'No matter what happens.'

'And how long might that be?' he said, raising his eyebrows.

'Who knows?' June said. 'How long's a piece of string?'

'It was a simple question,' Jimmy said, smirking.

June's eyes flashed. 'Don't be infuriating.'

'I'm sure he didn't mean anything, June,' Rook said.

'Oh, you don't know Jimmy,' she said. 'He *always* means something.'

Mildred laughed. 'You'll get used to it,' she said. 'It's part of his charm.'

Rook wasn't so sure. Jimmy seemed defined by his rudeness, by his determination to contradict anything anyone said. He felt the man's gaze on him as he chatted with another group of people, all artists or actors. Once they found out what he did, they had questions for him, about the war and what it was like to cover it.

'I couldn't do that,' a small woman wearing a feathered hat said. 'It's all so dangerous.'

'Not once you know what you're doing,' Rook said. 'It's really like anything else. Once you know the rules, it's easier than you'd think.'

The woman laughed. 'Maybe you need to believe that,' she said.

By ten o'clock, Rook was ready to leave. He went to find June, who was in a circle with Jimmy and another man, laughing at their jokes. He stopped and watched for a moment as Jimmy said something, his green eyes fixed on June, and she slapped him on the arm. He raised his camera and captured them.

In the taxi, June chatted away, high on the champagne.

'But how are you feeling, darling? Was it too much for you?'

'I'm fine.'

'You're quiet. Is everything all right?'

Rook looked into her eyes. Was this what her life was like when he was away?

'That man,' Rook said, 'Jimmy. I'm not sure about him.'

'Oh, he's harmless.'

'I think he likes you.'

'He does,' she said. 'He's dreadfully in love with me.'

'He told you that?'

June cupped her chin in her hand. 'He's always telling me. Every time he gets drunk. But he doesn't know what he's talking about.'

Rook felt an odd feeling prickle the back of his spine, the same one he felt in the field, when danger was approaching. 'I don't think I like you being around him.'

'That's a little difficult, seeing as he's my director. He gave me my first part, Rook. That's a big deal. So, he gets carried away sometimes. I'm perfectly capable of saying no.'

Rook observed her. 'I just don't like the thought of him creeping around you when I'm away.'

'Don't go, then,' June said, and Rook balked. 'I'm joking, Rook. Don't look so sad. I don't like the thought of you being in danger, either, but we just have to live with it. We have to have faith in each other.'

Rook thought of their argument on the day of his return. She was telling him she trusted him. And he knew, really, that he had nothing to worry about.

'You're right,' he said.

June smiled, leaning on his arm. 'You were jealous.'

'What's so funny about that?'

'Nothing. But it's made me a little bit happy.'

Rook kissed her.

EIGHT

Rook lets his son fetch him tissues, and dry his eyes. He can't look at him directly. He climbs into the bed and lets Ralph pull the covers around him, as if he is a child.

He shuts his eyes, afraid that blankness will elude him.

When he sleeps, he falls in and out of dreams.

He is in a car with June, rounding a cliff corner, the curve of the bay waiting before them. They walk through the sloped streets of the town, all leading towards the water. The beachfront: crowded with coloured deck-chairs. Children clutching ice creams, men with undiscovered burnt faces, women in sundresses with a bloom of pink at the neck. The flashing of legs running towards the water, shining solidly under the glare of the sun.

June buys a wide-brimmed white hat from a small souvenir shop, and they sit on the sea wall. He rolls up his shirtsleeves and trousers. Then Ralph is there, too. They hold his hands as he paddles, and they are smiling. June dabs at her forehead with a handkerchief: Rook reaches for his camera, catching them in the lens.

When he wakes, he is sure it really happened, as if the dream was a memory. They had so many days like that, after all, when they were happy. In the beginning, before they left Backton, Rook thought it would always be like that. It could have been, he thinks. He longs to go back there, to live those days again, to be happy within them. To make the most of them.

His son is there in the room with him, sitting in the armchair by the window. He is sleeping with his neck at an awkward angle, and Rook wants to wake him, to offer him the bed. But before he can, his mind shuts tight again.

*

When Rook wakes, he has slept deeply, despite everything. Ralph is still in the chair, tapping into the screen of his phone. When Rook pulls himself up in bed, Ralph looks up.

'Are you talking to someone?' Rook asks.

Ralph nods. 'Julia.'

'How is she?'

'She's fine. She wants me to come home.'

'You should go, Ralph.'

'Only if you'll come with me.'

Rook thinks of Tom, of Linh. 'There's something I still need to do.'

'What?'

'There's an old friend I need to see.'

'Is that why you came back here?'

'No. I didn't know he was here. I'm still not sure whether to believe it.'

'Anyone I know?'

'Tom.'

'Tom Mellor?'

Hearing Ralph say the name sends a tremor down Rook's spine. 'Did your mother tell you about him?'

'No. I read his book, about the war. Have you read it?'

Rook sees the cover flash before his eyes. That photograph, of them all together. He'd read a review in the Sunday newspaper. *A searing exploration of how one moment can change everything*. He'd chucked it aside, his anger still hot. 'No.'

Ralph looks surprised. 'There's a lot about you in it.'

'I'm sure none of it good.'

'Quite the contrary. He talks about your bravery, and your instinct for danger.'

Rook shakes his head. 'I don't believe that.'

'You should read it,' Ralph says.

'Tom and I haven't spoken in years.'

'It will be strange to see him, then.'

'Yes.'

Ralph watches him. 'I'll come with you, if you like.' Rook tries to find traces of pity in his expression. 'I'd like to meet him, to tell him I enjoyed his book.'

Rook tries to imagine Ralph and Tom in the same room. 'Does that mean you're staying too?'

'If you promise we'll leave tomorrow, I'll stay.'

Rook is tired of saying no. He doesn't want to face Tom alone. 'All right,' he says, and his son smiles.

*

They make it to breakfast just in time. There is little remaining in the vast metal servers, and the clatter of the room is diminished.

They take a table by the window and order a pot of coffee.

'This is some hotel,' Ralph says, looking around at the cornices on the ceiling, at the vast pillars.

'It wasn't always this grand,' Rook says.

'You stayed here, the whole time you were in Vietnam?'

'Five years.'

'It must be strange to be back.'

'It is. It's something I needed to do, I suppose.'

'Mum would have liked it,' Ralph said. 'All this luxury.'

Rook tries to see June here: one of the coiffured women with their pearl necklaces and pastel clothing. But he can still see only the war, and how none of them belong here.

'Julia and I were thinking of going away this summer, but I've rather blown our savings.'

Rook looks for the resentment in his son's words, but it is absent. Things between them seem calmer, more civilized, as if his breakdown last night has somehow neutralized things.

'Where were you thinking of going?'

'Italy. Julia loves the food there.'

'I don't think I've ever been,' Rook says.

Ralph smiles. 'I thought you'd been everywhere.'

'Not quite.' He pauses. 'I can lend you the money, Ralph. If you want to go.'

Ralph's face changes. 'I don't need your money, Dad.'

'I didn't mean it like that,' Rook says, as he feels eggshells begin to crack beneath his feet. 'I just meant – well, it's my fault you're here.'

'I wanted to come,' Ralph says.

Rook takes a breath. 'Thank you.'

There is an awkward moment in which neither of them can look at each other. 'Well,' he says. 'How is Julia, anyway?'

Ralph shrugs. 'She's all right. We've had a bit of a stressful year.'

'Oh?'

'We've been trying for a baby.'

Rook isn't sure what to say. 'I didn't know that,' he said.

'It's not been going very well.' Ralph smiles tightly and Rook feels his sadness, if only for a moment.

'How long?' Rook asks.

'Two years, almost. We're thinking of starting IVF.'

'I'm sorry, I didn't know,' Rook says. He wonders if June did.

'It's all right. We're not exactly close, Dad. We never have been.'

Something about his son's lack of concern makes Rook's sadness open up. He longs to make a connection with his son, though it all feels too late. 'It must have been hard,' he says.

Ralph nods. 'It is. It's part of the reason Julia wants me home. We had a doctor's appointment booked and I've missed it. She's been trying to get me to go for months. She thinks I came out here to avoid it. I suppose I did, in a way. I just don't want some doctor prying into our business. I wanted it to happen in its own time.'

Rook remembers June, standing in the kitchen of their London apartment, telling him she was pregnant. How the news had blindsided him, how he hadn't expected it. He wishes he could solve this problem for his son, to make up for so many other things.

'You should take Julia to Italy,' he says. 'Forget about the money, and the baby. Just do it. I wish I'd done the same with your mother. I always thought there would be more time.'

Ralph looks up and they hold eye contact.

'Maybe I will,' Ralph says.

1967

It was raining again when Rook left Vietnam for his fourth Christmas in England. Since September, when the monsoons had arrived early, perpetual wetness had soaked the country. Just two days ago, Rook had flown into the Con Thien base at the very north of South Vietnam, where the Communist fire was as relentless as the rain. The fortifications holding out the enemy were crumbling: the red dirt sodden, the dugouts and trenches collapsing in on themselves.

Rook had got his photos out yesterday, his last for at least two weeks. The *Sunday Times* had wanted six, but he'd sent the rest out on the wire, and *Time* magazine had bought one of a marine curled into his collapsed dugout, his hand over his head. Since he'd won the World Press Award for the photo of the burning man, his name was like a lucky charm, ensuring that most of the work he put out found a home. The fees he commanded had gone up, and editor responses had become more obliging.

June wasn't at the airport: he'd told her he was arriving tomorrow, wanting to surprise her at home. As he stepped onto the runway, the cold was like an assault, the act of drawing in his breath almost painful, his exhalations clouding in a way that reminded him of running home from school as a child.

From the taxi, he watched London emerge on the horizon, enjoying inevitably being swallowed up by it. Closer to the centre, the city was festooned with red and green and gold. The grey sky and dull winter light made him miss the heat and colour of Saigon, where Christmas was only celebrated half-heartedly. No decorations, except a lopsided tree in the hotel reception. They'd had a false, early Christmas dinner with the gang: all commenting on how odd the turkey tasted, laughing when they worked out it was scrawny chicken.

In other ways, he'd been glad to get away. Saigon was busy now, crammed with American soldiers and the industries that had sprung up to support them: the street sellers and the nightclubs, the prostitutes and opium dens. Journalists were common now, too: everyone wanting a piece of the story that kept on giving, that seemed determined not to die quietly. The TV men had been out at Con Thien, lugging their unwieldy equipment. Rook didn't envy them and their lack of mobility under fire, but he was strangely grateful to them, for bringing the war to life for people at home in America and around the world, for forcing people to pay attention.

'Didn't I tell you it'd be big?' Henry was always saying. 'I bet you're glad you stuck it out now.'

He was. The story had become theirs: they were the

experts, the old-timers. Rook, Henry, Tom and Hans: their names had become synonymous with the war, their coverage sought above all others. When they entered a bar, other journalists stopped and stared, approaching them drunkenly, complimenting them on stories they'd covered, asking for advice.

But being in the inner circle didn't mean everything was perfect. Sometimes, he still felt his relationship with Tom was fundamentally broken. He occasionally caught Tom looking at him with a sort of malice, which disappeared whenever Rook looked back. He heard the asides whenever he got a job: he wasn't stupid enough to think that Tom and Hans didn't talk about him, that they didn't try and get Henry to join in too.

'Some people make it look so easy,' Tom said when Rook heard back from *Time* magazine. They said he might make the cover.

'Yeah, Tom. It was a piece of cake.'

Tom knew as well as he did that even getting to the camp took guts: the American intelligence estimated there were over a hundred Commie guns trained on the camp, as well as tens of thousands of Cong hiding in the land surrounding it. Not to mention the rainfall, which made choppers rare and dangerous transportation. Rook knew that it was harder for Tom to leave Saigon: he was tied to the wire with its regular deadlines. Rook and Henry were freer to travel the country and search out stories, but he didn't believe he should be resented for that, not by someone who was supposedly his friend.

*

The taxi turned off the King's Road into their new street. They had moved again last year, to an apartment just north of the river in Chelsea, in a long row of white Georgian terraces, all with columns and tiled steps, and potted plants by the door. With his salary and all the additional freelance money, Rook was making enough for June to live very comfortably indeed. Last time he'd been back three months ago, he'd opened the wardrobe to an array of new clothes: all of them with neat designer labels inside. These days, the sewing machine was nowhere to be seen.

As he walked up the wide stairs to the third-floor apartment, he thought again how little this place felt like home. The carefully polished brass doorknob and the soft cream carpet made him feel dirty. He still preferred their first apartment in Crouch End, with its sticky floors and unreliable electricity; it felt more real somehow. But he knew that living here, near Mildred and her other friends, made it easier for June while he was away.

He paused on the second floor, looking at the closed door to their apartment, trying to conjure up the anticipation he'd felt the first few times he'd returned after being away. He remembered their early days in London with a sort of romanticism that he knew wasn't a true reflection of how things were: a time when they only had each other, when June's face would light up when he came home, when she meant everything to him.

Now, when he thought of opening the door and re-entering his other life, he felt exhausted. It wasn't just June he needed to readjust to now, but the life she had created: her crass, overbearing friends, who attended art gallery openings and kissed each other on both cheeks as if they were Europeans.

If he was honest, it wasn't just June's friends that had changed things. June seemed different too, both more and less herself. She had found a life here, and it wasn't one Rook was entirely comfortable with. It had exaggerated all the things about her that Rook was less sure about: her giddiness, her need for attention, her materialism, and obsession with her looks. He felt like the other side of June – her loyalty, her kindness, her natural beauty – was receding.

Rook shook his head to dispel the thoughts: he was about to see June, who loved him, and who was happy. He knocked twice on the front door. He wondered if she was asleep: it was still early. He knocked again. There was the sound of rustling from behind the door. When it opened, Jimmy was standing there, his dark hair dishevelled. He was wearing no shirt and loose corduroy trousers.

'You're a bit late for the party,' he said.

'Party?' Rook said.

'We got wasted last night. Crashed here. June didn't mention you were coming back.'

'It's a surprise.'

'She's not up yet,' Jimmy said, stepping out of the way.

The hall was stacked with old newspapers, and there was the smell of sleep. Through the living-room door, Rook could see a couple entwined on the sofa, semi-clothed. There were more bodies on the floor: a ginger-haired man was snoring, his mouth open.

'Where is she?' Rook asked Jimmy, who was standing against the wall with his arms folded.

He gestured towards their bedroom. 'She won't thank you for waking her,' he said. 'You know what June's like in the mornings.'

Rook pushed open the door to the bedroom. There were two people coiled around each other in the bed: June and Mildred, both fast asleep.

He went to June's side of the bed. 'June?' he said, softly. When she didn't respond, he shook her arm. 'June!'

Her eyes snapped open. She blinked slowly, then her eyes widened. 'What are you doing here?' she asked, her voice heavy with sleep.

'I'm home,' Rook said, and she threw her arms around him.

*

They went out for breakfast, to give the others time to leave. June took him to a crowded milk bar along the King's Road, the waitresses all dressed up in pastel-pink dresses with white aprons. They sat in a booth and June ordered a banana milkshake for them to share.

'I'm not hungry,' Rook said.

'More for me,' she said. She reached out and took his hand across the table. 'You look tired, Rook. I'm so glad you're home.'

She leant across, and he kissed her. She smelt of alcohol and smoke. 'So, what's been happening with you?'

Rook thought of the heat and the mess of Con Thien. 'Nothing much.'

June sighed. 'I'm sorry about the party,' she said. 'I wish you'd let me know you were coming.'

'How often does that happen?'

'Not often.' June looked at him with her big blue eyes. 'Are you annoyed with me?'

'It was a shock, that's all,' Rook said. 'I wasn't expecting to see Jimmy answer the door.'

June looked down at the table. 'It was just easier for everyone to stay over.'

'Don't they all live close by?'

'Yes, but we'd all drunk too much. Mildred and I went to bed before the others: I didn't know they were staying.' She sighed. 'I really wish you'd told me. I would have had the apartment all straight. Everything would have been ready. And now you're angry.'

Rook shrugged. 'I'll get over it.'

'I'm sure you have parties all the time in Vietnam.'

'It's not the same,' he said.

'Why not?'

Rook thought about this. She was right: the boys were always partying at the villa, and there were plenty of beautiful Vietnamese women. How was what June was doing any different? She had her friends, just as he had his. He knew he should be happy for her, that it was good for her to have things to distract her, that she wasn't lonely. But he couldn't help feeling resentful, even if he didn't understand it.

'I thought you'd fallen out with Jimmy,' Rook said.

'Did I say that?'

Rook was sure she had, in one of her letters. 'You wrote to me about it.'

'Well, I don't remember. I suppose we're always falling in and out with each other. All of us. We're all very emotional people.'

Could she hear herself? 'Are you still going to castings?'

June blushed. 'Not really,' she said. 'I was in that play last year.'

'Another one of Jimmy's?'

'It's not as easy as you think.'

'I didn't say it was easy.'

'You think I've given up.'

'Well, haven't you?'

'You don't know anything about what my life here is like.'

'The Ritz, all-night parties. It certainly doesn't look too taxing to me.'

June looked at him sharply. 'Look, I'm sorry about the party. But those people are my friends. This is what we do. I don't need judgement from you, or anyone else.'

'I'm not judging you.'

'It feels like you are. It's all right for you, coming back from being important, from doing something that matters, and picking holes in my life. Don't you think I'm doing my best?'

Rook didn't feel like sparing her the truth. 'No, June, I don't. I think you've been distracted from what was important to you. When I met you, you were the one with all the resolve. You were so sure of yourself that you made me believe it too. I just don't want you to lose that.'

'I've tried, Rook,' June said quietly, looking down at her hands as if trying not to cry. 'You don't know how much I've tried.'

She looked exhausted, and he felt his old guilt again. That all of this was somehow his fault. 'I'm sorry,' he said. 'But I love you, and I believe in you, and I don't want you to give up.'

'*Do* you love me?' June asked, looking up at him, her eyes burning.

Rook felt caught out. 'Of course I do.'

June paused, her next words coming out in a rush. 'I know we're not supposed to talk about this, but are you ever coming home?'

'I thought you were happy with things how they were,' he said.

'I was. I am. But I never expected it to go on this long.' June sighed. 'I shouldn't be saying this, but I'm not happy,

Rook, not really. I tell myself I am, that I'm keeping busy, that I have a great life here. That I'm lucky. But I don't always feel it. I miss you, sometimes terribly.'

His stomach turned over. 'You should have told me sooner,' he said.

'Would you have done anything about it? I know how important the story is. And every day, it only becomes more so. I'm so proud of you, of everything you've achieved. It just makes me wonder where I fit in. Is it ever going to end?'

Rook thought of the coverage of Vietnam, how it was splashed across newspapers worldwide, how it was only getting bigger. 'People are protesting against the war,' he said. 'It might end soon.'

'I don't think you really believe that. And I don't think you can walk away from it.'

Rook looked around the milk bar. Everyone around them seemed to be laughing, having ordinary conversations. June had just swung straight to the heart of everything, and he didn't know how to answer her.

She was still staring at him. 'Is this what our lives will be now? You away, and me here?'

Again, he didn't know what to say. 'I could give it up,' he said, 'if it really means this much to you.'

In the moment that followed, June's blue eyes examined his face. Finally, she shook her head. 'You'd resent me. And what would we do for money if you're not out there? We'd be right back at the beginning. This is why

I know we shouldn't talk about it. We're in an impossible situation.'

As they looked at each other, Rook let himself breathe out. She was right, he realized. Each time he'd been leaving for Vietnam, he'd been waiting for this moment, when June's patience would wane, and he'd be brought to this decision, and he was met with a crushing sense of inevitability.

*

They walked home in silence.

The apartment was empty when they got back, though the mess was still there.

'I'll clean up while you have a nap,' June said, so Rook pulled back the unmade sheets and slipped underneath them, turning away from the lingering smell of sleeping bodies.

The light crept around the edges of the curtains. As usual, now that he was finally in a comfortable bed, sleep eluded him. Listening to June collecting glasses, he longed to shut his eyes and forget everything, but he couldn't.

In the kitchen, June was standing by the sink, her back to him.

Rook wrapped his arms around her waist. She smelt so familiar: a powdery mixture of soap and sleep. Here she was: the essence of England, of home. He pressed his hips against hers, and she pushed back, turning and pulling him towards her, her hands in his hair. This was what they needed. This would make everything better again.

It didn't take long. When it was over, June stood looking at him.

'I've missed you,' he said, and in that moment, it was true.

*

They stayed in London for Christmas: the first time they hadn't returned to Backton to celebrate. When they'd discussed it, months ago, it had seemed exciting and grown-up, to spend the day alone in their own apartment. Since their chat in the milk bar though it had felt as if they were both wading through quicksand, their actions awkward and clumsy.

June roasted a goose that was much too large for two of them. She pulled it out of the oven, and set it on the counter for Rook to carve.

'It's perfectly cooked,' he said, as he slid the knife into the meat.

June smiled tightly.

They ate at the kitchen table. Rook tried to think of something to say, of some way to start a conversation. His mind was blank, and he was too aware of the drip of the tap, the sound of their cutlery scraping against china. He stood up. 'Shall I put some music on?'

June nodded.

In the living room, he tried to find a record they would both enjoy. Their collections had been shelved separately: hers all Dusty Springfield and Nancy Sinatra, his Rolling Stones and Cat Stevens. He pulled out an old Christmas compilation and placed the needle carefully.

When he returned to the kitchen, June was staring at her plate, her food untouched.

'What's wrong?' he said.

'Nothing,' she said, taking up her knife and fork again.

When they'd finished eating, it was only one o'clock. When June suggested taking a walk, Rook acquiesced too eagerly, pleased to have something to do before the darkness started in on them. They took a taxi to the edge of Hyde Park, walking amongst families and dog-walkers, all of whom seemed too cheery. The skeletons of trees, the brown earth, the frost that sparkled on the grass: it was all so different from the overwhelming lushness of Saigon, and Rook raised his camera to capture it.

He felt June's hand on his arm. 'Rook? What are you thinking about?'

'Just how cold everything looks.'

June scrunched up her nose. 'I hate winter. Everything's so dead.'

'I'd forgotten how much things change here though. When I was last here, the leaves had turned orange, and there was still greenery about. Now it's all gone.'

'Isn't it like that in Vietnam?'

Rook shook his head. 'There's two seasons: the wet season and the dry season. There's not much difference.'

'Does it rain all the time?' June asked.

'No,' Rook said. 'Every afternoon, at around the same

time. It's a different sort of rain: like a proper downfall, not a drizzle.'

'What else is different?' she said.

Rook thought. 'So many things.'

'I'd love to go there.' She looked wistful, as if she really meant it. And he longed then to take her with him, to make her a part of his adventure rather than a separate part of his life.

'You could come,' he said.

June laughed. 'And what would I do?'

As they walked, he wondered if this was the way things would be between them now. It felt like when he was a child, in the days and weeks after the accident, when everything hung in the balance, undecided. The altered way people behaved around him, as if what had happened had thrown him into a new relief.

*

They celebrated New Year at Mildred's house, only a couple of streets away. Rook knew most of June's friends by sight now, though new people were always moving in and out of their group. When the clock chimed in the New Year, Rook watched Mildred and June embrace, watched them all kissing each other's cheeks, and once again, he was on the outside of things. He longed, against his better judgement, for Saigon, for Henry and Hans and Tom. He longed to feel useful again, to feel needed.

For a few days, lying low in the apartment with June, catching glimpses of her unhappiness, he seriously considered giving up the job in Saigon and returning to London. He told himself that with his strengthened reputation he'd find work here. He should be putting his marriage first, shouldn't he? He resolved to go in to the office and talk to Tony as soon as he could, to see if anything could be arranged.

*

Tony wasn't in the office, but there had been a telegram for him. Standing on the office steps, pulling his coat around him, Rook read it, unable to wait any longer.

ROOK STOP WHEN ARE YOU COMING BACK STOP RUMOURS OF NVA SIEGE AT KHE SANH STOP WORSE THAN CON THIEN STOP SHIT HITTING THE FAN STOP HENRY STOP

For a moment, Rook was back in the Saigon office, listening to Henry clack away on the typewriter, waiting for some images to dry. Outside, the city held all its potential: of the evening ahead, of dinner at a noodle bar, of chats and laughter with the gang.

On the way back, Rook practised the words, over and over, trying to get them right. *This is something I need to do. Let me go back one more time.* June was in the living room, lying on the sofa reading a book. She looked up as Rook entered.

'What's wrong?'

Rook looked down. He was still holding the note from Henry. 'Something's happened,' he said. 'Something big. I need to go back.'

'What is it?'

'The Communists have besieged a big marine base.'

'How long would you be gone?'

'I don't know.' Ella Fitzgerald crooned from the record player. 'I need to see this through, June. All I'm asking for is a bit more time.'

He knew he had to give her some kind of reassurance he would be back one day.

'When will you be leaving?' she said.

'Soon. As soon as possible.'

As her face changed, resignation closing it to him, he had to look away. He heard her book close with a slap. 'I'll help you pack,' she said.

When she stood up, he made himself go to her. 'I love you, June.'

She nodded, her eyes flat. 'I love you too.'

NINE

They walk out into the streets. Away from the air-conditioned lobby, it is hot, and Rook stops, momentarily dizzy. Ralph takes his arm, and they move on together.

Now that Rook knows this is his final day, he is able to look around him without his fear of the past overwhelming him. Soon, this too will be a memory.

They find their way easily, the route as familiar as it always was. As they turn down the winding lane leading to Linh's house, Rook wonders what his son thinks of the real city, away from the sterility of the tourist areas. He turns to ask him, then something stops him. It's enough that they are here together, that they have come to some kind of agreement.

Soon, they are standing outside the yellow door, and he is knocking: there is the sound of footsteps slapping the tiles.

Linh pulls him towards her. 'You come! Tom.'

Rook feels his stomach drop as he steps across the threshold. There is a figure hanging horizontal in the hammock in the corner: it shifts as a man sits then stands, facing them. Despite his white hair, chaotic around his face, it is unmistakably Tom.

For a long moment, neither of them says anything. They stand with Ralph and Linh between them, taking each other in.

'You look exactly the same,' Rook says, eventually.

Tom smiles. 'You don't. You look ancient.' He looks at Ralph. 'Who's this?'

'My son,' Rook says. 'Ralph.'

'Now, he looks like you used to. The spitting image.'

For a moment, Rook thinks Tom is teasing him. But he is sincere, he must be. Rook looks at his son, with his black hair and green eyes. 'I didn't believe you were really here,' he says.

Tom grins. 'I never left.'

*

Linh gestures at the table, offers them beer. Rook and Ralph sit: oversized men, long-legged on low plastic stools. Tom helps Linh bring through the drinks from the small kitchen, and Rook notices that he knows his way around.

When they are all seated, Rook breaks the silence.

'I read your coverage of the fall of Saigon.'

Tom nods. 'It was crazy. People hanging from helicopters, desperate to get out. You must have seen the photographs. I had a way out, and I wanted to stay.' Tom laughs, and Rook sees his ambition, that fire, is still in his eyes. 'Everyone thought I was crazy: I pretended to be Canadian! But I couldn't just leave, not after everything we'd been through here.' Tom realizes what he's said. 'Not that I think you should have stayed. Here I go, putting my foot in my mouth again.'

'No, I get it. I would have stayed if I could,' Rook says. 'Everything was too different, though. It felt wrong, somehow.'

'You didn't say goodbye.'

'I couldn't.' He remembers staring out of the taxi window on the way to the airport, feeling numb.

'I tried to go back to America for a while, once the dust had settled,' Tom says. 'But I couldn't stand the silence. After the troops pulled out, it was as if they'd never been involved at all. It was someone else's problem. Somewhere along the line, it had stopped being home. I didn't fit in anywhere but here.' Tom swallows. 'Why did you come back?'

Rook looks at Ralph. 'My wife died. I didn't know what else to do.'

'I'm sorry,' Tom says.

'Did you marry?'

Tom shakes his head. 'I adopted a family.' He smiles. 'Linh's. We got a lot of them out, after the fall. To America. Linh was the same as me though, she never wanted to leave.' Tom is looking at Linh, her face alert: she knows he is talking about her. Tom explains, in Vietnamese. She nods, smiles. 'Tom help. Tom good.'

She is looking at Tom with such gratitude that Rook looks away.

'So how have you found being back?' Tom says. 'It's been a long time.'

'It's strange,' Rook says.

'It's different now.'

Rook nods. 'Some things are. The modern buildings, the cleanliness. But the people seem the same. So open. I didn't expect that, after everything.'

Tom's face changes: Rook sees again his passion for the story, for the truth. 'You're right. They talk about the war. They always have.' He pauses. 'Without that, I'm not sure I would have survived.' Tom looks at him, and Rook sees fear in his eyes. 'Did you read the book?'

'I couldn't. I'm sorry.'

'I understand. I needed to write it. It was my way of dealing with what happened, of saying sorry.' Tom is no longer smiling; he looks down. 'I was an idiot. I ruined everything.'

Rook shakes his head. 'You couldn't have stopped it. None of us could. I can see that now.'

Tom looks up, and there is a desperation there that Rook hadn't expected. He realizes he believes his own words, that he isn't trying to make Tom feel better. 'I'll try and read the book,' he says.

Tom smiles. 'I'd like that. I'm glad you came here, Rook. We should have done this a long time ago.'

Rook nods. 'I've wasted so much time.'

1968

Back in London, after the final trip to Vietnam, Rook woke in the night, sweating, his muscles tensed as if in flight: his fingers gripping his thighs. In his dream, he'd been in Saigon. The car, crawling towards them, emerging out of the darkness like a phantom. The muzzle of the guns, like black dogs' noses, poking out from the cracks in the rolled-down windows. The rush of adrenaline coursing through his body and the sound of Tom crying out. Then it was too late again.

He lay awake, telling himself there was nothing to be afraid of here, that he was safe. But his terror was like a fever that would not break. As if that one moment had released all his pent-up fear from his time in-country, as if it was finally catching up with him.

Beside him, June's breaths were calm and regular. Reaching out, he drew her sleeping body towards him. He needed to be close to her, to that peace and silence. Those few moments of escape, of forgetting. She murmured, and he held on to her more tightly, breathing her in. She pressed her back against him, turning so she could kiss him, her mouth wet and hot.

When it was over, he turned away, curling into himself. Her breathing slowed, and his fists clenched. He envied her: longing to be able to shut his eyes and meet only sleep, to no longer be afraid. He stared into the darkness, willing it to pass again.

*

London wasn't his city. The smoke-stained facades, the tired, drawn faces rushing along the pavements, disappearing into the dark mouth of the tube. He wanted to take hold of their shoulders and shake them until their teeth rattled in their skulls. Why couldn't they see how pointless it all was? How could they be alive when others were dead?

When he was alone, he'd walk until his legs ached and the sky turned black, trying to lose himself, as he had when they'd first arrived. Everything had been new then, and at every turn in the road, he'd found something that gave him that feeling, that made him want to lift his camera. Now, it hung around his neck unused.

When the city became too much, he'd take the bus to the airport. Under the huge domed roof, he'd watch the letters on the departures board. People checking their bags, bidding loved ones farewell, walking through the doors towards the gates. It was all so familiar to him. But the thought of walking up to the desk himself, of returning to Vietnam, was impossible.

He thought of Saigon constantly.

'I can never go back there,' he'd told June when he'd

returned this time. They were lying on the bed in their Chelsea apartment, the pressure of daylight pushing behind the drawn curtains.

'Are you sure?'

He shook his head. 'It's over.'

He turned away from her, onto his side, where he could see only the wall ahead of him. He didn't want to look at her face, to see the trace of happiness that was surely there. She'd got what she wanted, after all. He was home now, and he couldn't leave her again. He'd lost everything.

*

The first day of spring. June was humming in the kitchen, getting breakfast. As long as they were making love in the dark, she seemed to think everything between them was fine. As if his grasping after her in the night was a substitute for the long, tense silences that punctuated their days in the apartment. She'd sing to herself, as if she'd achieved something.

Sometimes, he'd remember momentarily how he used to feel about her: sharp, sporadic glimpses of feeling interspersing his numbness. Seeing her messy-haired and flushed in the mornings, as she made them coffee and climbed back into bed, wearing one of his shirts. Watching her read, when he'd told her he wanted to stay in the bedroom all day, when he didn't want to leave the apartment. The little crease between her eyes as she concentrated on the page. But other times he was angry with her, though he couldn't think why. What had happened wasn't her fault, after all. Maybe that was what annoyed him, that she couldn't understand it, the thing that had changed him so irrevocably.

Over breakfast, he watched her mouth moving as she talked, her apple cheeks as she smiled at him. She would be asking him what he wanted for dinner or what colour they should paint the bathroom. The old, itchy anger began to rise. The muscles along his jaw tensed: goose pimples ran up his arms and legs. Couldn't she see that none of it mattered? That this time next week, they wouldn't remember what they'd eaten for dinner at all? He knew, deep down, that she was trying to make things easier, that she couldn't stand the silences. But silence was exactly what he needed.

He saw a piece of lint on her nightie and focused on it as she gesticulated, her voice fading to a dull hum. A sort of blankness fell over him, a white noise, where he could exist for moments at a time.

Her voice eventually swam towards him. 'Rook?'

He realized she'd asked him a question. He shrugged. 'You decide,' he said.

'Decide what? I just asked you how you slept.'

He looked down at her empty cereal bowl, his half-full one, the cornflakes soggy.

'Do you ever listen to anything I say?' June said.

'Of course.'

'I don't think you do,' she said. She cocked her head to one side. 'Where do you go when you're like that?'

'Like what?'

She did a sort of impression: eyes glazed, mouth slightly open.

'I don't do that,' he said.

'You do. What are you thinking about?'

'Nothing,' he said, because it was true.

June's nose crinkled. 'It must be something,' she said. She took his hand. 'Tell me.'

He pulled his hand away. 'Really, June,' he said. 'There's nothing to say.'

*

They went out for a walk, to make the most of the good weather. The light bounced off the white terraces opposite and the leaves were out on the trees that lined the avenue. June reached out and took Rook's hand, and he willed himself not to shrug her off. His irritation had been growing all morning: she'd taken almost an hour to get ready, finally choosing a too-short shift dress and painting her face until he wanted to scream.

The kaleidoscope of the King's Road was like an assault. The whirl of colours: bright bulbous lettering, coloured railings, garish fashions trapped behind the glass. People everywhere, who'd all had the same idea as them: the girls like June in tiny dresses, big sunglasses and boots; kaftaned men with their jewellery and too-tight trousers.

Vietnam was everywhere. Splashed over news stands were photographs that he hadn't taken. Images of Saigon burning. The pinnacle of the war, the turning point: and none of them were there to capture it.

Rook walked fast, ignoring the feel of other people's bodies pushing past him. Their laughter echoed and he needed to get away from it. June shuffled to keep up with him: once or twice he almost lost her before he felt her touch his forearm again.

'What's the rush, darling?' she said.

As they drew closer to the centre of town, the streets became busier, until at last they turned a corner and were met with a wall of people. Singing and shouting filled the air; placards hovered. The crowd hummed: white men with long hair, headbands wound across their foreheads. Bare-faced girls in smock dresses and long skirts, hair unbrushed, chanting. *Save Vietnam. Go home Americans.*

Floating above the crowd was the red flag of the North Vietnamese, a gold star at the centre. Rook felt a searing vertigo, as if his two worlds had collided, as if Vietnam had come to London because he was here, as if it refused to leave him.

He found his camera, and then he was looking through the viewfinder, capturing the face of a singing man, eyes bright in his dirty face. Rook pushed his way into the crowd, jostling, searching. Again and again, the moments slid together. He was both there and not there. For a moment, he thought of the Aldermaston march, how he'd stood on the outside of it all. He had become a different man now: implicated and involved in what was happening around him, no longer an observer.

'Rook! Where are you going?'

He heard June call out to him, but he continued on into the mash of people, away from her, on his own at last. Up ahead, he could see the police blockade stopping people from entering the square: three black horses, waiting. He needed to get round the other way, to photograph the horses from behind, with the crowd ahead of them. He shoved his way through. The police pushed him back, but he held up his camera and shouted press. When they waved him on, he looked around for June, but couldn't see her.

The square was deserted except for the lines of police in riot gear. Rook took his photos carefully, cursing himself for not having more films with him. The crowd was growing louder now; people pushing against the barricade. A horse reared up, its legs dark against the white sky. Rook heard a scream as they began to enter the square. His camera glued to his face now, he smiled behind the lens.

*

When his roll of film ran out, he walked back through the streets, his head light. He held his camera as if to keep the photos inside it safe. The colours of the street, bright in the sunshine, had a strange charm now, and he wished he had another shot left to capture them.

When he got back to the apartment, he climbed the stairs and let himself in. It almost felt like the old days, when he would rush home to tell June what photos he'd taken, and which ones the paper had bought. He longed to see her excited face. At first, he couldn't see her, and for a moment he started to panic: maybe she'd become lost in the crowd. He was about to head back the way he had come, when he saw the outline of her bobbed head through the living-room door.

She was sitting in the semi-darkness, the curtains drawn.

'I thought I'd beaten you back,' he said.

She didn't say anything, and when he moved into the room, he could see her face. Dishevelled hair, mascara tracks running down her cheeks.

'June?' he said. 'What's the matter?'

'You left me,' she said, her voice choked with tears. Rook's breath tightened across his chest.

'What do you mean?' he said.

'You just disappeared,' she said. 'I tried to go after you, but – I couldn't. And then the people started pushing and I was on the ground, and I couldn't find my way back up. It was like drowning.'

Rook thought about that moment, when he'd followed his camera. 'I'm sorry,' he said. 'I was taking photos.' He wanted her to recognize how important it was, that he'd experienced that alchemy again. That after months of nothing but anger, he'd finally felt something else.

'It's always about the photos,' she said. 'You don't care about me at all.'

Rook looked into her watery eyes. 'It's not always about you, June.'

'I'm not asking for always. Just sometimes, just once, for you to put me first. You didn't even notice I was gone.'

He thought about his walk home, the happiest he'd felt for so long, how she'd been the one he'd wanted to tell. 'I do care about you, June,' he said.

'You've got a funny way of showing it,' she said. 'Sometimes, I feel like you don't want to be here at all.'

I don't, he thought, but didn't say it. He longed, every day, to be back in Vietnam, before everything that had happened. 'I just miss work, that's all,' he said. 'And today felt like work again. I'm sorry.'

June sighed. 'You need to talk about what happened, to at least try.'

Rook felt a wave of anger come over him, without warning. 'It's not as easy as that.'

She was still staring at him, wide-eyed. 'I want to understand.'

Rook tried to look at her, but couldn't. 'I need to go to the office. To develop the shots.'

'Go on, then,' she said, tilting her head towards the front door. 'Leave.'

He turned and walked away.

*

The darkroom at the *Sunday Times*' office was so much bigger than the cramped toilet they'd used in Vietnam.

The red light and the silence and the calm: he'd finally found it again. A place he didn't think about anything, except for the careful steps that led him to the images forming in black and white, undulating under the developing fluid. Each moment preserved, bringing back his exhilaration in the square, the feeling of things falling into place.

This, he thought, this is what I need to be doing. *This is what will save me from myself*. There were stories in other places, and they were what he needed. Catching sight of his eerie red outline in the mirror on the back of the door, he smiled.

'Rook?' Tony said as he was emerging from the darkroom. 'What are you doing here?'

'I got some shots of the Vietnam protest in Grosvenor Square. They're hanging up.'

'You're not supposed to be working. You're on leave.'

'I wasn't. We were out for a walk.'

'A likely story. You look terrible.'

'Thanks.' He wondered how to ask. 'Are there any foreign assignments at the moment?'

'Apart from the obvious?'

'Apart from that.'

Tony folded his arms. 'Why are you asking?'

'I want to start working again.'

'Do you really think that's a good idea?'

'Yes,' Rook said. 'I do.'

Rook felt his skin itch as Tony watched him. 'How are things at home?'

'Fine.'

'But you want to go away again?'

Rook's throat was dry. 'I think I need to.'

While he waited, he kept his eyes on the ground.

'I'll see what I can do,' Tony said. 'If you're certain.'

'I am. Thanks, Tony. I'll be in touch.'

*

When he got home, he followed the sounds of clanging pots and pans to the kitchen. June was reaching up into a cupboard, her bare calves stretching, the arch of her foot curved.

He wanted to step towards her and put his arms around her, but he couldn't bring himself to. He wanted to say he was sorry, that he felt he'd found the solution to their problem.

He helped her prepare the dinner, mashing the potatoes for the beef stew, laying the table. They even put out a tablecloth.

'I've got something to talk to you about,' Rook said, when they were finally sitting down.

'So have I,' June said.

'You first,' Rook said.

June looked down at the table, and then up at him. 'I'm pregnant,' she said.

Rook felt his face drop. 'I wasn't expecting that,' he said.

'I can tell,' she said. 'You can't be that surprised, though. You know we haven't been using protection.'

She was thinking about their late-night fumblings. Nausea turned in his stomach: a baby shouldn't be born out of that.

She took his hand across the table. 'Say something, Rook,' she said. 'I thought you'd be pleased. Now that you're staying, it's a good time for it, isn't it?'

Rook imagined them in the apartment, with a baby. He imagined late nights and no sleep and arguments over who was going out to buy the nappies.

'How long have you known?' he said.

'I went to the doctor last Wednesday.'

He thought of her, humming in the mornings. 'You should have told me.'

'There wasn't any point until I was sure,' she said.

Rook got up and walked towards the window. He looked out over the patchwork of roofs, the cram of the houses. His throat felt tight.

He heard June's footsteps behind him.

'Rook!' she said. 'You're crying!'

He put his hand up to his face and was surprised to find it was wet.

June was searching his face, looking for an explanation.

'I'm just so happy,' he said, and when she pulled herself into his chest, he desperately wished that it was true.

TEN

When they finally leave Linh's house, it is past midnight. Rook thinks of the curfew, and then remembers. It is all over now.

All evening, they sat around Linh's table, playing music from the old days, remembering. The Animals, Donovan, Buffalo Springfield. Songs Rook had been afraid to listen to alone, that he would switch off the radio or leave a shop to avoid. As the music played, they told stories. Rook had imagined that there would be nothing but his anger left for Tom, centred on that final night, which had been an accumulation of so many smaller clashes. But beyond their tension remained all the days and nights they spent together. All the good times: the danger and the excitement and the everyday. The things they'd lived through, the moments that would always be theirs. Nothing, even what happened, could take that away.

At some point, Tom pulled out a pouch of the old stuff and rolled a joint. Offered one to Rook, who nodded, smiling at Ralph's incredulity. Rook remembers returning from trips when Ralph was a teenager to the smell of smoke in his studio: his son's overt rebellion, which he had ignored. The taste of hash brought a rush of new feeling, of remembrance.

Rook feels strangely calm as they walk back through the palimpsest of streets. All these years, he has been so afraid to remember the bad that he's pushed the good away too. When he first saw Tom, getting up from the hammock in Linh's house, he had felt as if he'd been frozen in time, as if he might never move on from that moment. Then Tom stepped towards him, and it was really him: them, together again.

Tom was sorry. He'd been sorry for years. And there Rook had been, on the other side of the world, suffering too.

They had promised each other not to leave things so long next time, as if they were ordinary friends who had simply let life get in the way. But Rook knew that even if Tom never came to England, or Rook never returned here again, that something between them had been mended. That he would sleep easier tonight.

When they get back to the hotel, Rook and Ralph sit in the hotel bar, lost in their own thoughts. Rook is not ready to go to bed yet, to risk losing, overnight, this tentative feeling of rebirth.

Rook looks at his son, sitting across from him.

'How much do you know, about what happened here?' Rook asks.

'Just what I read in Tom's book.'

'So you know about Henry?'

Ralph nods. 'I'd like to hear it from you, though, if you're willing to tell me.'

Rook wonders if he is ready to tell the story himself. All night, he and Tom have been skirting around it. He wonders whether the words will make things better, or whether they will break something inside him. He thinks of Tom, of what he said about the American silence. He takes a deep breath.

'I suppose I should start with how I came to be here at all,' he says.

Ralph is waiting, so Rook continues. He begins with June, with the envelope she sent from Backton to the editor of the *Sunday Times*. Ralph has heard this before, and he smiles. He tells his son about their move to London. About Tony offering him a job overseas. His arrival in-country, where he met Henry and then Tom. Their little team: their treasure island, as Henry had once called it.

By the time he reaches the end of the story, they are alone in the bar, the square dark and empty outside the windows.

Ralph watches him pause, steadying himself.

'We can finish another time,' Ralph says.

'No,' Rook says. 'I want to. I'm ready.'

1968

At the airport, as he went through the doors to security on his final trip to Vietnam, he looked back and saw June waiting, poised on the edge of calling out to him. He turned away and kept going, despite something inside him repeating that he shouldn't go.

On the flight itself, guilt hounded him, but he pushed the thoughts out of his mind. Once he finally landed, taking a military bus across the damp runway towards the airport building, he couldn't help smiling to himself. He was back. He'd made it back.

On his first night, Henry and Rook went to the rooftop bar of the Rex, finding seats overlooking the square. Rook could see his hotel room: the balcony and the slip of trapped curtain in the patio doors.

'Tom's in hospital again,' Henry said.

'What is it this time?'

'Shrapnel. A POMZ mine exploded and blew the man in front of him to smithereens.'

'Is it bad?' Rook asked.

'Not really. The doctor said he was lucky. Tom was

turned around, joking with the man behind him. Flesh wound in his shoulder.'

Rook nodded.

'I'm worried about him,' Henry said.

'Don't be. He's a big boy: he can make his own decisions.'

The waitress smiled as she placed their whiskies on the table.

'He's getting reckless,' Henry said. 'He's taking risks.'

Rook shrugged. 'No more than usual.'

'That's the thing,' Henry said, sipping his drink. 'It *is* more than usual. When I first met Tom, he would only go on patrol if he knew the platoon. Now, he'll hop on any copter, go any place.'

'Anything for the story.'

Henry raised an eyebrow. 'We both know it's not about that. It's about winning. Ever since you got the World Press Award, he's been trying to match it.'

'He might, this year. That's what people are saying.'

'I sure as hell hope he does,' Henry said. 'Maybe then he'll calm down.'

'You know you can't do anything to stop him,' Rook said, turning his glass in his hand. 'Just because he's putting himself in danger, it doesn't mean you have to.'

'I know. He's got Hans now, anyway. For when I'm too much of a pussy.'

'Hans is nuts,' Rook said, grinning back.

*

A few weeks later, once he'd settled back into the city, Rook headed up to Danang, hoping to try his luck getting into Khe Sanh. The invisible men in the dark blue hills surrounding the base had finally made themselves known, pinning down the soldiers with repeated fire. As if the hills themselves had turned on the Americans, as if the jungle was rejecting them, the sounds of rockets like the footsteps of an angry God. Who'd known they had rockets at all, or how they'd positioned them in such impenetrable terrain?

Journalists had been trying to get out there since the siege began, but the overcast weather meant nothing was going in or out. The day after Rook arrived at the jumping-off point – Danang's coastal army camp – was the first clear day in weeks. It was what they'd been both waiting for and dreading: a chance to send in new recruits and supplies, and to bring out the dead. Rook was owed a favour and he planned to cash it in. The guy sighed, gesturing at a helicopter waiting on the airstrip, and Rook ran towards it before he changed his mind.

'You'd better be prepared,' the soldier yelled after him, his face contorted by the wind. 'There's gonna be a shit storm going in.'

The bird was rammed full of new recruits clutching weapons, with the darting eyes of those trying to hide their fear. Rook remembered when all the soldiers he'd flown with had been Vietnamese, but now the Americans were here, running the show. These lads looked like they were fresh out of school: they made Rook – at twenty-eight – feel old. He pulled his hip flask out of his pack and passed it around, watching the men's hands shake as they took big sips.

The helicopter rose, shrinking the tents of the base below them. The blue faded to mist around the horizon, but below them everything was clear, the battered land laid out. There were big areas of blank earth amongst the vegetation, as if the skin of the land was diseased.

They started to lower. The mirage of mountains ran around the orange rectangle of the base, dug out of once-green terrain. Blackened tree stumps, pockmarked earth: there were no longer signs of people farming here, their conical hats glinting like stars. As they spiralled down, there was the thudding sound of larger-calibre rounds being fired. Rook repositioned himself on his flak jacket, pressing his feet against the shaking metal floor. He shut his eyes and felt a wave of anticipation.

The whip of automatic fire. His body stiffened, his jaw tense. He checked his camera: he was ready, the first out, ducking and running for cover towards the command post. The shots rang through the air, ricocheting from the metal airstrip. *Welcome to Khe Sanh!* The sign flapped in the ground fire, the letters jumping. Fiery shapes flashed into black smoke, like flowers blossoming.

*

The next day, he got out of the base on the final stinking helicopter, full of the dead. Piles of dark-green body bags, with boots protruding from the unzipped ends, tread ingrained with sand. The smell, ripe in the heat, made Rook cover his mouth with his collar, closing his eyes and telling himself it was better than staying on the ground, pinned down under fire.

In the darkroom in Saigon, the pictures blurred into life and Rook was back there, arriving at the base. A photograph captured one of the new recruits, fallen on the runway. His face turned away from the camera, only his helmet and the hump of his body visible. It looked as if he was dead, but moments after he'd taken the shot, Rook had put his pack down and dashed out, pulling the man towards cover. There was another shot of him clutching his leg where a red stain spread, his mouth open in a wail that Rook could still hear. They'd got him to the field hospital.

There were photos of men in a bunker that he couldn't remember taking. He did remember running below ground through the deserted bricked-in corridors, the walls higher than his head and topped with sandbags, the sky above blue with little wisps of cloud. Crouching at the sound of incoming, he'd seen a rat running along the parapet and smiled at its bravery.

Fucking hell, fucking gooks, when's this gonna let up? The words poured out of a nearby bunker, red and fast and jumbled. He ducked in. In the dim light, he made out a group of men, sitting on their cots.

'God damn it, Rook,' one of the men said. 'We thought you were the lieutenant. How the hell did you get in here?'

In the photograph, the half-light made the man's narrow face ghostly. His eyes looked straight at the camera with a combination of fear and bravado.

'I flew in,' Rook said. 'Same as you.'

'I thought they'd stopped risking the choppers?'

Rook took a seat on the hard cot. 'New recruits,' he said. 'And they're taking out the wounded.' *And dead*, he thought, but he didn't say that aloud.

'New blood,' the soldier muttered. 'Fat lot of good that'll do. More men to be pinned down, stuck in bunkers.'

Rook had captured the next moment, when there'd been the roar and crash of incoming: the horrified look on the men's faces.

'I'm getting sympathetic with Charlie,' another man said. 'Putting up with our shit for so long.' He'd shaken his head. 'I can't believe you came out in this. You must be fucking crazy.'

Back in the darkroom, Rook thought about that. He wasn't crazy: he was doing his job. He'd had the opportunity to get onto the base, to capture the torment of those trapped men. He looked again at their terrified faces, the whites of their eyes in the dim dugout where he'd found them. The bucket of reeking piss and shit in the corner. *I'm not risking my balls to take a leak*, one of them had told him, when he'd complained about the smell. He wondered if any other journalists had made it out there.

*

At the hotel, the doormen grinned when they saw him coming. There were no letters from June waiting for him at reception: he hadn't received any since he'd left London. Usually, he'd have heard from her by now: a letter every few weeks was their standard, though he'd become rather lax at sending replies. He knew she was angry with him for coming back, but there wasn't much he could do about it now. Their conversation had given his work a sense of urgency, of making every trip count. He had a feeling that the next time he went home, he would have to stay, at least for a while.

The bar was already thronged when he crossed the hotel reception, fresh from the shower. Through the door, Rook could see the journalists: some of them were wearing partial khaki trousers and shirts, unofficial issue. Battered cameras were scattered across the bar, carelessly laid out without cases. So many of them these days, crammed two or three into hotel rooms across the city, arriving to cash in on the story of the decade. Rook still had the same room to himself: no one had ever suggested he share it.

He popped his head around the door, looking for Henry.

'Hey, Rook!' Hans was in clean fatigues, a red bandana tied across his sparse blond hair. He strode across the bar towards him. 'Can I get you a drink?'

'I'm still working,' Rook said. 'Maybe later.'

'Where've you got in from?'

'Khe Sanh.'

Hans's mouth dropped open. 'You're kidding me? They're not letting anyone in. We've been trying all day.'

'Looks like you're trying really hard,' Rook said, his eyes on the whisky in Hans's hand.

'Seriously, Rook. Have you really been there? Is it bad? We can't get a straight answer from the MACV.'

'Wouldn't you like to know?'

'Come on. Help a guy out. How long have we known each other?'

'Long enough.'

'Bet you'd tell Henry.'

Hans was right: Rook had been looking for Henry since he'd got back, hoping to catch him so they could write a story together. He wondered why he didn't want to share this with Hans. Maybe because he knew it would all be shared with Tom too. Was Rook punishing him, for teasing him, for his jealousy? He shrugged.

'Do you think there's any chance of getting in?' Hans asked.

'There might be,' Rook said. 'If the weather holds out. But I'm not sure you'd want to: it's pretty bad out there.'

'Really? I've heard they're totally hemmed in.'

Rook nodded. 'The men are terrified. They're being killed in their beds. The other night, they hit the ammo dump. Like the fourth of July, that's what one of the guys said.'

'Can't believe they're pulling this shit so close to the Tet holiday,' Hans said, shaking his head. 'It's supposed to be a ceasefire.'

'I know.'

Hans leaned in further. 'Who did you speak to? About getting in.'

Rook felt the eyes of the small group in the corner. 'Someone owed me a favour.'

'Mind telling me who?'

'Sorry, Hans.'

'Come on!' Hans moaned. 'We're all supposed to be in this together!'

Rook couldn't help smiling. 'I wonder if you'd be saying that if you were the one with the shots.'

'Give me a break, Rook!'

'Let me ask you something,' Rook said. 'Would *you* tell *me*?'

Hans downed his whisky, banging it down onto the bar. 'Fine,' he said, mock-angry. 'Be like that. Tom's going to go nuts when he hears this.'

'Isn't he otherwise engaged?'

'He's due out this afternoon. And he's not going to be happy.'

'That's not my problem,' he said.

Hans smiled. 'He might make it your problem.' He weaved his way back across the bar. The group leaned in as he told them what had happened, then groaned, looking over at where Rook was sitting.

'Come on, Rook!' one of them shouted. 'Help us out.'

'Come and have a drink,' another one called.

'Sorry, guys,' he said. 'Good luck.'

*

Rook's taxi circled the cathedral, the two turrets marked out against the sky. The streets were crammed with bicycles and people: visitors arriving from the Delta to celebrate the Tet holiday with family.

Rook liked this time of year, when the ceasefire started and he could catch a glimpse of the city as it was before the war. There were red lanterns strung across the road and outside important buildings. They passed the US Embassy, or what he could make out through the thick border wall. An impenetrable fortress, only recently finished after the last one was damaged by a car bomb in 1965. There were no lanterns here, only armed guards.

Tet at Linh's house was an annual tradition. Rook arrived a little late, and was greeted at the door by Henry, who was smoking a cigarette.

'Tom's not here yet,' he said. 'He's out though, and he told me he was coming.'

'I know,' Rook said. 'I saw Hans.'

'Where have you been?' Henry said. 'I was looking for you.'

'I went up to Danang,' Rook said. 'Thought I'd try my luck with Khe Sanh.'

'Don't tell me you got in?' Henry asked.

Rook nodded.

'You're kidding me?' Henry whooped. 'Your luck! Did you get some shots?'

'Yep,' Rook said. 'They've just gone out. We can write a story tomorrow if you like.'

Henry grinned. 'There's no rush. With the ceasefire, nothing else'll be going on.' He whistled. 'Tom's going to lose his shit over this one.'

Rook smiled. 'That's what Hans said.'

At that moment, Tom's golden head rounded the corner. He was limping slightly. 'What am I going to lose my shit over?' he said.

Henry was watching him. 'Want to tell him, Rook?'

'Not really.'

'What've you done this time?' Tom said.

'I just got back from Khe Sanh.'

'You're fucking kidding me!'

Rook shook his head. 'Sorry, Tom,' he said.

'No you're fucking not,' Tom growled, walking past them, into the house. Through his thin shirt, Rook could see a large white bandage stretching across his back.

Henry and Rook glanced at each other.

Tom barely spoke a word over dinner, eating his spring rolls and chicken soup with his head down. Rook felt his gaze on him a couple of times, but he refused to make eye contact. He wasn't going to let Tom ruin the occasion. It truly felt like a holiday: Linh's family were joking with each other in Vietnamese, and the food was stupendous considering the circumstances. As Linh made a joke, Henry leaned in and kissed her on the cheek: they looked so content, sitting next to each other, their hands entwined.

As usual, Linh's father stood up when they'd finished

eating to make a speech. 'We happy,' he said. 'Tet good. And Henry make Linh very happy too.'

Linh's face glowed under the electric light. Two weeks ago, just after he'd got back, Rook had gone with Henry to a backstreet jeweller to choose a ring. The stones were laid out in glass cases, hundreds of them. After viewing almost every one with a hand lens, Henry had finally chosen a pear-shaped diamond, the best he could afford. They'd celebrated his purchase with a drink at a nearby bar, clinking glasses.

'I'm thrilled for you,' Rook said.

'She hasn't said yes yet.'

'She will.'

'I hope so,' Henry said. 'I never expected this to happen, you know.'

'How could you?'

'I had everything mapped out. Make my name here, then get a job in New York or Washington.'

'You can still do that.'

Henry ran his fingers around the top of his glass. 'I'm not sure she'll come with me,' he said. 'All her family are here.'

'All yours are there.'

'But my family are assholes.'

'It'll work out,' Rook said, putting his hand on Henry's arm. 'The war's not ending any time soon, anyway.'

Henry hadn't proposed yet: he was collecting the ring next week, after the shops reopened. Rook couldn't wait for the party to celebrate, to see Linh's father's reaction to the news. Rook watched now as he raised his glass and they all downed their drinks, his eyes crinkled in laughter.

*

When they left, as full as they had anticipated, Rook was surprised by the darkness above the houses. A little unsteady on their feet, they made it out to the main street. It was deserted: no cars or bicycles or busy restaurants doing their dinner trade, all the shop fronts shuttered and dark. Today, the owners were with their families.

They didn't get far before they found what they were looking for: an open bar on Tu Do street, music escaping into the early evening air. A Vietnamese girl in a miniskirt and a short top held out a flyer to Tom.

Inside, the low-ceilinged room was poorly lit. Henry and Rook found a table next to the deserted dance floor, a disco ball throwing fading colours across the walls.

Tom went to the dusty Formica bar running along one wall: a mirror covered with photos of GIs smiling blearily at the camera. Scantily clad women sat on bar stools: Rook watched their backs straighten as Tom approached. Tom shook his head as one of them leaned over to say something to him, her lips pouting.

'I don't think he's coming back,' Henry said, as they watched Tom laughing at something one of the girls said, taking a glass from the barman.

'I'll get us some drinks,' Rook said.

At the bar, he stood a few people down from Tom and ordered a bottle of whisky and two glasses.

Tom swung round. 'For God's sake, Rook. Give me a minute. I'm just coming.'

Rook took the glasses and the bottle. 'Thought I'd save you the trouble.'

Tom slammed his hand down on the bar. 'This guy is a total ass,' he roared at the crowd.

Rook returned to the table.

'What was that all about?' Henry said.

'Just Tom,' Rook said. 'I can't do anything right.'

Henry sighed. 'I wish you guys could get along,' he said.

'I don't have a problem with him.'

'He shouldn't even be drinking. He only got out of hospital today.'

'Stop worrying about him,' Rook said. He looked around the half-empty room. 'Everyone must have gone to Hong Kong for R and R.'

Henry shrugged. 'It's early.'

Rook raised his glass and they clinked.

'Happy Tet,' Henry said.

*

Hans arrived later with a group of friends, bumbling over to their table and pulling out a stool, shaking everyone's hand.

'Have you heard?' he said, pouring himself a whisky from their bottle. 'The ceasefire's off.'

'What?' Henry said.

'The US called it off this afternoon. On account of Khe Sanh.'

'Surely it's too late?' Henry said. 'Tet's already started.'

'I know,' he said. 'I doubt it'll come to anything. The city's quiet enough.'

Rook looked at his watch. 'Is the curfew back on, then? If it is, we've broken it. It's half twelve.'

'No, curfew's still cancelled. The night is ours,' Hans said, raising his glass. 'I saw your photos, by the way. Everyone's sick about it. Great work.'

'Thanks,' Rook said.

The light outside had completely faded; most of the tables were taken. A beautiful woman stood on the low stage, surrounded by a small, tuneless band. She was singing old American love songs, and some people were dancing now, soldiers and bar girls leaning into each other.

*

By the time they left the bar, they had to fight their way to the door. Rook looked down at his watch, flashing up the multicoloured lights of the disco ball. Almost three a.m. His head felt loose and weak, the music thudding across his temples. He swayed as they reached the doorframe, grasping out with his hand to steady himself, pushing into Henry as he did so.

'Woah, Rook,' Henry said. His face was unruffled: he didn't seem in the least bit drunk.

Hans was still with them: he and Tom play-fighting

in the street. Tom's silhouette was tall and willowy, the slope of his shoulders bent forward; Hans's body was more robust, the faint line of his stomach visible in the reflected lights from the bar. The two men moved out of the way as a car, its headlights off, rolled down the street.

'Hey,' Tom shouted after it, waving his arm. 'Put your damn lights on.'

The car didn't slow down, moving steadily until it reached the junction. It turned the corner, and as it did, the lights from an opposing building shone through the windows. The back seat was full.

As it passed, there was a rumbling explosion, some distance away. They all dropped to the ground. It could have been fireworks, he told himself. But something wasn't right.

'What was that?' Hans asked.

No one answered. They listened. The thump of a drumbeat came from the bar, but beyond that, all was quiet. The road darkened into nothing just after the junction: without street lamps, the moonlight only allowed them to see so far.

Another explosion from the same direction, this time louder and accompanied by a flash.

'I think I can see smoke,' Rook said.

'We should check it out,' Hans said.

'We're drunk.'

Tom grimaced. 'But we're here.' He looked behind him at the bar. 'We heard it.'

Rook knew what he was thinking. There were other

journalists in the bar: they would have missed the sound of the explosion, masked by the music.

Rook felt a slow dread creep over him. 'I've got a bad feeling about this.'

Tom laughed, short and sharp. 'Don't be such a chicken, Rook,' he said. 'Not all of us have already scooped today.'

'I thought I saw gunfire,' Rook said, pulling at his camera strap.

Tom slid his hand into his jacket pocket and pulled out a Beretta 950. 'I'm not scared of their guns.'

'We're not here to fight, Tom,' Rook said.

'It's for self-defence,' Tom said.

Rook looked down the road where the car had gone. It was dark and unfathomable. 'We've no idea what's down there.'

Hans grinned, his teeth white in the moonlight. 'I'm up for it,' he said.

Tom looked at Henry, who was standing between them. 'What do you think?'

Henry looked at Rook. 'I don't think you should go alone.'

'Come with us then,' Tom said. 'Let's go, Hans.' Tom set off in the direction of the explosion, keeping to the sides of the street. Hans followed.

'I don't think this is a good idea,' Rook said.

The men were already disappearing. Henry stared after them. 'We shouldn't let them go on their own. Let's follow them to the corner.'

Rook sighed. 'All right.'

When they reached the junction where the car had turned, they paused, looking down the side road. Rook strained his eyes. In the darkness, he thought he could make out the density of cars, of figures moving. He heard Tom call out.

Henry set off again, running. Rook stood on the corner, frozen, his mind suddenly sharp. He squeezed his fingers into his palms, telling himself to follow. But a familiar fear spread through him, heavy and defined, as if he was standing at a height, looking down at something on the ground below.

Rook forced himself to take a few steps forward. He could make out the three journalists, stopped now, outside a building that looked familiar. It was the American Embassy. They were coming at it from the rear. There was the stuttering of gunfire from beyond the thick concrete border wall, which was taller than any man could possibly hope to scale. Now, there was a dark hole, low down at the base.

Rook centred the blasted hole in the wall in the lens of his camera. He moved around it, trying to maximize the light. When he looked around, Tom and Henry were further up the road, at the corner. Rook saw the car returning, crossing the junction, headlamps still off. The moon was reflected on the windscreen, a perfect circle. Then, too fast, solid black shadows appeared at the windows of the car. The gunfire started, and he watched Henry and Tom fall.

ELEVEN

'It's not your fault,' Ralph says, when he's finished talking.

'It shouldn't have happened,' Rook says.

'But it did,' Ralph says.

Rook nods. 'That's what I still can't get my head around. If we hadn't left at that moment, we would never have heard the explosion. If I'd spoken up more, we might have turned back. But I didn't, and Henry is dead. Even all these years later, I still feel like it hasn't really happened. That it couldn't have.'

'You need to accept it, Dad,' Ralph says. 'It will make things easier.'

'I have,' Rook says. 'I've moved on.' Rook is surprised to feel tears prickling. 'We moved to the countryside. We started a family. It was all supposed to go away.'

Ralph doesn't say anything. He doesn't need to. All this time, Rook has thought that by not talking about what happened he was preventing it from affecting him. But he realizes now he has been doing the opposite.

'Are you ready to come home now?' Ralph says.

Rook nods, and his son smiles.

1968

Rook pulled some strings and travelled back to the States with the body on a military flight, full of other dead men. Men who'd died in Khe Sanh and Hue, in Saigon. Henry had been afforded the same rights, honours and privileges as a soldier. He'd been there longer than most of them, after all.

As the plane took off, Rook watched the silver spread of the glassy river, coiling between the buildings of the city. There were smoke clouds rising above the downtown areas, where the fighting was still raging. From above, Rook could see the helicopters hovering like dragonflies, waiting to drop their cargo on the city that had been supportive of them for so long. To flush out the remaining Communists, they would need to destroy the homes of the friendly South Vietnamese.

Rook had spent the days since Henry's death holed up in his hotel room, listening to the fighting on the streets outside. A terrible numbness had overtaken him. He lay on his unmade bed, staring up at the whirring ceiling fan, unafraid of the sound of guns and artillery outside the window. Let them come, he thought.

He'd organized a sort of funeral for Henry in Saigon. They'd gone to Linh's family's villa out of the city, and had a ceremony by the river where they'd often sit and drink beer. Rook had held Linh's hand, watching her tears fall onto the dry red earth. Tom hadn't been able to come, still in the hospital, and Rook had been glad.

*

They dropped the body off at the funeral home near Henry's house in Oklahoma, Henry's brothers carrying it into the back of the building. Big men, muscular in rumpled checked shirts, rolled up over hairy forearms. So different to Henry with their blond hair: at the airport, Rook's eyes had glanced right over them, sure he was looking for a different family. But they'd made a beeline straight for him, grinning and shaking his hand, thanking him heartily for coming as if he'd arrived for a BBQ.

Once they were in the saloon, Rook had caught disorientating flashes of Henry: in his youngest brother's eager smile, the timbre of his father's voice, the way his eyebrows shifted as he waited for the line of traffic leaving the lot to disperse. Towns dotted around junctions, studded with bright advertisements, Laundromats, and liquor stores. As they drove on, the collections of buildings became smaller, older and more traditional: clapboard frontages and verandas, town squares with clock towers, dusty streets, ancient shop fronts. Then there was only the straight road, passing under the open fields and grasslands, on and on under a cloudy sky.

The house itself was as Henry had described it: a white wooden building, paint peeling, in a yard filled with discarded farm machinery. A big, creaking place, where the blinds were always drawn, even in summer. There was a shadowy kitchen with terracotta tiles and fake wooden cupboards. A dank living room with a TV in the corner, an ancient sofa and two armchairs turned towards it. A coffee table with a stack of magazines, the only reading material in the whole house. The place smelt as if it needed airing, as if a few days with all the windows open would do it good.

The bedrooms upstairs were brighter, with bigger windows that looked out over flat brown fields that stretched towards the horizon, scattered with distant buildings.

Two of the brothers still lived at home, and Rook was given Henry's old room. It was papered blue, strewn with faded squares where posters must once have hung. Rook longed to know what they had been of. He wondered if it was Henry who had stripped the place of his belongings, leaving only a low single bed and an empty chest of drawers.

'The bathroom's down the hall,' Henry's mother said. She'd kicked off her heels at the door and her blonde hair was escaping its neat chignon, ashy at the roots. 'I'd imagine you'd want to take a rest: it was a long drive.

Dinner'll be at seven.' She turned to leave, then stopped. 'I hope you don't find it odd, sleeping in his old room.'

Rook shook his head.

'It's not been his for a long time,' she said, turning and padding out of the room, pulling the door shut behind her.

Rook sat on the edge of the bed, avoiding the pattern of weak sunlight. It felt odd to be here without Henry. His head was pounding, but he didn't want to sleep. He didn't want to go downstairs and sit in the kitchen or the living room, or out on the porch. He wondered if he should have come at all. On the surface, things seemed normal: no obvious signs of the claustrophobia Henry had talked of. But Rook knew well enough not to be fooled by appearances, and he was angry with these people on Henry's behalf.

Through the window, he watched Henry's father mounting a tractor. Rook reached up and drew the curtain across, almost yanking it from its flimsy hooks. He lay down on the bed and turned his face towards the wall.

*

Henry's father – Terrence – collected burgers and fries for their dinner, handing them around the dining table in sweating paper bags. Rook wasn't hungry and he couldn't think of anything worse than eating, but the family hadn't lost their appetite. He watched as one of his brothers – 'Call me Tad' – demolished half a burger in one bite.

He wasn't sure what he'd expected of Henry's family, but it wasn't this. The brothers slapped each other on the back and made jokes, and the parents chatted about the price of wheat and when the new tractor would be arriving. He wondered how Henry had fitted in to these conversations, whether things were different when he was around. Would he join in with his brothers' laughter, or would he sit and stare out of the window as Rook was now, wondering when it would be acceptable to excuse himself?

He kept expecting them to ask him about how he'd known Henry, or what had led to his death. They didn't ask him anything at all. He'd told them in his letter – which had taken two agonizing days to write – that he'd known Henry in Saigon, that he'd been with him at the end.

Perhaps all the grief had already happened, before he'd got here. Perhaps Henry's mother cried into her pillow at night, when she thought no one else could hear her. Perhaps his brothers were masking their sorrow with the jokes and loud laughter. Or perhaps they had become so used to Henry's absence that nothing had changed now that he was gone for good.

Whatever the reason, as Rook tried to stomach a mouthful of fries, his fingers trembled with a hot, prickly anger. He'd thought about Henry every moment since his death. He remembered lying in his musty Saigon hotel room, unable to get up and cross the burning town even to visit Tom, who was still in the hospital.

He'd examined from every angle how things could have happened differently. He had thought there would be a limit to the number of times his mind could run over the events of that night, but it wouldn't let up, as if he was worrying a loose tooth that wouldn't come. Over and over he thought back to how they'd left the bar, and followed the car down the deserted streets. He saw the flick of Tom's moonlit hair, Henry's loping stride. He remembered checking his watch at one a.m. and wanting, for a fleeting moment, to leave, but then getting distracted, and staying. If he'd left then, would Henry have come too? Would they have never seen the car or heard the explosion?

His grief, and his struggle to rethink past events, felt strangely familiar. His sadness wasn't something he could help. These people – who'd watched Henry grow up, who'd known him in ways Rook couldn't even imagine – should feel something that was visible. Across town, Henry's body was lifeless in the funeral home, and they were eating fast food and laughing as if nothing had happened.

*

The funeral was held the next day in a small wooden church. Rook watched as Henry's coffin was lowered into the hard ground. There was a chill in the air and rain began to fall, resounding from the wooden lid as it disappeared from view. Rook glanced across at Henry's parents, and saw that his mother was crying.

As he watched her, Rook remembered the first photograph he had ever taken, with his grandfather's camera, of another mother crying at another funeral. He realized, suddenly, why Henry's death felt familiar. The aftermath of the accident at the old building when he was a child: the way one moment changed things, casting him as an outsider. Henry, who had offered him a reprieve from all that, who had accepted him, was gone now too.

There were refreshments at the house: little cheese quiches and sandwiches and cakes, and a big apple pie that apparently Henry's mother was famous for. Homemade lemonade and iced tea. A couple of the men were drinking beer. Rook was grateful he'd had the foresight to bring a bottle of whisky – Henry's favourite. The house was crowded: Rook went onto the porch and looked out over the gleaming hoods of the cars parked next to the house. The rain had stopped now, and the sun was making the stippled crops glow.

'You're Henry's friend?'

When he looked up, there was a man standing next to him, a wide chunky torso and doughy arms, wearing a vest and black trousers.

Rook nodded.

'I'm Siler,' the man said. 'Henry's uncle on his father's side.'

'Nice to meet you.' His voice felt rusty with disuse.

'I heard you were in Vietnam. Are you in the military?'

'I'm a photographer,' Rook said. 'Henry and I worked together.'

The man nodded, observing him. 'What's it like out there?'

Rook looked out across the fields. Two weeks ago, he would have told the man about the war. He'd picked up a few lines from Henry that summarized the escalation of the troops, how despite what the President was saying it didn't show any signs of slowing down. He would have struggled to keep the exhilaration out of his voice.

'It's a war,' he said, eventually.

The man nodded again, but Rook knew he hadn't given him enough.

'If you ask me, we need to get the hell out of there,' the man said. 'Why should our men die for no good reason? Get our guys out, and if the country falls, then good riddance. I don't see how it's any concern of ours.'

Rook sipped his drink, imagining what Henry would say if he was here. *It's not as simple as that.* Rook felt regretful that Henry's quick brain, his way with words, was gone. Rook was on his own now.

'Can I have some of that?' Siler asked, pointing at the whisky.

He poured a slug into Siler's outstretched glass.

Siler grinned. 'Thanks.' He smacked his lips as he drank.

They stood for a moment, watching a black crow descend on the field ahead.

'You were there, then?' Siler said eventually. 'When Henry got shot?'

Rook nodded. This man was the first person to ask

him. He started talking, quickly before the man moved away, explaining what had happened. The car, crawling towards them, emerging out of the darkness like a phantom. The instinct to run as the muzzles of the guns appeared in a crack of the window. The hot breaths, coursing through his body, his legs pumping against the pavement. He hadn't realized how much he'd needed to tell someone, that it was why he'd come. The man listened, looking out towards the bleary fields.

'It sounds like a scene from a movie,' the man said. 'I always liked Henry. He didn't fit in around here, that's for sure, but you couldn't fault him on being himself.'

Rook's eyes felt hot. 'You're right there,' he said, raising his glass to Siler's and finishing it in one burning gulp.

TWELVE

They arrange the flights through the hotel. Rook insists on paying, and Ralph lets him, stopping short of letting Rook reimburse him for his trip out here.

'I wanted to come, Dad,' he insists, and Rook doesn't push the issue.

When they are on the connecting flight to Singapore, Rook looks out of the window at the spread of the receding city. The eternal river, still coiling through new and old buildings. He knows, as the clouds finally obscure his view, that it might be the last time he ever comes here, that he is saying goodbye.

When they get back to London, they pass through the airport rituals in silence, exiting the terminal together into the crisp, bright morning. Rook wishes he had his coat, hanging in the hallway of the cottage.

'How will you get home?' Ralph says.

'My car is here.'

'You can't drive back now, Dad. It's a four-hour trip.'

'I'll be fine.'

'No,' Ralph says. 'You're exhausted. I absolutely insist you stay with us.'

'I'm sure Julia will love that.'

'She won't mind.'

'Fine. But I'm driving.'

Ralph shrugs. 'Suits me. Which way to the car?'

*

Rook is only planning on staying one more night. He knows he should get out of their hair, that he is delaying the inevitable return home. He even thinks about leaving early the next morning, when he wakes to a quiet house. He could walk out now, open the car door, and make his way home without bothering anyone. But something makes him stop, padding down to the kitchen in some of Ralph's pyjamas, making himself coffee and reading yesterday's papers at the kitchen table.

This is the perfect house for a family, he thinks. Semi-detached, in a quiet road of identical houses, all Victorian red-brick, with small front gardens and bigger back ones. Yesterday, Ralph had taken him for a walk around the block, having read somewhere that vitamin D exposure was a cure for jet lag.

There had been children playing out on their bikes, laughing. There was a young girl with a little white dog on a string. 'Hi, Mr Henderson,' she called, and Ralph had returned the greeting.

'A student,' he'd said. 'The school's only five minutes' walk from here.'

Rook wished, fervently, that he could solve this problem for his son. How unfair it seemed that Ralph and

Julia, who obviously loved each other, who obviously wanted children, were unable to have them. He thought again of the fear he'd felt when June had told him she was pregnant. How it had seemed inconvenient to him, when he thought he'd found the solution to his problem.

Last night, at dinner, Julia had roasted a chicken, and laid the table in the small dining room.

'We only use it for special occasions,' she said, as they took their seats.

'Thanks for having me on such short notice,' Rook said.

'That's all right.' She paused. 'I was so sorry, to hear about June.'

Rook hadn't known what to say. He still couldn't bear to think of June, who brought with her so many regrets.

'She was an amazing woman,' Julia said. 'Always so kind to me.'

Rook looked at Julia, but he saw June, smiling back at him. June who always tried so hard, who deserved everything. He nodded. 'She was. I was lucky to be married to her.'

There was a moment of silence: Rook heard a car passing outside the window. His longing for June was acute, and as much as he wanted it to pass, he also wanted it to stay.

Ralph raised his glass. 'To Mum,' he said, and Rook lifted his in response.

*

Rook hears the shower go on, and flicks the switch on the kettle.

'Coffee?' he asks, as Ralph emerges a few minutes later.

'That would be lovely. Hope you haven't been up long?'

'No. I've been catching up on the news.'

Ralph sits at the table. His hair is a little wet at the nape of his neck. Rook brings him his coffee, and they sit together.

'Before you go home, we should probably talk about the funeral,' Ralph says. He speaks slowly, as if he is addressing a horse that might bolt.

'Good idea,' Rook says.

'Where do you think Mum would have liked to have it?'

Rook thinks of the bell-ringing, the church meetings that took up so much of June's time. How she loved to moan about the others when she came home. 'The local church?'

'I was thinking of Backton,' Ralph says. 'Mum always said she wanted to be buried at that churchyard above the town.'

'Did she?' Rook says. He thinks of their walks up there, when they were courting. How they would look out across the town together. *I like it up here*, June had said. *You can see the wood for the trees*.

'I wasn't sure you'd be keen for her to be there: I know it's not your favourite place.'

When Rook thinks of Backton, he sees it in black and white. 'No,' he says. 'If it's what your mother wanted.'

'Great,' Ralph says. 'We can get planning then. Let's talk more when you're home.'

*

Two days later, Rook begins the drive to the cottage. Ralph has offered to accompany him, to help him get the house in order, but he knows it's something he must face alone.

The funeral is next week, and Rook has promised to make some calls.

As he pulls off the motorway, he slows his pace, the roads painful in their familiarity. He is afraid, of turning into the gravel drive, of finding the house just as he left it. As the stone building comes into view, he feels his desire to put his foot on the brake, to reverse. He remembers the first time they came here, so full of hope. A new start, that was supposed to cure so much. As he steps out of the car and opens the front door, as he walks from room to room, calculating all the things he needs to do, everything that must be packed away, he longs to go back to that first moment, to do everything differently.

But he can't, and he knows he must move forwards. Pulling some boxes out from the garage, he climbs the stairs, readying himself for the past, for everything he will remember.

*

He has put off the final phone calls, but once all June's acquaintances in the local area have been called, and he has accepted enough condolences to last the rest of his own life, he knows he must do what June would have wanted.

Under the *M*s in June's address book, Mildred's name is near the top. The handwriting is of a younger June, the letters looped and neat, full of hope. As the phone rings, he runs his finger over the letters.

'Hello?' the voice says when the phone is answered.

'Mildred?'

'Yes.'

'It's Rook Henderson here. June's husband.'

'Oh. Rook. How lovely to hear from you. It's been a long time.'

There is a pause on the line. He isn't sure what to say. *June's dead.* How many times has he said those words today, to people who loved June, but not in the way Mildred did.

'She's gone, isn't she?' Mildred says.

'Yes. I wasn't sure how to say it.'

'I couldn't think of another reason why you'd be calling.'

There is another silence. Rook knows he should give her the details of the funeral, but he can't quite bring himself to.

'I'm so sorry, Rook,' Mildred says, and Rook feels his throat thicken. So many people have said those words, and he's been able to respond with the appropriate: a thank you, a pleasantry. But the way Mildred says them tells him she knows how much he loved June.

'Shall I call around the old gang? When's the funeral?'

Rook breathes out. 'I'd really appreciate that. It's next Wednesday. In Backton church.'

'June would have liked that. She always talked about sitting at the top of the hill with you.' Rook is at a loss for words. 'I'll call and let you know who can make it,' Mildred says. 'There's not many of us left. Live fast and all that.' She pauses. 'Jimmy died a few years ago. Did June tell you?'

She knows, Rook thinks. 'No,' he says. 'She didn't.'

'So that's one off the list.' She laughs drily. 'Is this really what it's come to? I'll call you with the numbers.'

When she has rung off, Rook sits in the chair in the hallway, watching the light filter through the glass in the front door. He remembers the day they came to visit this house, after June told him she was pregnant, and they decided to leave London, to find a small place in the countryside where their money would go further.

He had taken to their house search with a sort of fervency, visiting estate agents and reading newspaper listings. He'd imagined a tiring search through the countryside, but two days after they visited the office they were in a car, heading back to the north. Under an overcast sky, heavy with the chance of rain, down narrowing lanes, enclosing the car in tunnels of foliage.

Hurtling around blind bends and through villages behind the wheel of the jerky rented car, Rook couldn't seem to slow down, his palms sweating.

The house was away from the road, through a gate, along a pebbled drive. It materialized out of nowhere, a small stone cottage with two crumbling chimneys. The day was windy, and Rook helped June out of the car and over to the front door where the estate agent was waiting. As he watched the man struggle with the keys in the old lock, Rook remembered being aware of the open countryside around them, of a feeling of calm. Perhaps, he remembered thinking, everything could be better here.

1968

Life in the new house started wonderfully, exactly as he'd hoped it would. They'd get up early and eat breakfast – porridge, first, before they got the chickens – sitting in sunlight at a pine table June had found in an antiques shop. Then they'd go outside, sometimes to the vegetable patch, where they'd work in silence, whatever the weather: pulling up and planting and watering. June had shrieked with excitement when they'd gone outside and seen the dark soil, punctuated with green: she'd hugged Rook and he'd felt her joy, as if it had been his own.

Sometimes, he'd work inside, on one of the bedrooms, painting the walls or making furniture in the small garage. Every plank of wood he sanded or window he cleaned made his mind go slow and clear in a way that was a remedy.

He still went out, some days. He'd pull his camera around his neck and walk out of the gate at the bottom of the garden, along the canopied lane towards the wood. He'd walk and walk and find photographs everywhere: the new buds on a dead-looking tree, the shadows of sheep on an open plain, the huge dark outline of a tree against a grey sky.

He shot them in black and white, and when he had his studio ready, he began to develop them. He sent a few to Tony.

'Love the shots, Rook,' he said. 'Isn't it funny how they look like war?'

'Don't be ridiculous,' Rook said.

Tony laughed. 'It's not a bad thing, old chap. We're using three this weekend. Some piece about bleak old England.'

After he got off the phone, he went back to the studio and looked at the images again. Tony was right: they were stark and caustic and bleak, and Rook wondered how that could have happened, how moments of inspiration and light could turn into something so dark.

Rook didn't even go out and buy the paper. June rushed in, having been given it by a woman from her choir.

'Why didn't you tell me?' she said, brandishing the *Sunday Times Magazine*, and Rook shrugged. He honestly didn't know. He couldn't muster up that feeling of excitement he'd felt in Backton seeing his pictures published.

June had found all sorts of activities in the village: she was out socializing almost as much as she had been in London. Rook didn't go with her often, realizing the less he saw of other people, how little he needed them.

He'd noticed a scaly patch of skin on his arm. When

it didn't go away, spreading like some unbidden fungus under his sleeve and up to his elbow, he went to the doctor in town.

'Are you under any undue stress?' he was asked.

'No,' he said, truthfully, 'none at all.'

He didn't tell June he'd been.

He wasn't stressed, but was he happy? He knew he should be. He had a gorgeous house, and a beautiful wife. He was an award-winning photographer: people had heard of him, and he was a bit of a local celebrity, according to June, who loved the attention, of course. Every morning, he'd look at his grey-skinned face in the mirror and tell himself these things, but his hard brown eyes were like the unmoving eyes in his photographs.

*

During the pregnancy, he photographed June's changing body every week, in the same position against a white-washed wall in what would soon be the baby's bedroom. She would stand patiently in the light from the window, while Rook took shot after shot, determined to get the right one.

The room was almost empty, with its sloping beamed ceilings and a low wooden crib that Rook made himself. June cried when she saw it: the beautiful intricate carvings along the headboard – a collage of fruit and animals.

There was a look of such gratitude in her eyes, he had to turn his face away.

June's waters broke in the chicken pen while she was

bending down to collect the eggs. She waddled across to the studio, where Rook was developing something in the darkroom. The moment he saw her perspiring face, he knew immediately.

They bundled into the car with her overnight bag. Rook had almost forgotten his camera, but he slung it around his neck at the last minute.

'How lucky I am,' June said, 'to have a professional photographer at the birth of my child. I'll have a perfect record of my agony.'

Rook's hands were clammy on the steering wheel as they left the cottage, along the uneven gravel drive, driving towards the city. He hadn't spoken to June, or anyone, about his fears. Sometimes, he tried to formulate the thoughts into words – *I'm afraid I'll be numb to this too, I'm scared I won't feel anything for our baby* – but none of the explanations he came up with sounded like something he could say aloud.

They had their own room in the hospital. June was huffing and puffing, her face pink as she leaned over the bed, working up the strength to climb onto it. Rook helped her, his hands sinking into the soft flesh around her buttocks. Pregnancy weight, June called it, an excuse to eat anything she wanted. Rook didn't care, he just wanted her – one of them – to be happy.

During the labour, Rook watched June, her tireless strength. In those long hours, he saw a glimpse of the girl he'd fallen in love with in Backton: the steely resolve at the very core of her. The same grit that had pushed his photograph into an envelope and sent it to the editor of the *Sunday Times*, that he'd seen in her eyes as she posed for those first photographs he ever took of her.

When he was ushered out to wait in the corridor, he wondered where that girl had gone. He wondered if it was his fault in some way: for providing her with enough money and security that she didn't need to strive for something more. He wondered if she regretted it.

In the final hours, however, he could only feel admiration. On and on it went, and still June stuck in, gritting her teeth, her hair damp with sweat, stringy around her glowing cheeks. She had never looked more beautiful. In that moment, as he took her photograph, ignoring her protestations, Rook truly loved her, for all that she was. She was bringing his child into the world.

And when it was over, and the baby's first sounds filled the small room, Rook's impatience to see his son became almost unbearable. When the nurses took the baby to clean him off, he wanted to push them out of the way, to look into his child's face. And when he did, as he was handed back to June, he felt a rush of love more powerful than he'd hoped he'd be capable of. He raised his camera, and through his wet eyes, he captured the face of his new son.

*

He hoped so much that it would be enough. Each day, as Ralph grew older, he expected things to improve, to stop feeling like he was outside his life, rather than living it.

It startled him, sometimes, to see a flash of dark hair running down the garden, or Ralph's small body in his coat in the hallway. The tiny fingerprints on the windows, the sound of him calling out at night. Every day that passed, Rook felt angry at himself, for all he was missing.

He walked the fields, through the wintry land: the skeletons of trees and the crunch of frost underfoot. He didn't mind the cold, enjoying his numb fingers and face. It numbed his mind too, like the whisky he carried in a hip flask. Sometimes, the moments of fear worked their way out, spreading through his body and making him freeze in the middle of the forest. He'd see Henry, running through the trees up ahead. He'd hear the dry leaves rustling. His heartbeat, too fast; his hands clenching, his whole body tensed as if he was poised to run, to fight. His sweating palms and tight jaw.

June seemed just as comfortable in her wellies and a battered winter coat as she had in her designer labels in London. Holding Ralph, wiping his snotty nose, she seemed more content than he'd ever seen her. He'd watch her looking at him with such love and it was as if he was seeing something he shouldn't. Their love was reverent, unbreakable, and once again, Rook was on the outside of it. She still had the opportunity to escape: to take Ralph to London for a few days, to visit old friends. Her old life still existed, whereas his was closed to him for ever.

*

One afternoon, he arrived back as the sky was turning deep blue behind the house. Tea-time, usually, but today all the lights were off. Inside, he stumbled from room to room, but June and Ralph were nowhere to be found.

Later, he woke up on the living-room carpet, his neck stiff. Outside the window, it was dark. How long had he been asleep? He sat up and looked around. June was sitting on one of the armchairs, fully made up, her red lips turned down, her arms folded.

'June,' he said. 'Where have you been?'

'Ralph's nativity.'

'That was tonight?'

'Yes. I see you had other plans.'

She was looking at the empty whisky bottle on the carpet next to him.

He remembered her sitting by the fire, sewing. And Ralph, in the kitchen, standing on a chair while June draped the costume over him. His excited face as Rook entered the room, as if he'd been waiting for him all his life. I'm not worth it, he'd thought.

'I'm sorry,' he choked, and then he was crying.

June's anger slid off her face for a moment. 'Don't, Rook.' She turned away from him. 'I'm so tired of this.'

Had he been emotional with her before? He couldn't remember.

'I'm sorry. You don't deserve this.'

'Stop saying that!' Her cheeks were pink under her make-up. '*Ralph* doesn't deserve this. This was his big night. He was so excited. And all the way home, all he talked about was you.'

'Where is he?'

'He's gone to bed. He wanted to come and see you, but I thought that wasn't a good idea.'

'I'll go and see him,' Rook said, trying to get to his feet.

'He's asleep. He's always waiting for you, Rook. Do you know that?'

'I'm right here.'

'You haven't been here for a long time,' she said. She looked down at her hands, then up at him. 'Are you happy, Rook?'

'What do you mean?'

She gestured at the whisky bottle. 'What do you think I mean?'

He looked at June, her eyes tired. She deserved so much better than this. A husband who could interact with his own child, who could at least talk about how he was feeling.

How could he explain without hurting her? He tried to find the words. *Something's missing. It's not enough. I'm scared.*

He took her hand. 'Yes,' he said. 'I'm happy.'

'You don't miss photography?'

'I still take photos,' he said. He had been doing advertisements, as well as his landscape work. The former paid well; the latter could be exhibited. He had an agent now, a man with ambition enough for both of them. The relocation had been easier than he'd thought, the power of his name and reputation carrying forward beyond Vietnam.

'But . . .' She paused. 'Don't get me wrong, they're beautiful. But they're not the same, as the ones you took in Vietnam.'

It felt odd to hear her say the word: they never spoke about it. He never let himself think about it, either. 'This is the life I want,' he said.

'You don't think you should talk to someone?'

'What do you mean?'

'A doctor. What happened—' She stopped. 'It's normal to feel sad, Rook.'

'I'm fine, June. You worry too much.'

June didn't say anything, and when he looked back, she was crying. 'What's the matter?' he said.

'I just—' She stopped again. 'Moving to the countryside was supposed to make everything better.'

Rook felt angry, though he didn't understand why. 'It has,' he said.

There was the sound of the clock on the mantelpiece, ticking.

'I'm not sure I can do this any more,' June said, eventually.

'What?'

'I can't go through all this again, Rook. I can't put Ralph through it. He's getting old enough to understand.'

'I'll get better,' Rook said.

'I've heard you say that so many times. And it only gets worse.'

He knelt on the carpet, taking her hand. 'Please, June,' he said. 'Give me one more chance.'

*

It wasn't always easy. He kept a bottle of whisky in his desk like a talisman, never to be touched, never to be opened. Sometimes, he would take the bottle out and turn it over in his hands. It felt as if he was flying through the air without the chance of pulling a cord to save himself. He missed the cloudiness of his hangovers, how they dulled the edges of everything, making him feel less, care less. But the denial felt right, like a punishment, a curse.

It was difficult, sometimes, in social situations. At the pub, with their local friends. Rook didn't find them a particularly interesting bunch, but they served a purpose: people he could chat with while June was off with her girlfriends, other mothers.

They'd learnt not to ask Rook about the football: he didn't have a clue. He knew he'd never truly fit in with them, not the way he had with Henry and Tom, but they tolerated him, and that was enough. He kept them at a distance, some part of him not wanting to find the intensity of his Vietnam friendships again. They never talked about politics or what was in the news, but that suited Rook.

He didn't want to be reminded of Vietnam, of what had happened. In order to move on, he'd forced the place out of his mind. He didn't even display the World Press Award, hiding it in a drawer, as if it was something to be ashamed of, something forbidden.

*

Their lives found a sort of equilibrium, holding each other at arm's length, each of them terrified of tipping the balance. Since the nativity, their conversations had been confined to practical matters: what they were eating for dinner, who was picking Ralph up from school. Rook busied himself in his studio and June with her various commitments, so that their entwined lives were more separate than they seemed.

One weekend, when Ralph was six, June took him to London, to see some children's show at the theatre.

'Do you want to come?' she said to Rook. 'We could make a trip of it.'

'I've got some commissions coming in,' Rook said.

They both knew he hated the city: that being around so many people made him claustrophobic and desperate for a drink. Once she left, Rook found some work to be getting on with. The morning flew by, and when he finally came inside the postman had been, a stack of letters on the doormat. Rook flicked through them, putting the bills in a pile for June to deal with. When he came to a handwritten envelope addressed to her, he stopped, turning it over in his hands.

Something about the sloping letters had made him stop. He had a sudden longing to see what was going on in June's head, to force open the doors that had been closed to him. Momentarily reckless, he watched his finger push underneath the gum and open it. Inside was a slip of paper, a few sentences scrawled on it.

I know you say it has to be over, but it isn't. You know that. I'm coming to see you in London. I presume you're at the usual hotel. Jimmy.

Rook's stomach dropped: he watched the letter fall from his hands.

You know what June's like in the mornings.

How many trips to London had she taken? To go to the theatre, to visit Mildred. How many times had he given an excuse? June always nodded when he said he had too much work on, never tried to persuade him. He'd always imagined that the love she had found for her son was enough, that it had smoothly replaced how she once felt for Rook. But perhaps there was something else, or someone, he hadn't thought of.

His mind went immediately to the bottle of whisky he knew was still locked in the bottom drawer of his desk. He walked across the garden. Inside, the photos he'd been working on were laid out on the table. He remembered this morning, how he'd worked happily for hours.

He pulled out the whisky bottle and took two long, deep swigs.

It has to be over. What did that mean? How long had it been going on?

He remembered the night of Ralph's nativity play, how June had threatened to leave him.

Rook drank some more. What was he going to do? He'd have to confront her, wouldn't he, when she came back from London? He'd have to wave the letter in front of her face, and ask her to explain herself.

It wasn't until he'd almost finished the bottle that he thought about Ralph. He was sitting cross-legged on the floor of his studio, the sound of Beethoven echoing into the darkness, when he noticed the photograph of Ralph on his pinboard, just born. His green eyes. Rook stood up and moved closer to the image. And in that moment, everything collided. His anger – replaying every moment with June, looking for clues – was replaced with a deep, frightening sadness.

He stood up. He needed further proof: more than the letter, more than an odd dislocated feeling he'd always had.

He headed back to the house. June's bureau stood in front of the living-room window. He imagined her, writing letters, paying bills, the curve of her cheek as she wrote. Had she written to Jimmy, sitting there, in their house?

He opened drawer after drawer. In the bottom one, he found a bundle of letters. His own handwriting: the haphazard letters spelling out the addresses of their various London apartments.

He sat back, leafing through them. Staccato summaries of his actions, reassurances that he was safe. A cloaked, secretive tone, as if they had been written in code. Scrawled in quick, jerky writing, like a child's.

Sometimes only one or two lines. *I'm safe. I'll call when I can.*

He tried to locate the moment he stopped telling her everything. He remembered sitting in his hotel room in Saigon, trying to find the words. The burn of the whisky, the tiredness. Suddenly, he missed it with an intensity that made his fingers tighten around the edges of the pages. The man he was then, lost in these dark places, unable to even pull himself out long enough to write a few lines home.

At the end of one – a small, hasty afterthought – he found a collection of words that made him freeze. He remembered writing it: on his final trip, before the Tet celebration. He and June had argued that Christmas, when he'd been at home: she'd asked him to stay, but he'd left anyway. Then she hadn't written, and he'd given in one night after a few drinks, writing her a note. *I'm sorry I didn't stay*, was all it said. *I love you.*

His eyes burned and he swiped angrily at his cheeks. Was that when she'd slipped, when Jimmy's patience had finally paid off? He tried to work out the dates, but his mind swam, refusing to focus. She'd told him she was pregnant after he'd returned from Vietnam for the last time. After they'd become caught in the protest in Grosvenor Square, at the same dinner when he was going to tell her he needed to go back to work. He'd given up everything – but then so had she, hadn't she?

He shoved the letters back in the drawer, continuing

his search. Everything was neat and ordered, which surprised him: June always seemed to be operating on the cusp of things, always last out of the house, always leaving something behind. There were bills in labelled folders. A stack of programmes of plays she'd seen, in date order. He flicked through: all the ones she'd claimed to have taken Ralph to were there.

Underneath the programmes was a folder marked 'Career'. Rook slid it out. A series of rejection letters: plays he remembered her auditioning for when they first moved to London, but many he didn't recognize. Sheets and sheets of them, moving beyond the dates when he'd left for Vietnam, up to the time they'd decided to leave the city. Rook sank back onto his heels. Had she really still been auditioning then? He remembered asking her once, how she'd shrugged it off. *I really don't have time these days*. Then he thought of the one time he'd pushed her on it, in the milk bar, when he'd accused her of giving up. *I've tried, Rook*, she'd said. *You don't know how much*.

At the end of the pile was a longer letter, the pages yellowed and the staple rusted. Royal Court Theatre, Sloane Square, stamped across the top. Rook scanned it, presuming it would be another rejection. *We are writing to offer you the part of Pam in our revival production of Saved by Edward Bond*. Rook stopped, and checked the date. January 1968. He'd been on his final trip to Vietnam. Shortly before he came back to London and they'd gone to the protest in Grosvenor Square. When he'd left her in the crowd. He heard her voice. *I'm not asking for always*, she'd said. *Just sometimes, just once, for you to put me first.*

Rook felt his head drop into his hands. This letter was June's big break, and she'd turned it down. Or perhaps she hadn't. Perhaps she had never told him about it, only giving it up when he returned home so damaged after his final stint in Vietnam. Two months later, she had told him she was pregnant and they left for the countryside. Had this thing with Jimmy been going on all that time?

He couldn't be in the house any more. Rook picked up his keys and went out to the car. He barrelled along the country roads, driving too fast, the engine roaring. As the headlights of other cars swung towards him, he pushed his foot down on the accelerator, forcing them to veer onto the verges, their horns blaring in the darkness.

Joining a bigger road, he increased his speed still further, drawing up close behind any vehicle ahead until they moved out of his way. He didn't hear the sirens or see the lights until they were almost upon him. When the policeman leaned into the window, the smug look on his face suggested he was happy Rook had done so many things wrong, that he'd found someone to assert his minuscule authority on. Rook refused to get out of the car.

'I'm going to have to ask you to accompany me to the station, sir,' he said.

*

The next day, June turned up in the middle of the afternoon. Rook was sitting on a bench in the holding cell, the hangover weighing across his forehead. His anger had burnt out, leaving a sort of blind numbness that dissipated for a second when he saw June's taut, made-up face.

They didn't speak until they reached the car.

'Where's Ralph?' Rook said.

'I left him with the child-minder,' June said. 'I didn't think it was a good idea for him to come and pick you up from the police station. What the hell, Rook?'

Rook pulled his seatbelt over his body. He wasn't going to say anything, not yet, anyway.

'You've been doing so well,' June said. 'I leave you for one weekend, and this happens. Do you really not have any self-control?'

'You're one to talk,' he snapped.

'What are you talking about?'

'What have you been doing this weekend, June?'

'I've been in London, taking our son to the theatre. You know that.'

'And that's it, is it? No chaste reunions?'

June looked confused. 'I saw Mildred. She came with us.'

Rook turned away from her. 'You're a better actress than I thought, June.'

*

It was as if his mind had been a dark and starless sky, blank and infinite – unnerving, but at least predictable.

Now, against his will, the stars had emerged at last – burning holes of gas and light, unavoidable, blinking in and out of view without warning. If he moved too close to those bright flashes, they would sear through his entire body.

He spent most of the time in his studio, keeping himself away from June, away from his family. Even in Vietnam, afraid to leave his hotel room, he'd never felt so alone.

His anger was difficult to control. One day, he walked into the living room and found Ralph's paper and coloured pencils abandoned in the middle of the carpet. Rook turned and saw Ralph, clad in dungarees and a checked shirt, his small hand curved around the end of an orange crayon, which was an inch or so away from the wall. Ralph looked up at him, and there it was, the naughty look in his green eyes.

Then June was there, her hand on Rook's upper arm. Ralph was crying, and Rook got up and stepped towards the whisky bottle. June got there first, clasping her slender hands around it as if it needed her protection. *No*, she said, as if to a disobedient dog. And Rook acted like one, slinking out of the room, pulling his camera around his neck and marching along the lane, towards the wood.

He walked and walked, his footsteps fast and angry. He needed to get away from that toxic house, which was turning him bad. What was he supposed to do? He turned over the letter he'd found in his pocket, pulling it out and reading the words again.

You say it has to be over, but it isn't.

How could she do this to him? Rook thought of the women in Vietnam, of their bodies swaying and how he shook his head. How he lived for years, waiting for June, waiting to come back to her. And all that time, there was Jimmy, moving in closer and closer, wearing her down, giving her what she needed.

When he returned, the light was fading and the night-time sounds had started up in the forest. Ralph and June were in the kitchen. June had her back to the door, humming as she sat facing Ralph in a kitchen chair. Ralph's face changed when he saw his father in the doorway, his mouth dropping open, his smile drifting away. He recognized the look, he had hundreds of photographs of other children, of other people, with the same expression out in his studio. His son was frightened of him.

June picked up Ralph and took him out of the room. Rook heard them on the stairs. The slosh of the bath-water, June singing softly. He sat at the kitchen table and he waited.

When June came back, she pulled out a chair and sat opposite him, her face hollowed out in the kitchen light.

'What's going on with you?' she said. 'I thought we were back on track.'

'We were,' he said. 'And then I found this.'

He pulled out the creased note from his pocket and watched June read it. A millisecond of shock suffused her features, before she smoothed them over. 'It's not what you think,' she said.

'Isn't it? What else could it possibly be?'

'It's about my career,' she said. 'He thinks I've given up. He can't understand that I'm happy here, with Ralph.' She realized her mistake. 'And you.'

Rook looked at the words on the paper again. *You say it has to be over.* 'I don't believe you,' he said.

'Well it's true.'

She stared back at him. He thought of the night they met. *Would you take my photo?* He wanted to believe her. 'I didn't even know you were still in touch with him.'

'He comes to the theatre with us, sometimes. And Mildred.'

'You never mentioned it.'

'I didn't want you to get the wrong idea.'

'Well, it's too late for that.' Rook paused. 'He's met Ralph, then?'

June wasn't looking at him. 'Yes,' she said.

Something wasn't right. 'I wouldn't blame you,' he said. 'I'd understand.'

'I don't know what you want me to say. I haven't done anything wrong, Rook. Have I ever given you any reason to doubt me?'

Rook shook his head. But he thought of those nights at the Ritz, of Jimmy's eyes on his wife. He couldn't look at her. 'I need to go back to work,' he said.

June's face changed. 'What do you mean?'

'I can't be here anymore.'

'You want to go back to being away all the time? How will that help anything?'

'I don't know, June. But this isn't enough for me. And it clearly isn't enough for you either.'

June swallowed. 'I thought we were happy here.'

'So did I.' He paused. 'I'm trying to tell you I understand. You need something I can't give you. That I'm sorry.'

'You're not making any sense. I don't want anyone else. I never have.'

'I've made up my mind, June. I think it will be better for both of us.'

'It won't be better for Ralph.' Rook thought of the boy, sleeping upstairs. 'You can't just run away, Rook. It won't solve anything. You need to get yourself sorted out.'

'I've tried,' Rook said. 'The only thing that makes it better is working.'

There were tears in her eyes now.

You've hurt me too, he thought. 'We're running out of money.'

June's eyes flashed. 'Don't pretend this is about money. This is about you, Rook.'

'I'm doing what's best,' he said, his voice eerily calm, at odds with his thumping heart. 'I'll be home when I can.'

'Ralph will never forgive you for this,' she said.

'One day, he'll understand,' Rook said.

After June left the room, Rook felt himself sink against the counter. *We are broken*, he thought. *This is the only way*. He imagined an airport, a plane, a new landscape. The moments flashing by, needing to be captured. June and Ralph, sitting at the kitchen table, content without him.

THIRTEEN

The night before June's funeral, Rook dreams of the jungle. The crack of dried leaves underfoot, the whir of insects. In every direction, glaring green.

Waking as dawn rises, he thinks he sees Henry, standing at the foot of his bed. It's only his suit, hanging up on the wardrobe door. The outline of the dresser, the moonlight catching the tines of a comb. He's in the cottage: an island, surrounded by fields that ripple like dark water.

His body's as stiff as if he's slept for weeks. He pulls himself up, walking carefully along the creaking floorboards, as if there's someone to wake. He showers and shaves, whittling out the pinpricks of light, filling the room with the scraping sound of razor against skin.

He pulls on his new suit and shoes. He went to a department store in the city for them specially, letting the sales assistant measure him to get the perfect fit, and thinking all the time of June. She would have wanted him to look his best.

When he's ready, Rook sits on the patio with a cup of tea, watching two birds dart between the trees that overlook the small garden. He watches the light creep above his studio, turning the sky from pink to blue.

When the doorbell rings, he finds his son, standing on the doorstep. 'Ready?' Ralph says. 'We'd better get going. Julia's in the car.'

Through the dim, reflective glass of the Volvo estate in the driveway, Rook can just see Julia, her frizzy dark hair pulled back.

They drive through the canopied lanes towards the motorway, crossing the black shadows the dense hedge-rows throw onto the tarmac. Rook catches glimpses of lambs, galloping unevenly towards their mothers. He is glad the day is so beautiful.

It feels strange, to be driving towards Backton. His brothers are dead now too, having battled through the miners' strikes and the pit closures. The last time he'd seen them was when he'd come up on assignment, to take photos of the protests. Peter was a big man in the union: Rook had got some shots of him looking tough with the pithead shadowing him. The men, massing on the picket lines. His father, in a wheelchair, his strong hands now limp in his lap, his wheezing breaths.

They walk through the town to the church, all dressed in black. Past the chemist's where he worked, which is now a dentist's surgery. The wide wooden window is still the same, though the cram of dusty products is gone. The newsagent's where June worked is boarded up and he's glad she isn't here to see that. He imagines her, for a moment, bending down to lock up the shop, a blonde curl neatly tucked behind her ear.

Retracing the steps he has walked a hundred times, they climb up to the small stone church on the hill. He remembers when this journey was an escape, a reprieve. Now, his stomach is a tight chrysalis of nervous energy. It feels as if something is unwinding, spooling backwards against his will.

The church's pointing is still dark with coal dust. There are people inside, a collection of shapes outlined by dim light filtering through the stained-glass window. As Rook's eyes make them out, he feels sure he will recognize them. But as they approach, he feels as if he's walking through an odd shadowy dream, surrounded by strangers. Dropping his camera onto a nearby pew, he watches Ralph kiss a woman's cheek. These past weeks, he's felt changed, and he wonders if people will even recognize him. They do: taking him by the hands, offering their condolences, the warmth and suddenness of their touch startling him.

Mildred is there, her red hair now white. She comes straight over, still looking and smelling expensive, in a royal-blue suit, pearls at her neckline. She pulls him into a hug, holding on for some minutes.

'I see you brought your old friend,' she says, gesturing at the camera.

Once the people have dispersed to their seats, Rook sees the photograph, standing on an easel. The same one

June kept beside their bed. She is wearing a white dress and arching back against a table, her smile too wide. The photograph he took the night they met.

As the vicar begins to speak, Rook feels his sadness, falling across him like a shadow. He looks down at the order of service: seeing the dates of June's life and death, and the same photograph, repeated. His hands begin to shake, the edges of the paper fluttering. He sees her, with greying hair, reaching up to pull something out of a kitchen cupboard. Her hands, spreading over her pregnant stomach. Standing in the chemist, asking him to develop her picture. *I'm sorry*, he thinks. He wishes she was standing beside him now, that he could take her hand and squeeze it, that they had the chance to begin again.

When he looks up, Ralph is looking at him. He doesn't try to wipe away his tears, and he feels his son's hand, on his shoulder. Their eyes meet, and Rook doesn't look away.

1959

The night they met, the cold had a smell: a sharpness burning the back of his throat, forcing him awake.

Rook's brother Peter had come for him, after tea.

'I'm not going,' Rook said.

'You bloody well are. Get ready will you? We're late.'

'I'm not in the mood.' Rook had plans to fix the camera, and he didn't fancy the dance at the town hall, with the crowds of people and music. Listening to the other men talk about the pit, cracking jokes that weren't funny.

'You should go, Rook,' his mother said from her seat by the fireplace. 'You might get some good shots.'

Rook thought of the stack of blurry images he'd got the week before: how none of them had looked right when he'd developed them in the darkroom. Then he was on the stairs, in the bedroom that was now only his. His brothers lived further down the road: Rook couldn't afford to move out yet, not on his pay from the chemist. He brushed his hair and put on his hand-me-down brown suit. He pulled his camera from its hook and clattered back down.

Peter was checking his quiffed hair in the mirror above the huge black-leaded fireplace. He looked at Rook and grinned. 'At least you make us look good.'

Rook followed him to the car where Robert was waiting, the radio jumping through the chilly air.

They drove through light rain, polishing the cobbled pavements, passing long rows of identical terraces, net curtains softening the light. During the day, winter gloom dulled the grey stone and brick, but at night, under the glow of occasional streetlights, it was a strange sort of beautiful.

Peter tapped his coal-edged fingernails on the battered steering wheel. Robert turned up the music as they approached the town hall. The doors were open and the white light turned the wet steps black, darkening the edges of the gathered crowd. Rook wheeled down the window, ignoring his brothers' protestations, and centred the shot. Just as he clicked the shutter, four girls shimmied into the viewfinder.

Rook sighed; his brothers whistled.

'Oi!' one of them shouted, turning around. 'Pervert!'

Rook's brothers were laughing; he wanted to follow them and explain, but he knew it wouldn't do any good.

Outside, Rook distracted himself from the chill, taking photographs. The men in suits, a string or skinny tie at the neck. Pointy, shiny shoes, winking like black beetles. Their hair, like manicured hedges he'd seen in photographs of London. The girls: narrow-waisted, big skirts poking out under their coats, stockinged legs and little white socks. An American film set, except they were in England: the girls pale and plump, the men grey-eyed from the mines.

The jumping beat of the music from inside, the chatter of other people. His brothers around him, jostling and joking. The pent-up energy from the working week jumped between them, almost visible: a sharpness to their actions; a need to move, to make each free moment count. They passed around a bottle of vodka. Rook took a burning sip when it reached him, but only to keep warm: he didn't drink when he was taking photographs.

Then, the moment itself. One of his brothers whistled, pointing ahead, into the crowd above them. There was a glimmer of brighter white there, and he looked away from the camera, trying to make it out. A girl. She wasn't wearing a coat, and Rook wanted to offer his. She stood alone, without the usual gaggle of friends. Then the crowd realigned, and she was gone.

*

Inside, people thronged. Spotlights threw yellow circles onto the parquet, catching the edges of a dusty chandelier hanging unlit from the domed ceiling. Tables and chairs stood around the dance floor, most already taken. The band was set up on a stage at the far end, in front of a shimmering wall of tinsel, playing cover songs of some whining American singer. It wouldn't be long until they were bullied into playing something more upbeat.

His brothers went straight to the bar. How many

times had Rook been here or in the pub, waiting for a space to open up where he could feel at home? Sometimes, when he thought hard enough, he could remember a time when he hadn't been outside things, when he and his brothers had been like some six-legged animal, racing through the town.

He got up. He'd slip out the back without telling the others, walk the mile or so home. The streets would be quiet, the pavements shining with the now-past rain.

As he turned, his camera jolted into something: the girl from the steps, in the white dress.

She smiled, her teeth neat and straight. 'Are you leaving?' she said.

'I was thinking about it.'

'I've been looking for you,' she said, the words stiff, like a line from a film. 'You're the photographer, aren't you?'

Rook looked down at the heavy metal object on his chest. 'I have a camera,' he said.

She put her hand on his arm. 'Would you take my photo?'

Rook glanced around. A crowd of girls was watching. 'Now?'

She shrugged. 'Why not?'

He positioned her in the viewfinder. Close up, her blonde curls were stiff and dry. She was wearing too much make-up: powder on her forehead, her cheeks the wrong shade of pink.

She looked down at her hands, straightening the bow on the front of her dress, preparing herself. In that moment, she was beautiful. As she looked up, he clicked the shutter.

She froze. 'Did you take it?'

Rook nodded. 'It's a good shot,' he said.

'I wasn't ready,' she said, pouting. 'Can't you take another?'

She leaned against a table behind her, arching her back and looking coyly at the camera. The girls around her stared, whispering behind their hands. Rook hesitated.

'What's wrong?' she said.

'I think the other one will be better.'

She leant back, further. 'What about this?'

'No,' Rook said. 'The other way.'

She changed her stance again. It still wasn't right, but Rook took the shot.

She relaxed. 'Thanks,' she said, lovely again. Rook clicked the shutter before she changed. She put her hand up to her face. 'What are you doing?' she said.

He wound on the film and took another.

'Stop,' she said, covering the lens with her hand.

He lowered the camera. 'I'm sorry.'

'You shouldn't have done that,' she said, taking out a small compact, checking her face in the mirror.

He needed to explain himself, to tell her she was beautiful without trying so hard. 'Trust me,' he said.

She shoved the compact into her bag, turned, and walked away from him.

*

First, the darkness of the background, around a strip of white. Then her lips and her hair, the flowers on the table behind her, leached of colour. Her back was reflected in the mirror: the exposed skin made him want to put his hand there, to feel the warmth of her body.

He carried the photograph with him, sliding it out as he sat behind the chemist's counter, or in his bedroom at his parents' terraced house. He loved the feeling it gave him: a hot white hope, as bright as the girl's dress. That something might change, that his future was really waiting for him, away from Backton, away from everything he knew. He wanted to cup his hands around it as if it were a flame that might gutter out.

*

His brothers, barrelling in for tea at six, bringing a blast of cold air. Peter, his ruffled orange hair, his ruddy cheeks hiding his freckles. Broad torso, strong arms: from shovelling coal and the football. Then Robert, with his darker hair and quiet smile.

His father wasn't far behind. He pulled off his cap: his hair was threaded silver at the temples, his face lined; then shoved his hands in his pockets.

'You lads coming back to the pub after?' his father said, taking the beer their mother had poured for him.

Peter shook his head. 'I've got footy practice,' he said.

'Suppose you need all the help you can get,' his father said. 'Going in for the cup again?'

Peter shrugged. 'Of course,' he said. 'We're in the league, aren't we?'

'Well, you can try. How many times have you finished bottom now?'

'It's not bottom. It's bottom half. We're climbing slowly.'

Their father held up his glass. 'We won the league in '48.'

'As you keep reminding me,' Peter said. 'I'd love to see you try now.'

'All right then,' their father said. 'I can get a team together from the lads at work. We'll give you a run for your money.'

Peter sipped his drink. 'I was joking, old man,' he said. 'I wouldn't want to embarrass you.'

His father was chewing with his mouth open. 'Cheeky bugger,' he said, laughing. He turned to Robert. 'You're not too busy for the pub, are you, lad?'

Robert shrugged. 'Nothing better to do,' he said.

'Are you going to go along, Rook?' his mother asked.

His father looked up at him, blinking as if only seeing him for the first time.

'I've got work to be doing,' Rook said. He had photos to sort, from the chemist.

His father smirked, looking down at his plate. 'All

work and no play . . .' he muttered, looking sideways at Peter.

Rook felt himself push his chair back. He walked to the sink. His father was still talking, about something else now. Closing his eyes, he still saw his father's stupid, smirking face, and felt himself kick out, at the bottom of the skirting board. When he turned around, it was only his mother who was looking at him: the others had moved on to some other joke. He avoided her eyes.

His father stood up, slapping his hands together. 'Thanks for tea,' he said. 'Coming, lads?'

His brothers got up and followed their father out: Rook could still hear them laughing on the street.

'You shouldn't let him get to you,' his mother said, as they started to clear the table.

'Who?' Rook said, keeping his eyes on the pile of plates.

'Your father.'

'I don't know what you mean,' Rook said.

He ran the water, sudding up each plate, stacking them on the draining board with a clatter. He knew his movements were too fast, too rough, but he couldn't slow down. As he rubbed one plate with the cloth, it broke apart in his hands.

'Leave it,' he heard his mother say behind him.

But he finished the plates on the rack, and the roasting tin and pans, and put them away. When he was finished, he hung the dishcloth over a kitchen chair.

'I'm going out for a walk,' he said.

His mother nodded.

His boots clattered against the pavement; sweat prickled under his clothes. He remembered again the day he'd gone to work in the mines. The walk to the pit-head. The smell of the coal in the yard. Waiting for the lift, the whoops and songs of other men.

The lift creaked, swinging on its chain as he crammed in next to Peter, Thomas and his father. Their work clothes were faded and worn-in: Rook felt like an impostor in his newly issued ones.

As the light at the surface began to slide out of view, Rook felt the darkness beneath them. Eventually, the metal cage opened and they poured out into a wide cavity, the men heading off along narrow tunnels. Peter took him to the beginnings of the belt that pulled a huge heap of coal towards the surface. Then they got to work, picking at the rock face with their tools, the men behind them shoring up the tunnel.

By dinnertime, Rook's chest was full and tight. The sandwiches his mother had made for him tasted of coal, even inside the snap tin. Peter and his father laughed and shoved each other, a real comedy duo: they had half the men in stitches.

At the end of the day, when Rook stepped out of the lift, stretching his back, he knew he wouldn't go back down. When he told his father, he only shrugged, his eyes skimming over Rook in a way that was familiar. Rook had been ready with his reasons, but he wasn't asked for them. It was one more thing that separated him from the others.

It was easy, he thought, to think himself above them: to know that his father and brothers' lives between the pit and the pub and the television were pointless. He shouldn't care about what they thought of him. But he did.

And after all, how was his life any better? He took photographs, yes, but no one saw them, except his mother. He worked at the chemist's; he lived with his parents. He was wasting his life. He touched the edges of the photograph in his pocket. In the dark, he couldn't make out the girl's face.

He stopped walking. All around him were the shadows of the terraces: the looming heaviness of other people's lives. The weight that dragged on those who lived here day after day, making it hard for them to lift their heads to say more than a few words to each other, words that weren't about the weather or that didn't poke fun. He thought of his father's jokes, and what hid behind them: the empty space that he couldn't confront.

As he walked past his old school, he remembered running out of the gate, along the pavements. He remembered the way people looked at him after that terrible day in the abandoned building: the way his own brother crossed the school corridor to avoid him. He picked up a brick from the pavement and threw it, hard, over the railing. He hadn't expected it to travel as far as it did, and when he heard the smash of glass ring out, he didn't move, didn't run away. But no one came or seemed to care, so eventually he started back for home.

*

He was sitting behind the counter, flicking through the new *Life* magazine, sent over from America. When he looked up, she was there, near the dusty make-up stand, trying lipstick colours on her hand: a glossy rainbow of reds and pinks. They caught each other's eye: she looked away. Something about the way her lashes brushed her cheek, the delicate skin of her eyelid, made Rook's nerves tingle. The same feeling he got when he wanted to take a photograph.

He tried to go back to his magazine, to examine a set of images with the headline – *Castro's Mob Assembles to Castigate the Yanquis* – a huge crowd massing in front of a grand, flag-dressed building. It couldn't hold his attention. The girl's silhouette was moving across the far wall. A glimpse of her patent heels as she turned the corner, and then she was at the counter with a lipstick in her hand.

'Hello,' she said.

'Hello.'

His fingers were heavy on the till buttons. When he looked up, she was smiling. A blue skirt and a green cardigan, pulling at her chest. Less make-up, her hair still curled neatly. Rook thought of his mother's rollers, and how she had to sleep on her back with her head straight.

He handed her the lipstick in a paper bag.

'You don't remember me, do you?' she asked.

Rook struggled to keep his face blank.

'From the town hall? You took my photograph.'

Rook nodded. 'I remember.'

'I wanted to ask if you could develop one for me.'

Rook thought of the photograph he'd already developed – in an envelope under the till. 'It wouldn't be ready until tomorrow,' he said.

'That's perfect,' she said. 'I'll come in on my lunch break.'

She clutched the bag to her chest and held out her hand, which was warm, the skin surprisingly calloused. Her nails were neat, painted bright red. 'I'm June, by the way.'

'John,' Rook said. 'But everyone calls me Rook.'

'What a marvellous name!'

'It's a nickname,' he said, feeling stupid again.

'Well, Rook,' she said, sounding out the K carefully. 'It suits you.'

Now he knew he was blushing.

'I'll see you tomorrow,' she called. And then the bell rang out, and the shop was empty.

*

The next morning, each time the bell tinkled, Rook felt himself sit up straight, against his will. But it was only Mrs Edith collecting her prescription. Then Mr Reynolds the grocer, asking if he had change for a pound. Rook saw his fingers shaking as he counted out the money, and told himself to calm down.

When the bell rang for the third time, she was there, pushing open the heavy door, heels clacking on the tiled floor. A pink dress drawn in at the waist, and beige gloves that looked like they'd seen better days. She was carrying a matching umbrella, despite there being no rain.

'Afternoon,' Rook said.

'Sorry I'm a little late,' she said. 'The shop's always busy when I've got an errand to run.'

'Shop?' Rook asked.

'I'm working at the newsagent's along the way. We're always busy in the school holidays.'

'I wondered why we were so quiet,' he said.

June leant on the edge of the wide stone counter. 'Did you get a chance to do the photograph?'

Rook pulled out the envelope and passed it to her. She slid out the photo, frowning. Perhaps she could see his fingerprints, could tell how many times he'd looked at it.

'This isn't the one I meant,' she said.

'It's the best one,' Rook said.

She looked at him for a moment. 'It's lovely. But I need one where I'm looking at the camera.'

Rook thought of the intense, pouty look she'd held in the other shots. 'I only developed one,' he said.

He was surprised to see her blush. 'Sorry to have put you to so much trouble.' She paused. 'There's no way I could have a look at them, is there, so I can see which one is best?'

'We could use the enlarger,' he said. 'It's in the darkroom.' He gestured to the doorway behind him.

'Are you sure that's all right?'

Rook nodded. 'I'll just have to close up for a minute,' he said. He stepped past her, turning the lock. He held open the door to the darkroom and flicked on the red light.

She followed him inside: so close, her arm brushed his in the semi-darkness. It was odd, to have someone else in this space. Rook busied himself, rummaging through the old negatives with the slow care of someone being watched. Her breathing: he slipped the strip into place, pressed the switch on the side. A blurry outline of June leaning against a table appeared on the flat surface below. Rook turned the focuser, feeling June lean in.

She gave a quick intake of breath. 'It's wonderful,' she said.

Rook smiled. Was this the first time he'd shown someone his images, other than his mother? She did look beautiful, but in a studied, unnatural way. Her top leg, crossed over the other, looked long and slender, her neck slim; her back was arched, her lips pouted. Her eyes were big and round.

Though Rook could appreciate it, he didn't like it. It felt like a false version of the June standing in front of him now.

'You're really good,' she said.

Rook was glad the light was red. When he looked up, her face was inches away from his. The gap between them, though small, felt impossible to cross.

'May I have that one developed?' she said.

Rook felt himself nodding.

*

They started meeting after work, walking up the hill towards the church. The first time, the light was heavy: they were out of breath when they reached the top. June's face glowed and he wanted to take a photo, but instead, he leant forward and kissed her, their lips brushing for only a second. It was the first time for so long that his body had moved without his mind allowing it to, and when their lips touched he was startled, as if it was her who had kissed him. But when he pulled back, the light was honey-like and she was smiling.

Each night, the summer offered them a little more time. The town was laid out below them, a golden patchwork of fields spreading around it towards the coast.

'It makes me feel better,' June said, 'to be up here. Like I can see the wood for the trees.'

Sitting on a bench, she'd pull off her heels, their legs almost touching. Sometimes they'd hold hands, sometimes not – talking about anything and everything. She told him about her childhood: the darkness after her father left, how hard her mother had worked to keep them afloat.

'I can't do that,' she said. 'Stay here and wait for life

to wear me down. I look at her, and it makes me so angry.'

Rook nodded.

'Sometimes,' she said, 'I want to shake her. Why did she marry him? How did she get herself in this position?'

June's voice was tired. Rook didn't say anything, but his chest was clouded with the same feeling. He kissed her again.

He loved to watch her talking about acting, about the theatre. The way her face changed, as if she forgot to hold it in place, as if she could focus only on what she was talking about and not what she looked like. She would fiddle with something on her clothing: the only time she seemed less than completely composed. Once, she told him how she'd skipped school to go into town and watch a production of something he'd never heard of but that sounded important, getting the cheapest ticket.

'My seat was so far back, I needed binoculars to see the stage,' she said. 'But it was so exhilarating. There was just this *feeling*, you know, in the whole room. Everyone's eyes trained on the stage. I want to make people feel that.'

Sometimes, Rook showed June some of his photographs. His boss at the chemist's only allowed him to develop one a week as the paper was expensive, and he'd pore over the negatives, knowing it was teaching him to be selective. He loved the careful way June slipped them out of the envelope, lingering over each one: pointing out things in the background or the composition that he hadn't even noticed himself. It was strange to be watched so intently, to feel so exposed, when for so much of his life people had been trying to pretend he wasn't there.

'These are really special, Rook,' she'd say. 'You should show them to someone.'

'I'm showing them to you,' he said.

'Someone important.' She paused, looking out over the fields below them. 'What does it feel like, when you take a photograph?'

No one had ever asked him that before. He looked down at his hands, unsure how to answer.

'I've watched you,' she said. 'And you get this look on your face. So focused. Like you've seen something and you have to move quickly to catch it. I just wondered what you're thinking.'

Rook put his hands on his camera. 'I suppose it is like that,' he said. 'It's hard to describe, but it just feels right. Something about the light, or the way the things are in that moment. It's like there's more there than I have time to think about. I take a photo to save it, so I can examine it again later.'

June was nodding, as if she wanted him to continue.

'In a photograph, everything's contained.' He paused. 'I hope that makes sense.'

June nodded. 'It does,' she said, reaching for his hand.

The sun sank, sending lower angled shafts of light out across the fields, casting the town into silhouette. They started back as the sky faded, everything below them in shadow. Sometimes, as they rounded a bend on the path,

June would disappear, and Rook was sure that when he turned the corner, she would be gone, like a spirit evaporated into the warm air. But there, he could make her out, just ahead.

After he dropped her at her house, Rook walked the few streets further to his own, already thinking of the next night. When he was away from her, he'd struggle to remember the way they were together. He remembered the things he didn't like: how she would laugh too loudly in the cafe or on the bus; how people would turn when she passed them, staring at her clothes and hair, everything so careful and stylized. She drew attention, coveting it, whereas he wanted to sink into the background, to be invisible.

But when she was there before him, he didn't think about any of that. He'd watch her: the way she moved, looking down before she spoke, the perfect curve of her lips. She had no shadows, everything was bright light and white teeth. She'd lean in when he was talking, as if to catch every word. He never felt like the youngest with her, the one always running after the others. He could imagine a life that was different, newer and fresher than his parents' life, where they would laugh and be happy together.

*

It was weeks before Rook found out what June wanted those photos for, the ones that had brought them together in the first place.

They'd taken their lunch break together. Walking along the High Street with June – her platinum hair, her red lips, her small tottering steps – had felt like something reckless and wild. The low-ceilinged cafe was crammed with tables, tablecloths chequered pink and cream. The eyes of the other patrons followed June as she swayed across the room in her tight red dress, bumping a table with her hip.

She ordered straight away: a teacake and a pot of tea.

'Teacakes for lunch?' Rook asked, once the waitress had gone.

June shrugged. 'Why not?'

'No reason,' Rook said. 'Do you come here a lot?'

'Never,' she said. 'I'm saving money.'

'So only if someone else is paying?'

'It's the only place to go in this whole town.'

'What are you saving for?' Rook asked.

'I want to move to London,' she said. 'To be an actress.'

Rook stared at her. 'On your own?'

She nodded, pouring the tea.

Rook wasn't sure what to say.

'That's what I needed the photo for,' she said. 'Head shots. For castings. I've been working to get my Equity card.'

'What's that?' Rook asked.

'I need it to act in London. I have to show I've been working here first.'

June glanced across at the people next to them: two

elderly ladies in high-necked faded dresses and cardigans, rings flashing on their fingers. They ate their sandwiches with knives and forks.

June grinned, leaning in. 'How old do you think they are?' she whispered.

Rook stole a look at their creased faces.

'At least eighty,' he said.

'Imagine staying in this town your whole life,' she said. 'I'd rather die.'

Rook thought of his mother, in the terraced house across town, washing something that would only need to be washed again in a few days. He nodded. 'I know what you mean,' he said.

June reached across and grabbed his hand. Rook looked around the cafe, but no one had noticed. 'Let's make a pact,' she said. 'We'll never end up like them. We'll get out of here.'

Rook squeezed her hand. 'All right,' he said.

That afternoon, in the chemist's, he couldn't think about anything else. London. He couldn't narrow down his feelings about it, and about June. On the surface, he was relieved, that there was someone else in this town who felt trapped in the same way he did, who felt there was more to life than the pit and these narrow terraced houses. But underneath that, he felt a frisson of irritation towards June, though he couldn't work out why.

Finally, as he was cashing up the till, he realized. Although he'd known he wanted to get out, to do something bigger, he'd never thought of London. Or if he had, he'd imagined himself disappearing into it as if it was a molten pool of quicksand. June had not only imagined herself there, she'd actually started preparing – saving money and getting her photos done. While he'd been stewing in his anger and resentment, she'd started taking small steps towards a solution. And she made it look easy.

He met June at the corner for their walk up to the top of the hill, which was becoming shorter and shorter now that winter was drawing in. She filled the silence, telling him about her day, about the customer who had berated her for twenty minutes for running out of the *Telegraph*.

'I told him I don't make the orders, but he didn't want to hear it,' she said.

He looked at her: her carefully applied make-up and big eyes, and for the first time, he was looking past all those exterior things to what was beyond them, to what was actually at the core of June. How determined she was, how sure of herself and what her life would be. She was so much more than a pretty girl who took good care of herself. Even this was a way in which she was making the most of herself, preparing herself for the future. How had he not seen this before? He felt a pulse of admiration for her, taking the place of his desire.

'You're very quiet tonight,' she said. 'What are you thinking about?'

'You,' he said, and she blushed.

On his walk home, as he passed the glowing working men's club and laughing children making the most of the last sliver of daylight, his mind began working differently too. What could he do to propel himself forward, to find a way out of here? If June could do it, he thought, so could he. Perhaps they could do it together.

FOURTEEN

After the service, they walk towards the town hall. Rook tells his son he will meet him there, that he wants to walk by his old house.

'Do you want me to come with you?' Ralph says.

'I won't be long.'

The sandwich of terraces is the same as it always was. The pithead has long since been removed, the town oddly naked without it. The front steps of some of the houses are cluttered with rubbish bags, the small yards untidy with discarded toys and piles of bricks. There is graffiti, covering the wall at the bend into Rook's old road.

Rook stops for a moment at the corner, looking down the street at the row of identical doors, stretching away from him. Seeing the cracked pavement, he remembers his feet clattering along it towards the railway, where they weren't supposed to play. Were they freer then, or was it an illusion? He remembers the bomb-damaged houses, like pulled teeth: the unlucky things that had happened before he could remember. The smell of rubbery gas masks.

Outside the house, he stops. The brickwork has been

cleaned here, and without their old net curtains the windows look strangely empty, as if they are hanging open. Rook is glad there is no rubbish in the yard, that someone has planted some roses which curl up the outer wall. There is a small patch of grass, and one neat flowerbed. As he stares at the door it opens, and for a moment, he sees his father's lumbering frame, watches him blinking into the brightness of day.

But it is an old lady who stands there in her carpet slippers, looking down at him. Rook thinks of his mother. They sold the house after she died.

'Can I help you?' the woman asks.

'I used to live here.'

'I thought you were one of those God-botherers,' the woman says, peering down at him. 'You're not one of the Henderson lads, are you?'

Rook nods. 'I'm John.'

The woman nods. 'The youngest,' she says. 'I'm Marjorie. I was at school with your brother.'

'Peter?' Rook says.

'Yes,' the woman says, smiling. 'He was quite the heartthrob, back then. There aren't many of us left, are there?'

'No.'

'Survivors,' she says. Then she seems to remember something. 'You're not the lad that was involved in that accident, are you? In the old building?'

Rook nods slowly. 'It's a long time since I've thought about that.'

'Tragic,' she says.

Rook thinks of that feeling he'd had of being on top of the world, standing on the top floor looking down at Larry. How it had felt to fall. 'It felt like it was my fault at the time. It was all anybody could remember about me.'

'That's the trouble around here,' Marjorie says. 'Nobody lets you forget a thing. Or at least they used to.' She looks up and down the street. 'Not like that any more.' She folds her arms. 'Do you want to come in for a cuppa?'

'I'm at a funeral,' he says. 'I'd better get back.'

'Who died?'

'My wife,' he says. 'June Jacobs.'

The woman's face changes. 'I remember her,' she says. 'Quite the glamourpuss. Didn't she move to London?'

'We both did,' he says.

'I'm sorry to hear she died,' Marjorie says. 'Next time you're around here, pop in and see me. It'd be nice to chat about the good old days.'

I won't be back here, he thinks, as he turns and walks on down the street, towards the town hall.

1947

Running out of the school gate, along the pavements past the sliced rows of rain-slicked terraces. Streets and streets of them, on and on, like his reflection in the fun-house mirrors. The sky was fading and he ran to beat the darkness, his cheeks hot. Through the town centre where the street lamps were already lit and the shop windows glowed: the click of the last heels of the day along the pavement. He ran like a bullet, the world shuddering around him. Greying brick, yellow light and smoke. What if – he was invisible, if no one could see him and he could see them? But he caught himself, grinning, in a shop window, his messy-haired reflection like a mad thing.

The early shifters were heading back along the main road, white eyes in dark faces, whooping with the delight of being back above ground. He winced, thinking about what it was like down there, in the darkness, with the weight of so much earth above them. Only the damp coal and the warm stuck air, the sounds of picks and coal tumbling into carts to go up to the surface.

Always, above the town hung the pithead: high steel, spindly black lines against the twilit sky. Only standing just below it could you see the strength of the metal and the chains that pulled the coal up. From here, it looked frail: the struts like twigs, swaying in the wind. Below that, the shadow of the pit buildings and the beginning of the railway.

He was panting now, his breaths fast. The peeling paintwork of the door to the terrace: the sound of a splash inside, a grimacing shout. The light behind the net curtains. Inside, his father, bent over the rag rug next to the tin bath; his mother, scrubbing at his back with an old sponge. His meaty spine, arched over folded knees: thick skin and hard flesh like the pig carcasses hanging in the butcher's window.

*

His father's shadow, standing in the doorway.

'Get in here lads, now!'

The smell of cooking from someone else's house. Darting about, playing football, their shoelaces trailing. Robert with the ball, dribbling it between grimy ankles, his shorts getting too small. Peter: orange hair glowing, dashing like a fox across the cobbles, face rigid with concentration. His leg going out, and Robert tripping, a grazed knee, blood trickling down towards his sock. Larry was there too: another neighbourhood boy with a sharp, waspish face and long gangly limbs. Always scuffed knees and a runny nose.

They ran home together, losing Larry along the way.

His father was wrapped in a towel, the hairs on his

torso glistening with bath water. He was blinking, strange without his flat cap, his wet hair smoothed down and face exposed.

His mother looked up from the stove, clapping her hand over her mouth, her curls like wisps of cloud. 'Steve,' she said. 'Will you get back inside – dressed like that?'

A grin, spreading across his father's face. He flapped his towel open, stuck his tongue out, stepping towards her, his hands around her waist, kissing the side of her mouth.

Boiled eggs and soldiers for tea. The soft, buttery yolk; steaming Bovril that burnt his mouth. Later, his mother singing, soft and low, darning. Songs of miners lost in disasters, of lovers leaving lovers. She looked pretty, he thought, in the warm firelight, her face turned towards his father's sock, her hair loose.

His brothers were clean and flush-cheeked from the bath, playing cards in front of two beige armchairs. Behind them, the small kitchen with the dining table and the battered, blackened range.

*

The next morning, his mother hummed in the kitchen, making porridge. She was going out to see her sisters.

He raced his brothers through the town. His breaths and body moved in time like a metronome. He passed the postman's cart, dodging prams. They stopped at Larry's house on the edge of the town, where the buildings fell away into the scrub around the railway line. He was waiting for them in the front room, his face pressed up close to the window, made foggy by the impression of his breath on the glass.

They all ran towards the bombed building, battered by the war. Hide and seek, amongst the fallen beams. He found Larry easily, inside a barrel, ripe with the smell of decaying wood.

'Not fair,' Larry whined, swiping at the underneath of his nose.

'That's a rubbish place to hide,' he said.

Larry's dark hair was getting too long: he blew it out of his eyes. 'Let's find the others.'

Where were they? He and Larry clambered over debris, ran their hands along the sweating brick walls. There had once been a second floor: above them hung the edges of floorboards, swatches of old-fashioned stripy wallpaper, an empty window frame. Larry followed him, and he was pleased, finding a chair, balancing a stool on top. He clambered on, stopping when it began to rock. There was a narrow moment when the stool wobbled beneath him and he was sure he was going to fall. He could feel Larry watching him from below. Standing with arms outstretched, his breaths began to slow. There was a strange calm on the edge of falling.

He looked up: there was a hole in the second floor, letting in rainwater and birds. There was something clear and bright about the sky above, framed by the edges of the floor. The clouds, skirting across the weak sun. The look of it made everything stop, made his insides clear and calm and quiet. As if it was all frozen still just for him, waiting.

Then he grasped the edge of the floor above and pulled himself up. He stood, looking down at where Larry was standing below him. The outline of his dark, messy hair.

'Come on,' he said.

Larry paused. 'Are they up there?'

'I don't know yet, do I? Come up and we'll look together.'

Larry took hold, stepping up first onto the chair and then tentatively lifting his left foot to reach the stool above. It wobbled, and he paused.

'Come on. It's easy.'

He watched Larry's head from above as he moved closer, the muscles in his scrawny arms tensing. Slowly, he raised himself to a standing position. He looked up, putting out his hand.

As Rook reached forward to take his hand, Larry's foot slipped. The stool wobbled and then he was falling, calling out, his body plummeting through the air and landing on the ground. When he stopped, he wasn't moving; his arms and legs lay oddly.

When Rook called out for his brothers, no one came. Slowly, he sat down on the edge of the exposed floor, and let himself drop.

*

His father's face, looming over him where he lay on a cot. The silver-domed ceiling of the ambulance. The strong, sour smell of old alcohol and sweat. The siren. They were moving: he flung out his arm to steady himself and pain ran up into his chest.

The bottom half of his father's face was dark with stubble.

'Where's Larry?'

'Never you mind,' his father said.

At the hospital, he was offered a wheelchair.

'It's his arm that's hurt,' his father said. 'Not his leg.'

The nurse tutted. The long grey hospital building swam away from him. He forced himself to stay standing, shutting his eyes until he was ready.

'How's the pain, lamb?' the nurse asked.

He looked at his father. 'Fine.'

'We'll get you something for it. Is his mother here?'

'She was out,' his father said.

They led him to a side room. His plaster cast was applied by the same nurse.

'You're a quiet one. Does it still hurt?'

'It's all right now. Where's Larry?'

The nurse looked at him, then looked away. 'He's gone to another part of the hospital.'

'Is he all right?'

'We're not sure yet, lad.'

His head rang. 'What do you mean?'

'He's in a bad way. What were you boys doing in that building?'

'Playing hide and seek.'

'It was a nasty fall.'

Under his cast, his arm went cold. Something wasn't right. 'Where are my brothers?'

'They've gone home,' she said, starting her daubing again. Behind her glasses, her eyes were clear blue with little veins, magnified.

*

His dad was in the waiting room, tapping his foot on the linoleum.

'The cast will need to come off in eight weeks,' the nurse said.

'It's broken, then, is it?'

The nurse nodded.

'And how's the other lad?'

The nurse turned her back, so that he couldn't hear her properly. 'It's not looking good.'

'What do you mean?' his father said. 'He'll be all right, won't he?'

'They said his neck was broken.'

His father's face went white.

'We'll keep you posted,' the nurse said. 'Get your lad home now. He needs plenty of rest.'

His father's footsteps were too quick. At the bus stop, he turned. 'What were you doing in that building?'

His heart, like a jackhammer. 'Playing.'

'You'd better hope to God that Larry lad's all right, or you'll never hear the end of this.'

*

His mother, fresh from the city with her sisters. When she saw his arm in the cast, her smile dropped. 'What happened?'

For a long moment, his father didn't say anything. His quiet anger was like a clock, ticking in the background. 'Where were you?' he said.

'I went to see my sisters. I told you I was—'

'These boys are running riot. They were messing about by the railway. Him and another boy. They fell.'

'Is he all right?' his mother asked.

'They're not sure the other boy's going to make it. He's broken his neck.'

His mother's hands flew up to her mouth.

It felt like a story they'd read at school, not something that was really happening. He pictured Larry with his runny nose and messy halo of dark hair. *Come on*, he heard himself say, *it's easy*. Then he saw Larry's silhouette laid out on the ground below him, unmoving.

He sniffed, wiping at his face. His father swung round. 'Don't start on the waterworks,' he said. Then he turned back to his mother. 'What kind of a mother are you?'

She looked down at her hands. *It's not your fault*, he wanted to say.

'We'll talk about this later,' his father said. 'That boy isn't to leave the house.'

There was silence after he slammed the door.

His mother was still looking at her hands. He was afraid she was crying.

'I'm sorry, Mother,' he said.

She looked up as if she'd forgotten he was there. 'Does it hurt?'

'It's not bad.'

'Is it broken?'

He nodded. His mother, bent down on the rug with him, looking at his cast closely, as if she could see beneath it.

'What's going to happen to Larry?' he asked.

His mother wouldn't look at him. 'I'm sure he'll be fine, lad,' she said. 'Where are your brothers?'

'Playing outside.'

His mother put her hand on the crown of his head. 'You'd better stay here with me,' she said. 'I'll make you some Bovril and light the fire.'

*

He woke up in the darkness, his heart jumping. There was a strip of light under the door. Then the sound of heavy footsteps and pans clashing together. Vaguely, he remembered a clatter swimming towards him through sleep.

His mother's voice travelled through the ceiling, then his father's, rough and low. Then silence, for a long time, and he started breathing again. But then there was another clatter and a muffled cry, and he squeezed his eyes tight shut.

The tension, the boiling in his temples, every muscle in his body tight and strained: his fists clenched at his sides. His stomach dipped lower. Was this his fault? He felt Robert's hand reach out for his: they squeezed and squeezed until his fingers ached.

*

He went back to school and found he was a sort of terrible celebrity. Kids would cross the corridor to avoid him. He even caught his own brother hiding behind a pillar until he had passed.

In the classroom, he looked across the neat heads of the other children, bent over their desks, towards the stencil of the roofs outside. Using his left hand made his writing wide and loopy, like a child's or a mad person's, and his other arm got in the way, hanging in its sling.

At home, things were different too. Everything was oddly still, as if they were all waiting for someone else to break the silence. The sounds of the house became louder and almost unbearable: the clatter of knives and forks on china over dinner, or the click of his mother's knitting needles, the crackle of coal in the fireplace. His father was there, too, more than he was in the pub. Sitting in his chair, his hands hanging over the arms, staring at the fire with a far-away look in his eyes. It made him nervous: the waiting for something to change, for something to happen.

On his first day back from school, the kitchen was quiet. There was the sound of splashing water in the yard: his mother crouched on the cobbles, scrubbing clothes, even though washing day was almost over. Her hands were below the water, her eyes fixed on next door's wall, and when he asked if he could help, she jumped.

'You're all right, lad,' she said, lifting out one of his father's work shirts and twisting it between her fists.

'It's cold out here,' he said.

'I'm just getting it done.' She tried to smile, but she looked afraid.

He sat on the steps. His mother stopped the washing, came and sat beside him. Her apron brushed his bare knees.

'Is it always going to be like this now?' he said.

His mother looked at him. 'What do you mean?'

'Different,' he said.

She was trying to smile. 'It will all blow over, once the boy gets out of hospital.'

'Is he going to get better, then?'

His mother nodded, slowly, and Rook was reminded of the puppets at the fair.

'It was an accident,' he said.

'I know.'

'People are acting like I pushed him.'

'It's all right,' she said. 'Everyone knows it wasn't your fault. Sometimes, an accident is the scariest thing of all.'

His mind ran over her words, but he couldn't find the meaning. He wondered if he would understand, one day.

*

When the school holidays finally came, he was relieved. He could stay at home and play with his brothers, and things could go back to normal.

But on the first Saturday of freedom, when his brothers made for the front door after breakfast, his father grasped hold of his arm.

'Not you, lad,' he said. 'You stay here with your mother.'

'Why?'

'Because I say so,' his father said. 'Can't have you running wild with that boy lain up.'

He felt like the animals they'd seen in the zoo, pacing their cages. His brothers would come in, mucky-socked, and a heaviness would turn through him, of being the one left out and left behind. They'd talk about their day over tea, some game they'd been playing, and he was unable to join in. He longed to go back, to the days before the accident, to change what had happened.

'I'm bored,' he moaned.

'Only boring people are bored,' his mother said.

She started sending him on errands: to the baker's and the butcher's. One day, when he came back with a loaf under his good arm, there was a cardboard box on the kitchen table.

When he looked inside, he saw an expensive-looking

camera. It was heavy and black: he pressed the silver button and the front opened up. Inside was a glass circle surrounded by numbers, on top of something like the fire bellows.

He lifted it out with his good hand, resting it on the table and looking through the viewfinder. There was the chair, and the window with the little pot of dried lavender. He noticed the light skimming along the windowsill, catching the uneven paint. He'd marked them out.

'That's for you,' his mother said from the doorway, her arms full of washing. 'My sisters gave it to me. It was my father's.' She paused. 'I was going to wait until you're older. But I thought it might give you something to do.'

He looked into the viewfinder again, turning it around until it was pointing at his mother's face. She was smiling, and he wanted to keep her there, happy in the frame. 'Don't tell your brothers,' she said.

*

He practised, holding the heavy camera, playing with the silver dials. Looking through the viewfinder at the blackened terraces from the back window. It took his mind off things, searching for that feeling that made everything stop.

His mother, outside, pegging up the wet clothes on the line. He clambered onto a wall at the back of the house, and got the yards, all crammed together with their identical washhouses. One of his brothers, playing by the fire.

His father, pulling the sack of coal around to the back of the house on his day off.

'Give it a rest,' he'd said covering his face with his hands. 'You're like a bloody rook, always peering at us with that thing.'

His mother laughed, over at the stove. 'Our little rook,' she said. 'I like that.'

He loved the feel of the world around him, how far away things felt when he was looking through that metal frame. It made the house seem new and different, the familiar unfamiliar.

He didn't press any of the buttons or turn any of the knobs, not yet brave enough. He wished there was a way to find out how to use it properly, to get the images out of the camera. He'd asked his mother, but she'd shaken her head. 'No idea,' she said. 'You could try the chemist. They do developing, don't they?'

The next morning, he was at the shop before it opened, peering in through the rows of small, thick-glassed panes, beyond the crowded blur of dusty products laid out on tissue paper, and into the dim interior of the shop.

Mr Timmins looked surprised to see him. 'You're one of the Henderson boys, aren't you?' he said. 'John, is it?'

He nodded. 'Everyone calls me Rook now,' he said.

Mr Timmins had a beard. He was wearing a shirt with a jumper over the top, and he looked smart and not-smart at the same time. 'What can I help you with?'

He held out the camera. 'I was wondering if you could show me how to use this.'

'Bring it here.'

Mr Timmins turned the machine over in his hands. 'Nice old one this,' he said. 'Rolleicord. Where did you get it?'

'It was my grandfather's.'

'There's a film in it,' Mr Timmins said. 'So you're all ready to get started. I can give you a demonstration, if you like?'

He listened hard as Mr Timmins showed him the small metal lever that you turned to wind the film on. 'After you've taken a shot, of course,' he said. 'And you do that by pressing down this one. But before you do that, you need to get the shutter speed and the *f*-stop right, and there's the light to think about. And there's the focusing.' He smiled. 'It's not as simple as it looks, is it?'

He didn't think it looked simple at all.

Mr Timmins handed him back the camera. 'Tell you what,' he said. 'I could use a hand with the developing. If you come back after lunch, I'll show you how it's done, and then you could come in one afternoon a week. In return, I'll teach you to use that machine of yours.'

He grinned. 'Really?'

Mr Timmins nodded. 'That way no one's getting something for nothing, eh?'

He ran home and bolted his dinner.

'Where've you been all morning?' his mother said. 'Your father said you weren't to be out.'

He swallowed a mouthful of bread. 'I was at the chemist,' he said. 'Mr Timmins said he'd help me with the camera. If I help him with his developing. Can I go, Mum?'

His mother looked at him, then shrugged. 'I suppose it's OK for you to go out if it's for work.' She smiled. 'Aren't you important? I'll have to pop in and thank Mr Timmins.'

He shook his head. 'Neither of us is getting something for nothing, Mum.'

He ran through the streets towards the chemist, keeping his head down in case his father was about. He didn't want to get his mother in trouble.

Mr Timmins was behind the counter, writing something in the big shop ledger. He looked up when he heard the bell. 'That was quick,' he said. 'Have you even had time to eat?'

'Yes.'

'We'd best get this show on the road, then,' he said, holding open the door to the developing room.

After they re-emerged, he couldn't have said how much time had passed. He remembered only the red glow, the row of bottles that glimmered like jewels. The tang of chemicals. The photo paper, sinking below the surface of the water, hanging on the line. He too felt suspended, floating away from the world outside: the world of uncertainty where everything could change in a moment.

Walking home, he still felt the calm of that place. He grinned to himself all through dinner. Mr Timmins had said he could come back tomorrow for his lesson: then perhaps he'd be able to make some images of his own. He wasn't sure if he'd be able to develop them: he knew the photo paper was expensive, but he was sure there was a deal to be made.

*

It was late that night when the knocking started, and the shouting. His brothers and he knelt on the bed, craning to see out of the window. There was a woman down there, Larry's mother, her hair wild and her arms gesticulating under the street lamp.

'This is your boy's fault,' she was shouting. 'He's dead. Dead. And there's nothing you can do about it.'

His mother appeared on the step, tried to draw her into the house.

'Don't you shush me,' the woman yelled. 'I'm not going in there, and I'll never let you forget this.'

*

He wanted to go to the funeral, but his mother had shaken her head.

'But he was my friend.'

His mother folded her arms. 'They don't want us there.'

'Just lie low, lad,' his father had said in an oddly quiet voice. 'Until all this blows over.'

He'd seen the crowds, walking like shadows towards the church. It was raining, and the umbrellas looked like vulture wings, held open.

He followed them at a distance, his new camera heavy around his neck. He wanted to be close to the black car that crawled slowly up the hill, carrying Larry's body. He saw again the way he had fallen, how the smile had slipped off his face.

At the edge of the churchyard, he stood behind the grey wall. Slowly, he moved around the edge, holding his camera to his chest as if it was a shield. With its protection, he felt like he could look without being seen. The people were clustered on the steps, their umbrellas shiny from the misty rain. A woman turned towards him, as if she could see him: Larry's mother, her eyes half-crazed with sadness. He felt his guilt, and before he had a chance to think about it, his finger clicked the shutter.

FIFTEEN

The town hall looks the same as ever: the wide stone frontage and steps leading up to the double doors. Inside, there is a table with a demure white cloth; plates of sandwiches and little blocks of cheese on sticks, some dainty cakes.

Rook goes over to stand with his son and Julia. 'Did you do this?' he asks Ralph.

'Julia did,' Ralph says.

Rook takes her hand, squeezes it. 'Thank you,' he says. 'June would have loved it.'

Julia smiles.

Ralph clears his throat. 'We've got something to tell you, actually,' he says. He looks nervous, and Rook is suddenly concerned. 'We're having a baby.'

Rook's smile spreads across his face. He pulls his son into an embrace. 'That's great news.'

He thinks of a baby boy, of holding him in his arms and feeling again the rush of love he felt for Ralph. Or a baby girl, who would have blonde curls and flashes of June.

When he pulls back, Ralph's face changes. 'Dad, you're crying,' he says.

Rook wipes at his face. 'Can't an old man be happy for his son?' He clasps the camera hanging around his neck. 'This calls for a photograph.'

Rook steps back, centring Julia and Ralph in the viewfinder.

'Wait, Dad,' Ralph says. 'You should be in it too.'

Rook lowers the camera. He looks at his son, with his arm around Julia. He imagines himself, standing next to them. Then he nods.

'I'll ask someone,' Ralph says, taking out his phone and switching on the camera, and before Rook knows what is happening, he is smiling and looking into the lens, his son's arm around him.

Acknowledgements

First of all, I would like to pay tribute to the sixty-three journalists who were killed during the Vietnam War (between 1955 and 1975) and those who survived. Their work captured the history of this extraordinary place, as well as impacting the direction of the war itself. Although none of the characters in *The Last Photograph* are based on real people, I was influenced by the early Vietnam correspondents, such as David Halberstam, Neil Sheehan, Peter Arnett and Horst Faas, as well as the band-of-brothers captured in Michael Herr's incredible *Dispatches*. I hope I have done justice to their experiences.

When I started writing this novel, I knew close to nothing about the Vietnam War, the country itself, or photography. Therefore, the process of writing has involved a huge amount of research, both from books and directly from experts. I would like to pay homage to certain titles which had a huge impact on me: *Once Upon a Distant War* by William Prochnau, the *Eyewitness History of the Vietnam War* by George Esper and Associated Press, *Page after Page* by Tim Page, *Two of the Missing* by Deane Perry Young and *The Quiet American* by Graham Greene. The photography of numerous photojournalists was an inspiration to me, among them Tim Page, Don McCullin, Larry Burrows, Malcolm Browne, Horst Faas, Nick Ut and Eddie Adams.

The idea for this book was planted in my mind by a play – *Safety* by Chris Thorpe – I studied as part of my AS Level Theatre Studies over a decade ago. I would like to thank Jen Baylis for introducing me to this work and for taking us to see it at The Royal Exchange in Manchester. Studying this play led me to discover Don McCullin's photography and his autobiography *Unreasonable Behaviour*. My Founders' Day book on leaving Withington Girls' School was a collection of his photographs, and I remain inspired and in awe of this brave man, who has survived so much and outlived so many.

I decided to write about the Vietnam War as it was the last major conflict where journalists were given a certain amount of freedom to explore the story and draw their own judgements. Armed with a Press Pass during the American war, it was possible to gain access to any army vehicle up and down South Vietnam. Since this conflict, and perhaps because of the impact of the journalism resulting from it, journalists are 'embedded' into groups of military personnel, which inevitably only offers them one side of the story.

I first visited the country myself in April 2012, traversing it with the aim of setting a book there. While visiting the Central Highlands, I was introduced to one of the kindest people I have ever met – an English teacher in a small town who had lived through the war. When I asked him how many native English speakers came to the town to help him with his teaching, he told me that the last time was twenty years previously. I returned to Vietnam in May 2012 for three months to help him with his school, and in return, he and his family taught me an enormous amount about the war and their country, and opened my eyes in ways I had never predicted. I will always be eternally grateful to them for their kindness: they have become a second family to me. Through the volunteer scheme I set up on my return (www.vietnamvolunteerteachers.com) I hope to repay some of this debt. I encourage anyone interested in learning more about the country to get in touch through the website. In return for teaching English for a few hours a day, you will be welcomed into a Vietnamese home, eat traditional foods, and enjoy a rare experience of this incredible country.

It is very easy for an author to claim all the credit for a work of fiction, but whipping it into shape involves more than one person. I would like to thank both Jamie Coleman and Antony Topping for their insightful edits and faith in the book, as well as my kind, super-smart editor Francesca Main and her editorial assistant Nuzha Nuseibeh, and the rest of the Picador team. I would also like to thank Nicholas Blake and Laura Carr for their eagle eyes: any errors remaining in the manuscript are entirely my own.

As far as writing groups go, I have people spread over three continents to heartily thank: Dawn Barker, Amanda Curtin, Petty Elliot, Sara Foster, Tom Feltham, Kat Gordon, Carolina Gonzalez-Carvajal, Lucy Hounsom, Rebecca Lloyd James, Liza Klaussmann, Natasha Lester, Anita Othman and

Annabel Smith. Other early readers include Tomek Mossakowski, Sally Knox (and the team at EWM Helmsley), and the photojournalist Tom Bradley. I would also like to thank Sophie Hoggard for accompanying me to Vietnam and for breaking the ice.

For their ongoing support, patience and belief in me, I would also like to thank my friends and family.

picador.com

blog
videos
interviews
extracts